C.F. Lascelles Wraxall

Life and Times of Her Majesty Caroline Matilda Queen of Denmark and Norway

From Family Ducuments and Private State Archives

C.F. Lascelles Wraxall

Life and Times of Her Majesty Caroline Matilda Queen of Denmark and Norway
From Family Ducuments and Private State Archives

ISBN/EAN: 9783741183584

Manufactured in Europe, USA, Canada, Australia, Japa

Cover: Foto ©Andreas Hilbeck / pixelio.de

Manufactured and distributed by brebook publishing software
(www.brebook.com)

C.F. Lascelles Wraxall

Life and Times of Her Majesty Caroline Matilda Queen of Denmark and Norway

LIFE AND TIMES

OF

HER MAJESTY CAROLINE MATILDA.

LIFE AND TIMES

OF

HER MAJESTY

CAROLINE MATILDA,

QUEEN OF DENMARK AND NORWAY,

AND

SISTER OF H. M. GEORGE III. OF ENGLAND,

FROM FAMILY DOCUMENTS AND PRIVATE STATE ARCHIVES.

BY

Sir C. F. LASCELLES WRAXALL, Bart.

IN THREE VOLUMES.

VOL. II.

LONDON:

Wm. H. ALLEN & CO., 13, WATERLOO PLACE, S.W.

1864.

CONTENTS OF VOL. II.

CHAPTER V.

SHARING THE SPOIL.

CHAPTER VI.

THE NEW GOVERNMENT.

CHAPTER VII.

WHAT THEY SAID IN ENGLAND.

CHAPTER VIII.

STRUENSEE IN PRISON.

CHAPTER IX.

THE QUEEN'S TRIAL.

CHAPTER X.

THE QUEEN'S DEFENCE.

CHAPTER XI.

A JEALOUS ADVOCATE.

CHAPTER XII.

A LUKEWARM DEFENCE.

CHAPTER XIII.

STRUENSEE'S APOLOGY.

LIFE AND TIMES

OF

CAROLINE MATILDA.

CHAPTER I.

A GATHERING STORM.

THE ANONYMOUS LETTER—INCENDIARY PLACARDS—THE SAILORS AT HIRSCHHOLM—ALARM AT COURT—THE FEAST OF THE BŒUF ROTI—THE CONSPIRACY—FALCKENSKJOLD'S ADVICE—STRUENSEE'S ALARMS—BRANDT'S LEVITY—THE SECOND LETTER—BRANDT'S RESOLUTION.

WHEN Brandt had got rid so cleverly of his oppressive duties in constantly attending on the king, it might have been supposed that he would have nothing to trouble his mind henceforth, but would take the goods the gods provided him in a happy frame of mind. But Brandt had one of those private skeletons which are said to be in every house, and his took the shape of an anonymous letter in French, which was sent to him early in July. Although the writer had disguised his hand, he had taken no great trouble to

remain unknown, as the seal bore the initial letters
of his name, and in the letter itself there were plenty
of allusions to enable Brandt to guess the writer.
This was Conferenz-rath Braëm, deputy of the College of the Generalty.

SIR,

Perhaps you may wonder to receive a letter without
a name on a matter of so great importance, from a
friend who formerly used to tell you the truth before
your face: but the times we live in now will not justify a man in exposing himself to danger, without
seeing any good arising from it.

The two last court days I sought for an opportunity
at Hirschholm to speak a few words to you in private,
but I found it was impossible. You might have observed that if you had been at all attentive: but I found
you so much engaged with another object that I could
not approach near enough to you to make you understand what I wanted, and I thought it inadvisable to
go to Hirschholm on purpose to pay you a visit.

Once, sir, you showed that you had the honour of
your master at heart.† It was then asserted that
neither zeal nor attachment was the mainspring of
your actions, but ambition and interest, because you
hoped that if you could bring Count Holck into dis-

* This and the following letter were found in Brandt's pocket-book when
he was arrested, and were first published by Dr. Jörgen Hee, in his account of
his penitent's conversion.

† An allusion to Brandt's letter to the king, intended to overthrow Holck.

grace, you might succeed him in the favour and honour he enjoyed. However, the bulk of the people thought your intentions noble and without self-interest. Perhaps the immediate consequences of this transaction have made so great an impression on you, that you think you dare not venture on such another. And yet the final issue of the affair has shown, that even your ill-success in it has been more advantageous than detrimental to you. Therefore, sir, do not think that this was the mere effect of accident, but rather that a higher hand has guided this matter. I do not know what your notions of God may be, or whether you believe in a God at all, or in a mere stoical fate. It would be very superfluous to discuss a matter of so great importance here. The time will come, when experience will teach you that there is a God, who sees and knows everything, who either early or late rewards virtue and punishes vice.

My intention is not at present to make you a Christian. It is only to remind you of your duty—that duty by which even an honest heathen thought himself bound toward his king, his country, himself, and his family. The heathen even demanded this of every subject and of every man who laid any claim to honour.

You see, sir, in what manner your king and benefactor is used. You see the indecent things that are done before his eyes, and in which you, yourself, are so much concerned. You see that in the whole kingdom everything is turned upside down. Consider,

1 *

sir, and recover your senses, and you will not be at a loss how to act. If it be true (and it is but too true) that the life of the king is in danger, or at least that preparations are being made to take away his liberty, you certainly must know it. The sense of the nation on this head cannot be unknown to you, and that one time or another you will have to account for the life and liberty of your sovereign. You, sir, since you are constantly with him, and since you see and know everybody, be assured that your head will be answerable for it either sooner or later. Think of your own safety, I conjure you by the friendship I entertain for you. It is in your power to do it. You see plainly from the king's desire to avoid the place and company in which he is ill-used, and from his aversion to return to it, that he is sensible of the ill-treatment. Some day the king will deliver himself from you, or good fortune will rid him of you, and what will then be your fate? Would it not be best for you to save your head and do your duty at the same time? To build your happiness on a solid and noble foundation, which you will then owe to your zeal, your faithfulness and attachment to your king, who will reward you with riches and honour; and the nation will not think even this an equivalent for your services. You and your present welfare depend on the caprice of a wretch who will abandon you as soon as he is above your assistance. At present he makes the same use of you as the monkey did of the cat,

and I fancy you have found this out more than once,
if you will not impose on yourself.

If the king should come to town, I advise you to
act in the following manner: Prevail on him to go
to the palace, and persuade him to call for one or two
of his faithful servants, in order to consult on the
best way of proceeding. It is unfortunate enough
that the number of these faithful servants is so small,
and reduced, perhaps, to one or two persons; for the
best and cleverest men have been carefully removed.
You will easily guess who these persons are, without
my naming them. Perseverance, honesty, and experience, are characteristics by which you can know
them. I could name them, but would avoid the least
suspicion of self-interest. However, I must tell you
that it must be neither Rantzau nor Gühler, for both
are detested by the nation in an equal degree. You
will forfeit your head if you do not follow this advice,
which I give you as a friend, and a faithful servant of
the king. If you do not heed it, but neglect your
duty toward your king and benefactor, you may be
sure it will cost you your life, your honour, and everything that is dearest to an honest man; and, moreover, no one will pity you. If, on the other hand,
you do what your duty requires, and save your king
from those wicked hands into which he has fallen, you
may be sure that there is no honour or prosperity to
which you will not be entitled, and this with the consent of the king, and all his faithful subjects.

Perhaps you will think proper to show this letter to your friend Struensee, in order to give him a proof of your fidelity at the expense of those obligations which you have sworn to your king, and to induce him to grant new favours to the husband of Countess von Holstein; and perhaps he might do so, in order to deceive you, and keep you in his interest. But I assure you that when they have deposed the king, you will be wretched, and perhaps the guilt will fall on you.

I repeat again, that your head shall answer for the safety of the king. You are continually about him. You accompany him; you are entrusted with his person ; and lest you may plead ignorance, I assure you on my honour, that in such a case a copy of this letter shall be produced against you, at the proper time and place. And for fear you should mistake in this respect, I desire you to notice the seal of this letter, which contains the initial letters of my name, and which will also be produced against you.

The life and health of the king, together with the welfare of the kingdom, are in your hands : act in such a manner as you can answer for before your fellow-citizens. I do not say before God, for I do not know what your idea of God may be ; though I have reason to think, from what you told me once in your apartments at Christiansborg, and afterwards at Hirschholm, that your notions are not altogether what they should be.

You see I am not afraid of your guessing who I

am, and I assure you, that if you act in the way I expect from your birth, you will find me to be your
faithful and devoted servant.

July 8, 1771.

It had always been hitherto assumed as an historical fact that the Copenhagen Palace Revolution was
concocted only a few days before the catastrophe of
January 17, 1771, by the Queen Juliana Maria; but
it is sufficiently evident, from the above anonymous
letter, that six months previously a plot existed among
men of position, to overthrow Struensee at any cost,
and they seem even to have uttered the blood sentence, which condemned their victim to death and
ruin.   The threatening letter does not appear to have
produced the intended effect on Brandt; but he became very serious, concealed the contents of the letter
even from Struensee, and carefully kept it in his
pocket-book.   As he gradually became more and more
melancholy, he lost the king's favour to the same
extent.

With what boldness the conspirators dared to act,
even at this period, is evidenced by the numerous
threatening and abusive documents which were sent
to the cabinet minister's house, placarded on the walls
of the palace and the theatre, and even thrown into
the Hirschholm garden.   As a specimen of the tone
and contents of them, we may here reproduce a pla-
card, supposed to have been composed by Brandt's

father-in-law, Conferenz-rath Lüxdorph, which was found one morning posted up in the principal street of the capital.* The literal translation is to the following effect :—

" As the traitor Struensee continues to ill-treat the beloved king, to mock his faithful subjects, and to daily seize, with force and injustice, more and more of the royal authority which the subjects have entrusted to the king, the before-mentioned Struensee and his adherents are hereby declared free as birds (outlawed), and the man who puffs out this treacherous soul, shall receive as reward 5,000 dollars, his name be kept secret, and in any case a royal pardon be granted him."

The dissatisfaction of the people of Copenhagen, which was partially justified, being fanned in this way, began, ere long, to display itself actively.

The bomb-ketches intended to be sent against Algiers were not yet finished, and the sailors brought from Norway to man them roamed about the capital in idleness; moreover, the government neglected to pay them. The political creed of the Norwegians at that time was composed of two dogmas:—first, that the king is never-unjust; secondly, that the king must be blindly obeyed, provided that the order emanate from him. The corollary was, that acts of injustice were committed by the king's subordinates, and that by application to their master redress was certain.†

* The original is preserved in the Royal Library at Copenhagen.
† Reverdil, p. 283.

As early as June 10 many ship-carpenters had struck work, after in vain asking double wages for working on Sunday, which was considered necessary to get the fleet off. Two days after this event, a squadron of dragoons was posted in front of Hirschholm Palace; but, as no further excesses occurred, this picket was removed toward the end of July. On September 10, however, a band of from two hundred to three hundred sailors set out for Hirschholm; they had been waiting eight weeks for their pay, were almost starving, and had sent in repeated petitions, to which no answer was returned. As they now saw that no relief was to be obtained in this way, they formed the bold resolution of laying their request before the king personally.

When they arrived in the vicinity of the palace, a naval officer went to ask them what they wanted? "We wish to speak to our father," was the reply; "he shall hear us, and help us." The aide-de-camp hastened with this message back to the palace, but the whole court had already fled by a back-door to the estate of Sophienberg, about two miles distant. Here the question was discussed between the queen, Struensee, Brandt, Falckenskjold, and Billow, whether the flight should be continued to Elsinore. At this moment the sailors arrived here, and demanded speech with the king. They were answered that the king was out hunting, but the intruders did not believe it, and were preparing to force their way into the palace, when Colonel Numsen came up with a troop of dra-

goons and tried to drive them back.   The sailors laid
their hands on their knives, and declared they would
defend themselves if the soldiers attacked them.   Fortunately, some firmer and wiser gentlemen represented
that the men did not look like insurrectionists, and
that by signifying to them from the king through a
naval aide-de-camp that they must return and justice
would be dealt them, an odious and sanguinary scene,
perhaps a real sedition, would be avoided.   On the
pledge of the aide-de-camp the sailors went back to
Copenhagen as peacefully as they had come, and the
court returned to the summer residence.   Still, the
alarm the sailors had caused lasted all night, because
everybody felt persuaded that they would return furious and better armed.

The queen ordered that her horses should be kept
in readiness; she went to bed bare-headed and in disorder, had her riding-habit laid in readiness by her
side, and a moment after rose hurriedly to have her
jewellery packed up.   She also requested a colonel, in
whom she placed confidence, to sleep at the palace.
The dragoons, however, who patrolled all night, discovered nothing, and so the court became calm, and
did their best to hide the fright they had suffered.

Struensee gave way; the sailors on their arrival in
Copenhagen were treated with spirits, and temporarily
appeased by a payment on account, while the whole
arrears were paid up a few days later.   The chief of
the naval division, however, to which they belonged,

Herr von Rumohr, was dismissed the service, on the charge of not having attempted to quell the tumult.

The bad example which the Norwegian sailors had given, and the fact that they were not punished for it, soon induced other men to bring forward less just claims in a similar way. A fortnight later, some one hundred and twenty silk weavers proceeded from Copenhagen to Hirschholm to complain that they were starving, because the royal silk factories had been closed. This request was also taken into consideration by the alarmed court, and an order was issued to continue the work in the factories till the men obtained other employment. As these demonstrations, however, raised apprehension of others, from this time guards were posted round the palace, the manège, and the palace gardens, by Falckenskjold's advice, which naturally led to many bitter comments.

But the greatest fear was entertained at court about the dockyard-men, who were known to be still angry at their exclusion from the king's birthday rejoicings, and the loss of their perquisites. In addition to the sailors obtained expressly from Norway, there were generally five thousand more in Copenhagen, divided into five detachments, of ten companies each; some were intended to man the ships, while others were employed as carpenters, caulkers, and labourers of every description in the navy dockyards. These men were also dissatisfied with the new regulations introduced in the yards, as in every other department, and it was consequently resolved to give them a " festival of reconciliation," for which September 29 was selected. When the day arrived, all the dockyard-men went in procession, with their wives and children, to the riding-school of Frederiksberg Palace, where they were to be regaled in the open air.   Of course a roast ox again formed the staple dish; but as it was not sufficient to fill all the empty stomachs, six sheep, twelve pigs, and an infinity of geese, ducks, and fowls, were also roasted and distributed.   To wash this food down, upwards of thirty tuns of beer, and a quart of rum per man, were distributed.   Any one who liked to smoke received a charged pipe, and all were paid their wages as for an ordinary working-day.   Dancing and music concluded the festival.

Struensee, in his abject terror, had not duly reflected how uncertain is the permanent effect of popular demonstrations, or to what remarks they give rise.   But the mistake led to even more ugly consequences.   It had not only been announced that the court would be present at the festival, but the diplomatic corps, and all the dignitaries of the state, had been invited as well.   Fifty men of the flying corps of guards were to form the king's escort, and had been told off, when a rumour reached the court that a design on the favourite's life would be carried out at the feast of the roast ox.   In the terrible confusion which this rumour caused at Hirschholm, the advice of the experienced Falckenskjold was demanded.   Struensee was afraid of being murdered, and said in Brandt's presence to Falckenskjold, that the fate of Concini might be hanging over him.   The colonel advised him to mix among the populace at the festival, and display an undaunted demeanour, but took advantage of the opportunity to urge him to be more cautious, and not to arouse his enemies further.   He told him that the dissatisfaction with his government was now extending to his friends, and reminded him of the fate of Counts Corfix Ulfeld and Griffenfeldt, whom the court had been compelled to sacrifice to their enemies.

"Such is the fate," Struensee's best friend concluded his far-sighted warnings, "by which you are also threatened, and, if they can, they will drag you to the scaffold.   So, at any rate, take care that your papers are in order."

"My papers are arranged," Struensee coldly answered him; "from that side I have nothing to fear, if they will only behave fairly in other respects."

Brandt joined in Falckenskjold's warnings, and urged Struensee not to be so obstinate, but to give way, and yield to circumstances.

"No!" Struensee answered him, with considerable violence; "no! I will give up nothing of what, according to my conviction, promotes the welfare of the state."

"The time will come," Brandt said, prophetically, "when we shall be compelled to give way."

Struensee retired silently to his cabinet.   But, a few

minutes after, Falckenskjold received a note from him,
in which he asked whether he could be present at the
festival without risk. Falckenskjold answered him,
that he was able to stay away if he felt afraid.*

Neither Struensee nor their Majesties appeared at
the festival of the roast ox: the preparations for their
reception proved a farce. The proceedings passed off
tranquilly, with the exception that some of the sailors
remarked that it was not the ox that had been promised them—in allusion to Struensee's corpulence.
The citizens were very much annoyed at not having
been shown their king, whom they were growing accustomed to talk about as an automaton. They were
even more indignant when they learned that fear had
retained their Majesties at Hirschholm, and this distrust with which the king was inspired against his
subjects was a fresh crime with which the favourites
were accused. But though it is certain that the king
had nothing to fear, it is equally certain that he had
not been inspired either with fear or distrust; in the
whole affair he was passive and indifferent.†

There can be little doubt but that Struensee was
quite right in staying away from the festival of September 29, for there was a regular conspiracy; it was
formed under the auspices of Juliana Maria, and managed by the head man of the caulkers, Captain Win-
terfeldt, who was eventually rewarded for his good

* " Mémoires de Falckenskjold," pp. 151—2.
† Reverdil, p. 287.

will. In 1774, Baron von Bülow gave Mr. Wraxall
a detailed account of the plot to murder Struensee
and his partisans on this occasion.

The favourites were not at all reassured by the tranquillity of the people and the sailors, for a dull fermentation was going on, of which they could not be ignorant. Projects for leaving the country, and the results
which might ensue from obstinately despising the
danger, frequently occupied them.   The cabinet minister even one day mentioned his disgust to Reverdil,
who was in no respect his confidant, and the latter expressed his surprise that he put up with it. Struensee
replied that he had often thought of retiring, and was
only prevented by his devotion to the queen, who had
ever been before his time a victim of the intrigues and
malice of the favourites, and would be so after him.
On another occasion, when he assured Reverdil that
the king was the sole author of the reforms he had accomplished, he added, " I will not say otherwise under
torture."   Brandt, who frequently complained of his
lot, said, with respect to some reproaches he received
from the queen, " that alone is a hell."   Brandt, who
pretended to be seriously affected by an anonymous
letter, confirmed his friend, however, in his resolution
of remaining.   " To what place could you go," he said
to him, " where you would be prime minister and favourite of the king and queen?"

On other occasions, Brandt's incredible levity inspired him with jests as to the fate they had to fear.

One day, after making some rather malicious remarks about the marshal of the court, he added: "After all, though, Büilke is the wisest of us, for he is taking advantage of the present time to settle down; he is making a wealthy marriage, and when we are in prison, I flatter myself that he will have pity on us, and send us every now and then some good soup." At another dinner, Brandt began talking about the proposition of September 29 of all flying together, and asked each of the guests what profession he would choose to gain a livelihood. The queen said that she would turn singer; and, indeed, she had a very agreeable voice. Struensee said that he would take a distant farm, and live on it as a philosopher. Brandt proposed to carry on, on his own account, his trade as manager of a theatre; "and you, my fair lady," he added to one of the guests, "cannot fail to succeed; with your form, you need only offer yourself as a model at an academy." The lady was certainly very beautiful, but hid with a great deal of art a defect in her shape, which she thought no one knew.[*]

Still, these anxieties which Brandt treated so gaily in company, affected him, nevertheless, in secret. "I wish all this would come to an end," he said one day to Falckenskjold, "for I have a foreboding that this government will speedily be overthrown."

[*] Reverdil, p. 290. Though these details may appear trivial, they are worth notice, because Brandt's caustic manner procured him many enemies, and rendered the efforts made to save him of no effect.

"You will fare badly if it is," Falckenskjold answered.

"Oh!" said Brandt, with a flash of his old levity, "as far as that is concerned, I have studied law, and shall be able to answer for myself." *

About this time, Brandt received another anonymous letter in the same handwriting as the first:—

Well, sir, what I foretold you has happened, and you feel already the effects of your bad conduct. You have been faithless to your king, and you are now treated by others in the same manner. They use you as the monkey did the cat. You are deceived, and since they find they can do with you whatever they please, they laugh at you now, and it will not last long before they send you with contempt about your business, and lest you should tell tales, they may very likely imprison you for life, or send you by some means or the other into another world. This will be the due reward of your treachery, cowardice, and mean actions. I prognosticated all these things to you in my last letter of July 8: since that time my friendship for you, of which I have given you undeniable proof, has grown very cool. You do not deserve that it should continue, since you have been unable to follow good advice, and to do what your honour and your duty require of you. You have, on the con-

* "Mémoires de Falckenskjold."

trary, chosen to persevere in your wicked course of
life.   If you at that time had followed my advice, you
would have set the king at liberty, by saving him, and
your praise would have been immortal.   You would
then have satisfied the duties of a good subject, a
faithful servant, and an honest man: you would have
gained the applause not only of your countrymen, but
even of all Europe: they would all have united to
procure you rewards according to your merit, and pro-
portionate to the services done to the king and to
your country.   And certainly nobody would have been
more deserving of rewards.   But now you are detested through the whole kingdom, and are everywhere
laughed at.   Much was expected from your loyalty,
your love for the king, and from a sense of your own
duty; but people were mistaken.   You are now punished.   You are infamous among the whole nation,
and your name is mentioned with horror.   At court
you are laughed at and entertained with vain hopes;
an imaginary greatness is shown you.   You are treated
with the empty title of Count, which will remain a
monument of your want of faith, your weakness, your
meanness, and your reproachful conduct.   In the
meantime, Struensee insults the king and the whole of
the royal family, not because they have offended him,
but only to show his unlimited power.   He arrogates
all honours to himself; he makes himself master of
the kingdom, the concerns of the government, and of
the king, whom he dishonours before the whole world;

he disposes of the revenues of the kingdom in a despotic manner, and against all order. This wretch dares to place himself on a level with his master by drawing up an order, by which the signature of his name acquires the same authority that, by the constitution of the kingdom, only belongs to the signature of the king. Your meanness and unwarrantable conduct have assisted to raise him so high; you could have prevented this, and, therefore, you will be answerable for the consequences. He commits crimes and assassinations, and he does it to retain the reins of government; but you contribute your share by obeying the orders of this Cromwell, who is ready to sacrifice the life of the king a thousand times over, if possible, so that he may obtain his wicked ends, and provide for his own security. Instead of acquainting the king with things which nobody knows better than you (for you are cunning enough when it concerns your own interest), you assist this Diedrich Slagheck* in arrogating to himself royal authority; in keeping his master under guardianship; in degrading him in the eyes of his subjects, that their love may cease, or at least decrease; and, lastly, as every one says, " in using him personally ill in the bargain."

' You who can prevent all this and save the king from the hands of this good-for-nothing wretch, and

---

* The uncle of Diaveke, the mistress of Christian II., who induced the king to commit the massacre of Stockholm, under circumstances of the greatest treachery and barbarity.

yet are not willing to do it—you, sir, are accountable for it, and deserve greater punishment than the
traitor himself; and believe me, as sure as that there is
a God, you sooner or later shall pay for it with your head.

You see how preposterously business is managed;
everything is overthrown and jumbled together in the
strangest manner and blended with the highest incon-
siderateness, of which there is no parallel instance to
be met with in history. The most honest people who
have served the kingdom such a long while, and so
faithfully that even envy itself could not blame them,
are removed to a great distance; they are turned
away in the most shameful manner if they will not
fall in with the measures of this doctor of physic. As
if he were afraid of their honesty, their places are filled
up with wretches who know nothing of the constitution of the kingdom and the situation of affairs; who
know nothing of the business annexed to their offices;
in short, people of whom nobody so much as dreamed
that they were acquainted even with the first principles of the art of government.

For God's sake! what is the meaning that an Oeder
and a Struensee, professor of mathematics at Liegnitz,
are placed at the head of the board of finances? These
men enjoy an annual salary of 3,000 rix dollars, while
others who have served forty and fifty years without
blame, are now starving, because they could not betray
the king and their country, and would not be employed
in promoting bad and destructive ends. Yet these

ignorant men dare to take on their shoulders a burden under which, particularly in these unhappy times, a man of courage, ability, and experience, would have trembled.   However, the wise man knows the danger, and therefore will not hazard the welfare of the nation and his good character, but the ignorant man, who has nothing to lose, does not perceive the unhappy consequences of his inability and ignorance.

You see, sir, that the nation is acquainted with the wretchedness of this present administration, that it feels the bad consequences of it, which will drive it at last to extremities.   You may be the more assured of the truth of this, as discontent discovers itself in a public and alarming manner.   You know all this, but you conceal it from the king, though you are the only man that converses with his Majesty, while access to the throne is denied to all the rest of his subjects.   You, alone, can inform the king of the dangerous situation himself and his kingdom are in, and the inconceivable indifference wherewith the best and worthiest of his Majesty's subjects are treated.   I hear that a certain kingdom (Norway) may soon become alienated: so that in a short time everything may be hopelessly lost, if the king continues to listen to such bad advice.

You see, sir, how the department of foreign affairs is managed, and how, by the intrigues and incapacity of our great prime minister, who has the audacity to interfere, everything is confused, so that the name of the Danes is now a subject for ridicule.

You see, sir, and you know how arbitrarily his excellency, our great prime minister, Count Struensee, disposes of the finances,—the pure blood of the poor subjects.

You, sir, are a Dane of noble extraction, beloved by our king, to whom you and your family owe so many favours, and yet you keep silence! Do you not blush? and are you not convinced in your conscience that you ought to fall the first sacrifice of such conduct, since you might have prevented it, or had, at least, a thousand opportunities to set matters to rights again? If tumult and rebellion (which God forbid) should be the consequences, whom do you think the exasperated populace would attack first? Would they not secure you first, as you are at least as culpable as Struensee? And do not you expose your life, sooner or later, to the greatest danger by this conduct, which is not consistent with the character of an honest man?

Reflect, sir, and return to your duty: I conjure you by the ashes of your father, whom you never knew; by the tears of your virtuous mother, who weeps, perhaps, already on account of your approaching untimely death; and what is still more, I conjure you, by the tears which may some day be shed on your account by the king, the royal family, and your afflicted country.

You are not afraid to disagree with the doctor prime minister when it concerns your private interest: but you are mean enough to be reconciled by a present of 10,000 rix dollars, of which he had robbed the king and the nation to give them to you. Are you not ashamed of such a meanness? and are you not afraid of this man in matters that concern the welfare of your king and your country? These traitors and villains who defend a bad cause, would not have the courage to oppose you, through fear of endangering their heads, which already sit loosely on their shoulders. You would save your king and your country: you would deserve rewards, and would have a right to claim them: they would follow you, of course, since nobody would refuse them: I, myself, who write this letter, would be the first to contribute toward loading you with riches. With what tranquillity and inward satisfaction would you enjoy your fortune, your prerogatives, and your honour, if you should gain this by the consent, and even agreeably to the wishes of your king, your country, and your fellow-citizens. I desire you, sir, to consider this well, though I entertain a better opinion of your generosity, than to suppose that you can be instigated to perform noble actions only by mercenary motives.

In my opinion, you must begin this most important business in the following manner: You are frequently alone with the king: you take a walk in the evening with his Majesty, as I was informed last Wednesday, at Hirschholm: you have found that the king is weary of the guardianship he is kept under. Make use, sir, of such a favourable moment, or occasion it yourself, since you have sufficient understanding for it. Represent to him the unhappy situation he is in, and how inconsistent it is with those obligations under which his royal dignity lays him. Tell him that he, by signing the order of July 15, has divided the throne and his royal authority between himself and Struensee: that he himself, the royal family, the kingdom, all his subjects, his revenues, the life and the property of every one, are left to the arbitrary disposal of this arch-grand vizier, who is a man without experience, honour, religion, or fidelity: who does not regard laws, who is a master over all, even over the life of the king. You know that great crimes are ofttimes productive of still greater ones, or that we may at last fear that it might happen. When you have explained this to the king, then represent to him the despair his subjects are in, and to what they might be driven by such a destructive administration, and by such misery. Show him what danger threatens him and his kingdom, if this wretch has time enough to turn everything upside down. If you should have put the heart of the king in emotion, and have convinced him how absolutely necessary it was to think of the preservation of his royal person, his family, and his kingdom, then propose to him to go directly to Copenhagen, where he will be quite safe: to go to the palace, and send for two or three noblemen who can give good advice, according as the circumstances require: that he might not take false steps (which could be of consequence) at the

time when the nation should attempt to revenge itself,
and to show its hatred against the authors of its misfortunes and its miseries.   I could name these persons,
but the nation will do it for me; they ought to be
persons acquainted with government, that they may
advise according as the present situation of affairs
requires: but it must not be Rantzau, or Gähler, or
Von der Osten, for these three the nation equally
detests, and they, therefore, would frustrate the whole
design.

For God's, your king's, your country's, your family's,
your own sake—consider all this well; and do not
delay any longer to hasten to the assistance of your
unhappy country.   Save the nation, the king, and
your own head.

The contents of this hypocritical letter are in so far
of importance, because they comprise all the charges
raised by Struensee's opponents among the higher
officials.   The writer of the two threatening letters
was not publicly considered a man of bright intellect,
as indeed his Jeremiads sufficiently prove; but still
he was supposed to be thoroughly honest.   Although
he proved himself the contrary, as the result will
show, still Brandt appears to have paid some attention
to his repeated efforts to save his Danish countryman.
The letters, the alarm at the late tumult, and his own
melancholy forebodings, at last made Brandt form a
desperate resolution.   He determined openly to im-

part his feelings and wishes to Struensee, and hence addressed the following appeal to his noble col-league.*

* The letters contained in the following chapter, the originals of which are in the Copenhagen secret archives, have not been published before. Only some passages of them were quoted by Fiscal General Wiwet in his prosecution of Brandt. Hence it is probable that Struensee returned them as requested, and that the letters were found among Brandt's sealed-up papers.

CHAPTER II.

THE SINKING SHIP.

Brandt to Struensee.

REPROACHES often convert love into mere friendship,
and equality often friendship into coldness. But this
shall be no obstacle to my considering myself bound
to pour out my heart before you, as an old friend from
whom I am seeking counsel. For the last five or six
weeks I have incessantly felt unhappy. With the same
strength as I was tortured by melancholy considerations, I tried to appease myself again, but did not
succeed. Every night I walk weeping up and down
my room till four in the morning. With your remarkably healthy common sense, you, whom I do not know

whether I dare call a friend, may condemn me; but
you must feel yourself exactly in my position, which
you will probably have a difficulty in doing.   It must
be most oppressive to a man possessed of delicate feelings, through his earlier associations, to be the daily
companion of a king, who, far from loving this man
(myself), regards me as a burden, and does everything
in his power to liberate himself from me.   But you
force the king to live with me, and in order to complete my misery, compel me to treat the king harshly,
according to his own confession.   If this is in itself a
hell, it is far from being all.   I have at the same time
been exposed to the laughter and ridicule of the whole
nation.   In the provinces I am compared with Moranti,* and justly so.   I have not the slightest influence, and no more power than the first street boy,
chosen hap-hazard.   My position could at least have
an appearance of reputation, and thus flatter vanity,
but it has become ridiculous, contemptible, and almost
dishonouring, through the rivalry of the negro boy.
I am obliged to tell you disagreeable things, but they
are true.   I alone speak frankly to you.   You have
inspired everybody with terror: all tremble before

* Moranti, a negro boy from the Danish colony existing at that day on the
Gold Coast, who, with another lad and Chamberlain Brandt, had to dress and
undress the king, and a negro girl of ten years of age, formed the daily society
of the autocrat Christian VII., who, according to the anonymous correspondent
just quoted, was so inexpressibly beloved by the whole nation.   He and his two
playmates led so wild a life, that there was not a bust or statue in the palace
or the gardens, which they had not converted into a target, or was safe from
being destroyed, or, at least, mutilated by them.

you. No despot has ever arrogated such power as yourself, or exercised it in such a way. The king's pages and domestics tremble at the slightest occurrence; all are seized with terror; they talk, they eat, they drink, but tremble as they do so. Fear has seized upon all who surround the minister, even on the queen, who no longer has a will of her own, not even in the choice of her dresses, and their colour. Could you but see yourself in this position, my God, how startled you would be at yourself! Neither in my head nor in my heart has a wish been aroused to conduct the affairs of state, but it suited me to regulate the court and society. For this I am better adapted than you, and would have managed the business more properly: for, only to mention the liveries, they are not liveries, but uniforms. This would have spared you much hatred, and relieved the queen of considerable embarrassment, as she would have arranged the court parties more easily with me than with you. That would have given me a real existence, and saved me from becoming an object of mockery. But with all this it is now too late; for this evil, like so many others, is incurable. If you were now to entrust me with the management, it would only be apparent, and cause me a thousand annoyances. Only one as a specimen. I had a couple of suits of clothes made for the king, and they have been terribly criticised. You find the expense of two suits in three months a little too much, although the king,

as a rule, changes his dress thrice a day.　Had I not
been so firm, which is certainly a difficult matter when
opposed to you, I must have engaged, instead of real
actors, a lot of impostors, Crispins and Harlequins;
and instead of good comedies, we should only have
had farces, of which people would have grown tired
at the end of three months, after we had made ourselves ridiculous in the eyes of foreigners.　Martini
and Paschini, whom you tried in the queen's name to
induce me to engage, would have been of this description.　The orchestra would have been reduced one-
half, and have only consisted of pothouse fiddlers from
the regiments, who would have cracked the ears of
everybody.　It would have been the same case as at
the balls, which, owing to the eternal repetition of the
same dances, which, as you said, were performed by
the queen's desire, became in a short time unendu-
rably insipid, as I prophesied.　I only mention this to
show you what a part I play, and what I could have
played, and to request you, if possible, to place me
in a position suitable for a man of sense, information,
feeling, and decent and proper pride.　Even Warnstedt's
situation was not so unworthy as mine; and I have
cause to apprehend the contempt of all persons, which
in my present position would fall on me not unjustly.

Three months ago I wrote you a letter almost to
a similar effect, but since then love has made me
blind; with love in his heart a man closes his eyes to
the truth; he becomes blind, and falls asleep in this

blindness. When reason afterwards comes to his help,
when love has become friendship, then he sees things
in their true light. Now, I ask myself, what would
have afforded me any consolation in this unhappy position? and have only the answer—Struensee's friendship and kind conduct towards me. The former no
longer exists, for you treat me with rusticity and
arrogance. No mortal man has ever before dared to
behave to me in such a way. At the play table, in
company and everywhere, you decide everything yourself, and are only satisfied when you have humiliated
other men. You really should not have behaved thus
to a friend who has ever loved you so dearly, and even
at a time when all his companions and daily associates
reproached him for his intercourse with you ; and
though it might injure him, always praised you,
confessed his friendship for you to everybody, and
formerly employed all his skill in persuading Holck
and quieting Bernstorff. Ah, my friend, how dangerous life at court is to the character! Would to
Heaven you had never made acquaintance with it !
I cannot possibly comprehend why your fine feelings
have not been aroused against the unworthy and disgraceful game of loo. If you were to be so unfortunate as to win a large sum from a friend or a man
unable to afford it, you would not be satisfied till you
had introduced a loo, a *campion*, or a *trente-et-un*, of a
less dangerous character. For me it is a terrible reflection how much I have lost at these games in two

months.   There have been months in which I lost
1,800 dollars, and I am now obliged to sell some
of my shares.   And then, to be obliged to submit
to reproaches for at times losing less than formerly!
Could not a man blow out his brains for vexation
at it ?

If you desired to make a concession to a feeling
and cruelly-wounded mind, I have lately thought out
a plan whose fulfilment would render me perfectly
happy.   It would be the greatest pleasure to me to
be able to go to Paris, and live there decently.   In
order to realise this wish, I require a yearly revenue
of 20,000 species.*   The whole city daily expects to
hear that the king has given you estates, and people
mention Wallö and Wemmetofte, while others are
said to be intended for me.   It is considered strange
that we counts have no landed property, and if the
king gives you Wallö and Wemmetofte, which produce 21,000 species annually, and me the county of
Rantzau, which produces 15,000, no one will be surprised at it, and I shall thus be enabled to make an
annual trip to Paris, and reside for some months on
my estates.

Still this plan, however flattering it may sound for
me, and even if you concede its fulfilment, cannot
tranquillise me, for my imagination alone has sought
a vain refuge in it.   Fortunately there are three men

---

* Or about £5,000 a year.   It must be confessed that the count wished to
live "decently," especially when we take the value of money at that day into
consideration.

here who are all gifted with sound sense, and honest
and united, for whom I will answer with my head—
Reverdil, Falckenskjold, and Düval. It will, therefore, solely depend on you, whether I shall entirely
retire from court, and shortly undertake the post of a
theatrical director, which, if it is to be properly conducted, will require my constant presence. We shall
then love each other more, and you will find in me a
man who, sooner than allow himself by madness and
desperation to be drawn into a cabal against you, even
if it promised a successful result, would not hesitate to
free himself from his misery by poison or steel.

Hence I beg you to release me, to continue to be
my friend, to reflect on the contents of this letter for
a week or a fortnight, and then return it to me with
your answer. For it is written solely for you, and I
declare that I would despair if it accidentally fell into
other hands.

BRANDT.

Strange that Struensee, a man of sense and experience, could continue to trust in Brandt after the
perusal of such a letter addressed to him. Not only
does the letter contain a series of insulting remarks,
and the direct assertion that intercourse with Struensee
had been dishonourable to the writer, but it also bore
the stamp of incipient insanity, and a temper that
might easily become dangerous. But Struensee's self-
confidence was so great that he did not apprehend de-

sertion or attack from this quarter. Besides, he was sincerely attached to Brandt, and did not forget the services the latter had rendered him. His reply to Brandt's petulant letter may almost be called a state paper, though of the *doctrinaire* school :—

Struensee to Brandt.

Persons are always unhappy who possess an imagination rich enough to invent everything that makes us unhappy and yet wish to render us happy. When a man is gifted with such a temperament, and combines with it a natural levity which produces a liking for change, he will never arrive at a quiet enjoyment of the moment, but constantly find reasons to wish himself in a different position. But a man must sacrifice himself when he wishes to perform meritorious actions. For no one will give us credit for actions which cost us no trouble, or which we undertake for our own pleasure. The satisfaction which it will cause the queen if you succeed in your task, and the unmistakable proofs of it which you have already received, will be your reward. All that you say in addition would cause me no suspicion, if I were only convinced that it merely emanated from your zealousness; but I am morally convinced that it flows from an entirely different source. Since your amour (with Frau von Holstein), you have altered your principles, mode of thought, and views. From that moment, you have

deserted and neglected me, and only granted me a
few spare minutes.   I have never reproached you for
this, although it was done to please a person who has
a mean opinion of me, and often treats me improperly.
I have had the greatest respect for your inclination,
and done all in my power to please you, although it
has cost me trouble to overcome the anger with which
Frau von Holstein inspires me.   She is to me the
most disagreeable of her sex, and has become even
more so since I have been obliged to share your friendship with her.   I request you to compare this confession with my conduct, and then to judge whether I
have made a sacrifice for your sake.   You must also
take into account the queen's aversion for this lady,
which I had even to overcome at the moment when I
reproved her while dancing,—all of which, up to the
present day, has been occasioned by her.   This mis-
understanding has often embittered my happiness; but
I have never spoken to you about it.   Whether this
may be called a mistake or a reserve, the effect
remains the same.   You can yourself decide how
great my confidence in you must be, as neither my
feelings nor my conduct toward you have undergone
any change, although I saw you allied with a person
whom I dislike; whose society is disagreeable to me;
and whom I mistrust.

I request you to reproach me and to oppose my intentions, in case you see that matters are going badly,
or that I render the king unhappy.   But if they suc-

ceed, I do not permit you to examine the means I have employed. You object, that I cause everybody terror; you should, on the contrary, praise me for it, because it is the sole correct means of curing an enervated state, with an intriguing court and people, and a king who has the same liking for change as his nation. You ought to pity me, because it is necessary for me to make myself feared, as I can only find affection through the fulfilment of my duty. I challenge you to mention anybody whom I have rendered unhappy. A yielding minister, who does not know how to act, is only a charlatan, a harlequin; for if he is also compliant in his acts, the state will always have to pay the price for securing adherents in that way. Denmark furnishes the most melancholy instances of this.

The persons who have spoken to you about the suffering of the pages and lackeys are assuredly intriguing, mean men, of no character, who only aim to make everything sink once more into the old chaos. If a man has to reform an intriguing court, and bring it to order, he cannot treat it with the mildness with which the late Söhlenthal* managed his household. You, yourself, were a witness of the disorder that crept into the king's apartments during my illness.†　Good-heartedness and concession have ever been the true cause of Denmark's decay. I have saved the

---

* Brandt's stepfather.

† Struensee was thrown from his horse in September, and confined to his room for some time.

king from slavery, and done everything to render him
happy. As regards my conduct toward his Majesty,
I allow you no opinion about it, least of all when you
express it in such a tone as your letter displays. You
desire to arrange the king and queen's company? but
I cannot hand over to you this decisive way of acquiring influence. I could mention other reasons why the
court parties and balls have become insipid and tedious,
—the arrogant and imperious conduct of Frau von Holstein; the readiness to oblige which you imputed to the
other ladies through assisting in concerts, &c.; your
attempt to introduce tragedies, and thus overcome the
king's tastes; the composition of the dances contrary
to the queen's inclination, and the dislike for the *tour*
which she is fond of, and a thousand other trifles, which
I could mention to you, if I were equally inclined with
you to listen to complaints which persons wished to
bring against you. But I have constantly refused to
listen to such complaints, and have striven to convince
people of the injustice of their accusations, without
saying a word against you. If I liked to repeat
everything of this sort which has been said to me,
you would be astonished to find that as many complaints have been made against you as your so-called
friends have brought against me. I regard both the
one and the other as a thing that deserves no attention,
and hence does not cause me the slightest anxiety;
and I had expected the same from you.

As, besides, all these disputes have no ulterior effect

on the king and the state, and solely affect my person and yours, we should strive to remove them, for they do not merit that on their account men should select a different road, when they, in a consciousness of higher and nobler motives, occupy a place like yours and mine. Personalities must not be taken into consideration, or, at the most, be regarded as a matter of secondary importance. A man can change his situation when he does not feel happy in it; but he ought to go to work sensibly, and be tranquil under all circumstances, just in the same way as it is not permitted to change the cards because they are not good, or a man does not give up the game at once because he has been unfortunate for a time. A practised player does what he can, and waits patiently for a change in his luck.

I feel all possible gratitude for what you have done to place me in the position I now occupy. I regard you as the first man who helped me to it, although in politics it is not usual to reckon what any man has done to produce our good fortune by distant steps, but only what that person has done for us who also possessed the means to do it, while we value the former for his good intentions, which is a matter of friendship. After I had acquired the confidence and favour of the king and the queen, and gained respect with the public, through my own strength, and all the difficulties and dangers which are connected with such an enterprise, I summoned you, and shared with you all the results and pleasantness of my position, so

that you at once found yourself in the same fortunate situation as myself. But you are not willing to
thank me for this, but insist, on the contrary, that I
should owe everything to you, make way for you, and
share with you the honour which I have acquired
neither accidentally nor through favour, but solely
through my own exertions. You insist on my taking
the second place, so that you alone may be in possession
of the favour, confidence, and respect, and I execute
your orders. But let me tell you, once for all, that a
division is impossible through the character of the
king and queen. You must, therefore, either take
the whole authority, or be satisfied with the confidence
of being informed by me of everything that takes
place. I ask you to reflect, only for a moment, what
use I make of my dignity, and whether I apply it to
my personal profit? I have no court, no party, no
personal distinction. You enjoy the same privileges
at court as myself. And are my friends, if I have
any, the most distinguished? Can you not be satisfied with being at a court where there is somebody
who stands above you in respect and power? and if
you can be so, are you not glad that this man, whose
conduct is irreproachable, has invited you to join him,
and procured you the place you occupy?

You request that the management of the court and
all that appertains to it should be entrusted to you.
What else is this than that you wish to deprive me of
the sole means by which I can compel subordinates to

pay me external respect, as in the opposite case, they would openly express their dissatisfaction with me, owing to my proper opposition to them? But, leaving this point out of consideration, business would be impeded if it were believed that my influence was weakened, which would be so serious a matter to me, that I cannot allow any one to touch it, because in that case I should soon become powerless.

The sole cause why you desire a division of that nature is, because you think you play too insignificant a part in public. But who has told you so? I suppose some of your friends, or those who flatter you, and hope to profit by the change, if your influence were increased. But, at the same time, those who call themselves my friends, and probably with the same intention, have said to me, " You allow Brandt too much power; he and Frau von Holstein manage everything, if not by straight ways, then by crooked. It is better to cling to Brandt, for all whom he protects prosper better than those protected by you."

I have never refused you anything. You desired the Holstein, and I consented, in spite of my repugnance. Her husband has rewarded me badly for it. It is not his fault that the finances have not fallen into utter confusion, and I have even found myself compelled to resist the appearance of possessing influence which he has given himself. You have power over everything which agrees with the principles and with the system accepted by yourself, and have no cause to complain so long as I do not alter, either because my own interests might demand it, or for the sake of another person, whom I am forced to take under my protection. Everything you bring forward only leads to the conclusion that your ambition and vanity are not satisfied. You desire an immediate influence over my mind and my heart. You want to pull down the house because you did not build it, and refuse to inhabit it because it does not belong to you, and you are obliged to share it with another man.

You are the only person who is in possession of all my secrets, and in whom I have in every case confided without reservation. I have no necessity to justify myself for this, for my heart gives me the testimony that I have neglected nothing to prove that which you too would have recognised, were not your heart engaged elsewhere. I do not complain because I have not succeeded in meeting with reciprocal feelings, for it cost me no self-conquest to be devoted to you.

What folly that there can be men who speak of a rivalry between you and the negro lad Moranti! The livery is an insignificant subject among the arrangements I have made. It would have been better had you, instead of withdrawing from the hatred and discontent of the persons by whom you are surrounded, and who represent the court and the public, not mixed yourself up in this matter, for it is wise to be unpleasant to such persons, and this ought to be managed even in an unfair way. I have always striven to produce the king and queen contentment, and have, at least, partially succeeded. If you, on the contrary, strive to please others, you will stray off the road, like your predecessors. You know very well how necessary economy is, and that I request it on every occasion. The queen, though a lady, is not angry with me when I recommend retrenchment as regards her wardrobe. It is of the greatest influence on the general welfare that no paying of fees should exist, and yet you wish that the valet should retain his fees, although I took them away from him, and exposed myself to the risk of having enemies in the king's *entourage!* I have deprived the king's servants of a lucrative source, and you wish to restore it to them, so as to render yourself popular with these people. These are certainly only trifles, but every sensible man is aware that slight causes frequently produce great effects. We ought, perhaps, to have paid a little more attention to buffoons; for the king would, probably, have applauded farces more than tearful tragedies, and if you had been reproached on that account by foreigners, but had amused the king, would not that have been a sufficient reward for the sacrifice of your taste? If the queen has been mistaken in her opinion about Martini and Paschini, she possesses sufficient good sense to recognise her error, and the whole affair only cost 2,000 dollars. You ought to have dismissed these *soi-disant* artistes, as I advised you. If the regimental " pot-house fiddlers " had been properly trained and

practised in accompaniment, the expenses for flute and
violin players would have been saved, who look like
beaux, and drive about with four horses.   If the balls
had been carried on as they began, they would have
breathed a natural merriment instead of all the affectation which the dancing-master, favoured by Madame
de Holstein, introduced, and which rendered them insipid and tedious, because only a few danced well
enough, and the others, the protectress included, were
obliged to take lessons of the dancing-master ere they
could take part.   It was not the monotony but the
affectation that ruined the balls; for the king has never
been able to learn a set dance.   You prefer to gain the
applause of the public instead of pleasing your friend,
and humouring the whims and peculiarities of the king
and queen.   The comic element has always been most
in demand, because we could not expect to find trage-
dians.   I have explained to you the causes of this a
thousand times.   That desire is founded in the character of the king and queen, and the relations in
which they have always lived.

All your complaints are based on the passion
which possesses me at times when at the card table.
In other respects, however, I am not aware that I
have ever offended against the rules of good behaviour.
Your caprice alone has detected such failings in me.
If I have insulted you, it occurred through careless-
ness, and I beg your pardon for it.   I will, in future,
be more attentive to myself, for it would grieve me

were I to offend on this head, though I must confess
that I am not happy in the matter of small attentions.
As a compensation for this, I may be allowed to boast
that I have never neglected any opportunity to please
my friends that presented itself to me. Up to the present I was not aware either that persons had found
your intercourse with me blamable, and that you run
a risk of injuring your character by it. Such an expression ought never to have passed the lips of a man
who boasts of his susceptibility and fine feeling. It is
hard to hear such things from a friend, although it has
not insulted me; for I do not regulate my respect for
others on the opinion of strangers; and I do not remember a single moment when you had cause to be
ashamed of my acquaintance. And then, too, what
would have become of you if I had followed the advice
of my friends?

You accuse me of despotism? Well, if I am a
despot in business, your despotism goes much further,
for you wish to rule the taste at the theatres, and that
of dress, balls, and parties. Loo is the only game that
amuses the king; the queen, too, is fond of it, and
neither cares for any other game, for I have often proposed it to no effect. That you and the Holstein lose
at it, and that they refuse at once to begin another
game, is sufficient to set you in a fury. In order to
gain access to Frau von Moltke, I lost from 20 to 30
dollars nearly every evening, at a time when I had
only a salary of 1,000 dollars. But I did not grumble

at it, for I thought a man must regulate himself by the company he associates with. How many persons utterly ruin themselves at other places, in order to be able to live at court, and belong to the circles of the king and queen! The easy manner in which you obtained everything you desired, has led you to consider even those exalted personages as nobodies. My " delicate feeling " is not affected because you lose at play; for, in the first place, I do not always win; and, secondly, you are not without resources by which to recover your losses. However, these are but trifles when the point is to amuse the king and queen; but it is always a dangerous thing to undertake changes in their mode of life. After your return to court, you raised the stakes and bet heavily on the cards. I remember one evening when you won and I lost, but I did not, on that account, recommend more moderate stakes. But it is not you who wish or speak so, but the Holstein, and on that account I am vexed.

I ask you now, whether you do not consider your proposition (about the estates) indelicate and selfish? How have we deserved such great rewards, that we might amuse ourselves in Paris, because we are weary of Copenhagen? For my part, I would not accept such gifts, even if the king entertained the most insane and blind devotion to me, and therefore will not promote such a thing in the slightest degree, but always oppose it.

I shall be very cautious about proposing a friend

to the king.   He may choose one for himself, and I
leave him perfect liberty to do so.

I also beg you to reflect, whether, when engaged
with other people, either on business or pleasure, it is
possible to avoid all unpleasantness and arrogance?
But the more important the object of our action is, the
less must we care for such vexations.   If I had made
some slight concessions, I could have made my fortune,
but I declined the chance; for, if I succeed in introducing order into the government, I shall be sufficiently rewarded, although I must now put up with
daily ingratitude.

I greatly regret that, in spite of my zealous exertions to render you happy, and thus afford you a proof
of my friendship, I have effected exactly the opposite.
Still, I beg you to calm yourself, to give no heed to
ear-wiggers, to examine your position and what at-
taches you to it, to weigh the comforts on one side,
the unpleasantness on the other; to compare the present with the past and the future, and to draw a final
conclusion.   I have spoken to you frankly and perhaps
rather roughly.   From the latter, you must not conclude that I am prejudiced against you: for I only did
so because I felt convinced that Frau von Holstein is
the cause of your dissatisfaction.   You can say far
more bitter things to me without arousing me.   But
so long as you maintain your connections with that
lady, you will always find me reserved and susceptible,
whether it is that I do not like the woman, or because

I am jealous at being obliged to share your friendship with her. I'my reflect what a self-conquest it must have cost me to pay her such attention, or even to allow her to remain in Copenhagen.

Finally, I request you not to take any precipitate step, but to speak to me frequently about your affairs, so that we may discover a way to satisfy you. I will willingly sign any proposition to that effect.

STRUENSEE.

From the above answer of the cabinet minister, we see that he was most anxious to remain on good terms with Brandt, although he could not suppress his disgust about the liaison with Frau von Holstein. Yet he would scarce have treated his supposed friend so generously, had he had an idea of the odious design which Brandt undertook soon after against him.

A few days after the festival given to the dockyardmen, at the beginning of October, Brandt proposed to Falckenskjold to go through the garden to the king's sleeping apartment, induce the monarch to get up, take him privily to Copenhagen, and then arrest Struensee.

"What?" Falckenskjold exclaimed, in amazement and disgust. "You would effect the ruin of your friend, the man to whom you owe everything?"

Brandt replied that Struensee could be conducted to Kronborg, whence he could pass over into Sweden, and that as much money as he desired could be given him.

" And the queen ?" Falckenskjold enquired.

" Oh, I will take charge of her," Brandt answered. " I understand the art of amusing women. I will direct their pleasures: I would convert this court, where we now lead a very wretched life into a place of delight. As for the government, that can be carried on how they please, for I do not propose to interfere in that." *

Falckenskjold replied, that there was a good deal to lose and nothing to gain by the affair, and asked Brandt how he supposed they would both fare if they fell into other hands.

" Bah !" Brandt exclaimed; " I have studied the law, and will be able to answer. I only wish to have an end of this: I long to see this government overthrown."

Falckenskjold finally gave him the sensible advice to keep such ill-digested plans to himself, and kept the affair secret from Struensee.

About the same time, another man meditated designs of a similar nature against Struensee. This was Von der Osten, who, though overwhelmed with favours, did not mean honestly by his protector, and could not conceal his dissatisfaction. Von der Osten had a separate interview with Reverdil and Brandt:

* Reverdil tells us, in confirmation of this, that Brandt had thought of giving Struensee a successor in the queen's favour, as he believed that the minister's power and place depended on her, and he had turned his attention to those courtiers whom he considered most seductive, through their face or other advantages; but, in the end, his imagination growing more exalted, he conceived the plan of pleasing the queen himself.

to the former he spoke about overthrowing the favourite,
but could make but little capital out of the honest
Swiss. What he proposed to Brandt will be best seen
from the latter's report to Reverdil:—

"Osten," Brandt said to Reverdil a few days after
the interview, "is a coward and a villain, who would
like to employ you and me in pulling the chesnuts
out of the fire. Some days ago, he gave me a midnight interview, and finding me well disposed through
the anonymous letters I had received, he represented
to me the public distress in such lively colours, that I
entered with him into the project of arresting Struensee, and this is the plan I proposed to him:—

"In one of your (Reverdil's) drives with the king,
you would lead him to Rudersdahl (an inn on the
road to Copenhagen). Osten, Colonel Numsen, and
other persons would be assembled there: the king
would be induced to go on to the capital, after signing
the order, which would be entrusted to Numsen, to
convey Struensee to Kronborg, and arrest the queen
in her apartments. Numsen would be able to get
back to Hirschholm almost at the same time as the
king arrived in Copenhagen, and before the queen
suspected our interview and the removal of Struensee.
Besides, I should remain there to divert attention,
and prevent them learning too soon what had become
of him. Struensee, once arrested, would be allowed
to escape to Sweden, and I would soon find means to
console the queen.

"Osten approved the whole plan, except that he refused to go to Rudersdahl; he, therefore, was willing to have the entire power placed in his hands, if it could be done without danger to his own person, and so I would not undertake anything."[*]

Osten had the meanness to report the whole proposal to Struensee, but the latter said to Brandt very nobly, when alluding to Reverdil in the course of conversation: "Reverdil is so honest a man, that if he led the king to Rudersdahl in order to hand him over to my enemies, and they procured my arrest, and, probably, my execution, I could not help esteeming him; because, in acting so, he would believe he was promoting the public welfare."

While intrigues were being privately formed against Struensee, public attacks were also made upon him. Repeatedly when the king changed horses at Sorgenfrie, on his journey to Copenhagen, petitions and calumnies were thrown into his coach. The number of caricatures and placards posted up constantly increased; and in pamphlets their Majesties were attacked, and the man accused and ridiculed to whom the freedom of the press was owing. The sailors' feast also gave scope for the most unbridled attacks upon Struensee. He was said to be a traitor to the nation, and his reforms entail the ruin of the state. The well-known historian Langebeck published an anonymous pamphlet, under the title " New Specimen of the Liberty of

<hr>

[*] Reverdil, p. 295.

Writing, printed in the Golden Age of the Press," which was, in truth, a specimen of press impudence. In this wretched pamphlet he warned the king " to sit firmly on his throne, and not suffer any one to tear a jewel from his crown;" and his boldness went so far that " he pitied the king, who could have converted the spot of earth confided to him into a paradise, if he had only liked to have done so."

The cabinet minister regarded all this with equanimity, and remained calm even when Falckenskjold and Brandt urged him to take precautionary steps for his personal safety. To Falckenskjold he replied that the latter had grown accustomed in Russia to see conspiracies everywhere, and it was assuredly more glorious to reform a state than to win a battle. To Brandt he said bluntly that his warnings were tiresome, and that he would not allow himself to be disturbed in his undertakings. In short, Struensee was so busied with his plans, that he heeded neither warnings nor threats. Although he was well aware that he had attracted the hatred of the queen dowager and her son, by destroying all their influence over the king and court, he did not deign to concern himself about their cabals. The old queen was not supposed to trouble herself about affairs of state, and was not credited with any bold spirit. As for the hereditary prince, he was only eighteen years of age, and equally poorly endowed in mind and body. He had just received a terrible insult, as he considered it, from Falckenskjold, who did not order his regimental band to cease playing as Prince Frederick rode past, and who was said to have answered the adjutant who proposed to him to stop the performance—" No, not even if *le bon Dieu* were to come along !"   The queen dowager, too, had felt very much annoyed because the king and court had merely sent two pages to congratulate her on her last birthday on September 4.

It is true that Struensee, by Falckenskjold's advice, made an effort to effect a *rapprochement* between the two families, by inviting the king's two relatives to Hirschholm twice a week.   But he soon grew tired of this ceremonial politeness, and told Falckenskjold that he was sick of the visits of the king's stepmother and half-brother.   In October, Struensee was informed that the hereditary prince was at the head of a party, which meditated the seizure of their Majesties; but, although it appears incredible, the menaced minister paid as little heed to this news as to the warnings of his friends : he merely answered : " The purity of my views is my protection."[*]

About this time, several respected officials of high standing were dismissed.   The aged Privy Councillor Gram and Amtmann Dau lost their posts, and the master of the hunt, Chamberlain von Levetzau, became the successor of both.   Two assessors of the Supreme Court were also dismissed, but with large pensions.   At court, Privy Councillor von Staffeldt,

[*] " Mémoires de Falckenskjold," p. 166.

the chief equerry, lost his post, and only received as
compensation a small farm near Copenhagen, that produced 500 dollars a year. The management of the
royal stables was entrusted to Struensee's friend,
Baron von Bülow. Lastly, although Rear-Admiral
Kaas was acquitted by the committee that investigated
his conduct as commander of the squadron sent against
Algiers, and the unsuccessful attack on the piratical
city, he received no compensation for the loss of his
post.

CHAPTER III.

WHILE Struensee thus continued to augment the
number of his enemies, he, however, began to take
some measures of security. The palace guard at
Hirschholm which had hitherto been commanded by a
non-commissioned officer, was raised to thirty-two
men of the flying corps, who were fed from the royal
kitchen, and received a day's pay of five schillings,
which, at that period, when the line soldier only received three schillings a-day, was very high. When
the king and queen, in whose vicinity Struensee remained as much as he could, proceeded to the capital,
their carriage was always surrounded by a powerful
escort, two men riding on either side, and when they

remained in town, either at the palace or the play-house, the guards were doubled.

At Sorgenfrie policemen kept the people from pressing too closely upon the royal carriage, and these guardians of the public peace were also ordered to tear down each morning the pasquinades and caricatures posted against the houses during the night. In addition, their Majesties drove from their summer residence to Copenhagen at an unusual rate, and hardly any one in the city was aware of their arrival till they passed through one or the other gate. If they passed a guard, the latter usually shouldered arms, but did not offer any of the usual honours. Their Majesties and suite, when they visited the French plays, did not enter the theatre by the grand door, but went up a flight of stairs on the side, and never before had the royal couple been seen with so heavy an escort as on the night of October 17, when they proceeded from the theatre to Rosenborg gardens, in order to witness the fireworks.

The disbandment of the flying corps of two squadrons, which had been suspected of insubordination, also gave rise to ugly rumours. Shortly after, their commander, Colonel and Chamberlain von Numsen, a man who was known to be talented and powerful, but is represented by Suhm as given to drink, and amours, and of a treacherous character, was transferred to Jütland as commandant of a dragoon regiment, and ordered to set out at once. Among the public this removal aroused

the greater attention, because the colonel was regarded
as a faithful adherent of Struensee, and seemed very
necessary now as a courageous defender of the count.
A part of the men were sent to Jütland also, and the
rest were placed under Major von Adeler, but were
disbanded early in November.   It was rumoured that
Struensee was suspicious of the flying corps, though he
had founded it himself, because not only the officers,
but also a majority of the Guardsmen, were Danes.   The
regiment of Zeeland dragoons, commanded by Major-
General von Eickstedt, was selected to take the place
of the disbanded Guards, and in October two squadrons
of them marched into Copenhagen, under the command
of Major von Carstenskjold, one of which was told off
to Hirschholm to mount guard over the court.   The
other two squadrons followed shortly after.   The
report about the disbandment of the flying squadron
was, therefore, in all probability, purposely spread,
because the new regiment called in consisted almost
entirely of Danes.   To complete the military measures
of precaution, nearly all the Norwegian sailors were
sent on furlough.

Lastly, the government found it necessary to put a
check on the impudent attacks of the press. A rescript
was issued, in which it was stated that the government
saw with anger that evil-minded persons took advantage of the decree of September 14, 1770, to print
offensive documents, and thus make an improper use
of the liberty of the press which had been granted.

By royal order, therefore, Struensee on October 3, requested an opinion from the Danish Chancery as to what measures would be best adapted to keep down the licence of the press, and on the 7th of the same month an edict appeared addressed to the authorities throughout the kingdom, containing "Stricter Regulations for the Publication of Books and Pamphlets without Censorship."   In this edict the king declared that, as it could not be tolerated that a criminal use of the granted liberty of the press should be made in contravening other civil laws, all insults, pasquinades, and seditious writings would be subjected to legal punishments.   In order to prevent the misuse of the press henceforth, every author of a work would be responsible that it contained nothing contrary to the existing laws and orders.   Hence all printers would be for the future prohibited from printing books whose author's name they could not supply, or reprinting any work on whose title-page the name of the author or printer was not stated.   For it would be an utter misapplication of freedom from censorship if it were to be regarded as synonymous with perfect impunity for printed insults and offences.*

This restriction of the hitherto existing liberty of the press was carried out most humanely.   No prosecution for libels took place in Denmark or Norway during Struensee's ministry, and only in the duchies an exchequer process was instituted against Count

* The original decrees will be found in Höst, vol. iii.

Waldemar von Schmettau for the " Pages for the
Love of Truth," published by him.   Struensee's own
father, the superintendant-general of the duchies, de-
nounced the author to the chief consistory of Gluck-
städt as a blasphemer.

The new regulations at first kept the literary partisans in some check, and toned down the former coarse
and unbridled attacks on the government.   But the
libellers soon found out a way of employing their sati-
rical powers without fear of punishment, and the
sharpest pasquinades appeared in succession, whose
mere titles were sufficient to make the reader comprehend their drift.   Other pamphleteers contrived to
wrap up their attacks on Struensee and his ministry
in such an artful way as not to infringe on the new
regulations.*

Such were the precautionary measures which Struensee took in the autumn of 1771 to protect the royal
couple, himself, and his ministry.   In other respects, he
took all imaginable trouble to render the king's life
pleasant.   Reverdil was requested to keep his Majesty
au courant with French literature, and to be his regular
companion.   It was not Struensee's object, however,
to gain a support for his power in Reverdil; for
though he considered him a thoroughly honest man,

* As an instance of this, take the questions proposed for solution in the
" Magazine of Periodical Literature "—Is it possible that the lover of a woman
can be her husband's sincere friend and faithful adviser?   And if the husband
accepts him as his confidant, what consequences will result from it for all three
and for the children?

he kept rather aloof from him, as he feared his integrity and correct judgment. About two months after Reverdil's return, an ex-favourite of the king, Chamberlain von Warnstedt, who had been removed very suddenly, was recalled to court. This gentleman, however, did not succeed in regaining the king's favour, and Struensee, therefore, appointed a new page, in the person of Von Schack, to wait on the king, who pined for change.

In the meanwhile, Professor Berger continued to watch the king's health carefully, and ordered him to continue drinking the waters from September till December. On his morning visits to hand the patient his medicine he spoke but little, and when he noticed that these visits did not please the king, he left them off. As we have said, Berger had begun also to become cold toward Struensee.

The same servants still waited on the king who had done so before Struensee's appearance at court. The king's usual society consisted of the two boys, who were obliged to drive away ennui by all sorts of tricks, and certainly did not receive any confidence on the part of Struensee.* The king's immediate *entourage*,

* The reader is aware that the king was already quite imbecile, and had frequent attacks of mania. But, in order to remove the slightest doubts about Christian VII.'s condition of mind at this time, I will quote the following instances from Molbech's " Historic Journal for 1852 :"—

"One Sunday, during divine service, when the queen was diverting herself in the riding-house in the rear of Christiansborg Palace, the king was standing on the balcony over the gateway with his black and his white boys, and threw from thence logs of fire-wood, tongs, shovels, books, papers, and entire drawers, consequently, could hardly be regarded as instruments of the minister, and it was no more difficult than under the previous minister to obtain an audience of the king. There is no absolute proof that officials and others who could claim access to the king requested an audience in vain.

Hitherto it had been Brandt's duty to find the king amusement. But just as this gentleman was beginning to hesitate in his former friendship for Struensee, he now sank more and more in the king's favour. There had been a time when the king repeatedly said to Brandt, that no one knew him so well as he did, or was so like him. But this connexion was now greatly altered, and ere long a scene occurred between the two which, though apparently of slight consequence in the life of such a king, was destined to have the most serious results for Brandt. Christian VII. expected that those persons who were his daily associates should have their heart in the right place, as he used to say, and prove it to him. According to the king's will, however, this courage consisted in fighting and wrestling with their master, although the law sentenced

down into the court-yard, and at last wanted to hurl his favourite Gourmand and the negro boy over the balustrade. Among the papers thrown down was a secret list of the fleet and the condition of each ship, which the lackey of a foreign minister found and carried to his master. In the following June the king broke all the windows in his own and the queen's apartments at Hirschholm, smashed looking-glasses, chairs, tables, and costly china vases, and threw the fragments through the windows into the yard, in which his playmates helped him with all their might. At first such amusements on the part of the sovereign excited great surprise among the public, but they soon grew accustomed to them through their frequent repetition."

any man to death who dared even to stretch out a hand against his Majesty's sacred person. The king had frequently tried his strength with Holck and Warnstedt. As he had seen no proofs of Brandt's personal courage, although he had repeatedly challenged him, he one day in November insisted on Brandt trying his strength with him.*

At the queen's breakfast-table, in the presence of eight or ten persons, the king, who hardly ever joined in the conversation, after muttering to himself for some minutes, suddenly raised his voice, and imitating a favourite actor, said:

"I will give you a sound thrashing. I am speaking to you, Count, do you hear?"

This insult was unprovoked, and Brandt, as a thorough courtier, concealed the impression it made upon him. The hearers of it held their tongue. A moment after, the queen and Struensee, drawing the king aside, spoke to him very sharply. On a later occasion, when the favourite again expostulated, the king repeated: "Brandt is a thorough coward if he will not fight with me." He also said to Brandt, that if he had known what a cur he was, he would have hidden behind the door and killed him when he came in.

* One of the king's amusements was to fight with his young companions, and as he himself tried to hurt and even kill them, they generally leagued against him; but he was never beaten, except by his own express wish.— *Reverdil.*

Struensee and Brandt consulted as to what was best to be done. Struensee was of opinion that the wisest thing would be for Brandt to go into the king's apartment in the evening, and say, " As your Majesty is determined to fight with me, I am now here at your service. So if you want anything, come on."

On the day before the execution of this plan, Brandt incautiously concealed a riding-whip inside a pianoforte that stood in the royal ante-room, with the intention of frightening his opponent with it, but changed his mind.

In the evening, Brandt entered the king's chamber quite calmly, ordered the two boys to retire, and bolted the door after them. Then he turned to the king, saying, that his Majesty desired to have a specimen of his courage on his own person : he was quite ready. The king having declined pistols and swords in turn, they agreed to fight with fists. Up to this point it was an extravagance, authorised, to a certain extent, by the example of former favourites; but during the fight Brandt behaved cowardly. He forgot both the consequences his brutality might have, and the respect due to his master as sovereign : he beat him unmercifully, and bit his fingers. The poor king yelled for quarter, which Brandt at length granted him, and left him terribly bruised, and even more frightened.

Brandt proceeded to the queen's apartments, where the company were seated at the card table. When the game was over, he told Struensee what had happened, to which the latter replied: "Well, I am glad of that, as we shall be at peace for the future; but do not tell any one about it."

They were, however, compelled to inform the valet, who found the king's throat grazed, and the result was, that other persons soon heard of the affair. From this time, however, Brandt behaved more submissively to the king, in order to keep him in check. This did not please the king, and Struensee effected a species of reconciliation between them. As a consequence of it, Brandt was appointed, on November 26, Maître de la Garderobe du Roi, which satisfied his vanity, as it procured him the title of Excellency.

The instructions the new officer received from Struensee were to the effect that henceforth he would have, in addition to the direction of the theatre, the orchestra, and the court amusements, the management of all the king's household—the pages, valets, lackeys, hairdressers, &c—so that the servants might perform their duties with accuracy. In addition, the king's wardrobe would be entirely in his charge; and he would regulate all the household expenses, save in the matter of pens, ink, and sealing-wax, which would in future be supplied in kind from the expeditions cabinet. To such trivialities did the all-powerful minister condescend.

By this appointment Brandt was more than ever attached to a court which he desired to leave. It seems that Struensee tried to satisfy him in every pos-

sible way, for he offered him Von der Osten's ministry,
a post for which Brandt did not possess the slightest
ability; although that, after all, was of little consequence, as Struensee expedited all the foreign affairs
himself.

At the queen's court two new ladies-in-waiting, Fräuleins von Kalkreuter and Von Thienen, were appointed
in November, and soon gained Caroline Matilda's attachment. Frau von Schimmelmann, Generaless von
Gähler, Countess von Holstein, and Conferenz-räthinn
Fabricius, were the queen's most intimate friends toward the close of the year; and as a proof of her special favour, she presented Frau von Gähler with a set
of carriage-horses, Countess Holstein with a saddle-
horse, and Frau von Fabricius with a solitaire.

The court amusements were now arranged on a
settled plan for every day of the week. In September, there was every Wednesday at court at Hirschholm, and after the court, an Italian operetta. Twice
a week, on Tuesday and Friday, French plays were
performed at the Royal Theatre in Copenhagen, which
the king and queen were accustomed to attend, and to
which persons of rank and respectable citizens had free
admission. But by Brandt's orders there were separate seats for the nobility and the bourgeoisie. In
order to complete the troupe, Captain Duval was sent
to Paris to engage actors. Thrice a week there were
hunts, for the chase was the chief amusement of the
court, and the queen managed her horse like a first rate
equestrian. At times the royal party appeared on the

parade-ground of the dragoons; and in October they were present at the races, when a royal huntsman thrice won the highest prize. The royal couple also witnessed the fireworks given to the public at Rosenborg, under the management of Chamberlain Gabel; and went thence to the palace of Frederiksberg to see Bram-billa's "pantomimic games" and exercises in the "higher art of balancing."

We see that there was no want of amusements and diversions at court. But as the king was growing more and more averse to business, this was probably chiefly carried out for the purpose of cheering him up, although he evidently only vegetated from one day to the other.

On November 30 the court quitted the summer residence of Hirschholm, as a rather severe winter had already set in, but did not proceed at once to the Christiansborg, but in the first instance to Frederiks-berg Palace, outside the city. It was perfectly well known in public that the royal pair had selected this palace for their temporary residence, and that the reason they had not come to it before was, because a new road was being made from it to the city, and was only just completed; but Struensee's enemies saw in the length-ened residence at Hirschholm only a proof of the fa-vourite's fear to approach the capital.

At Frederiksberg there was a court every Monday, on Thursday and Friday a French play at the Royal Theatre, and on Wednesday an Italian opera at the Danish playhouse. At times there was a hawking party outside the Norderthor, at which the king and queen were often present on horseback with Struensee. At home the king played draughts, read novels, or walked about the park with his new page of the chamber, Von Schack, to whom he had taken a liking. The queen also frequently went out with the harriers.

At Frederiksberg, military arrangements were also made for the security of the court. A squadron of dragoons was quartered in the outbuildings, and not only mounted guard, but patrolled the surrounding country. When the king and queen drove to town, their coach was guarded by forty dragoons with drawn sabres. At the same time, Struensee tried to provide for the safety of the city.

The minister was not pleased with Colonel von Sames, the commandant, for he knew that he was an intimate friend of Rantzau-Ascheberg; interfered in many things that did not concern him; and, in addition, annoyed the favourite with all sorts of plans for improving the city, in which he proposed to pull down entire quarters. Struensee, also, did not consider it in accordance with military rules that a cavalry colonel should command a garrison consisting of seven infantry regiments, while the king had to pay seventy general officers. He therefore consulted Falckenskjold, who proposed to him the Prince of Bevern, governor of Rendsberg at the time, as commandant of the capital. But Struensee did not want so influential a man for the post, and was of opinion that a major-general of infantry should be selected. There was, consequently, only a choice between the two generals Schuell and Gude; and as the former commanded in Norway, the latter was chosen.*

At last Struensee saw that it was necessary to protect himself against the people, in the event of their daring to get up a tumult. He therefore gave the new commandant orders to hold everything in readiness, so as to maintain peace by force if necessary. The heaviest guns in the arsenal were planted on the walls in front of the guard-house and the town gates. The guns on the walls were pointed at the city every evening after tattoo. The soldiers had thirty-six cartridges apiece served out to them, and there was an extraordinary quantity of patrolling. Even loaded cannon were drawn up in front of the palace; and any one who had business to transact there was led in and out by two soldiers.

The king was surprised at this, and asked Count Struensee what was the meaning of these terrible preparations? He replied to the king that all this was done for the protection of his beloved person, as his subjects were aroused against his Majesty; hence it was feared lest the king might meet with the same fate as the unhappy Peter III. The king was terribly

* It is rather difficult to decide about this old soldier's character. According to Reverdil and other authorities, he was a regular old woman, and was solely appointed as a cover for Falckenskjold, who was the real commander. Still, Wiwet, in his indictment of Struensee, states that Gude was a man "who could frighten the whole city by his loud voice and savage looks."

alarmed on hearing this; he clasped his hands, and exclaimed, "My God! what harm have I done that my dear and faithful subjects should hate me so?" *

Unfortunately, these very precautions served as weapons for the favourite's enemies; and they did not fail to employ them. A report was already spread that it was his intention to dethrone the king, or get rid of him; that he would marry the queen, and be declared protector of the kingdom. The display of loaded guns was regarded as a threatening arrangement, intended to intimidate the people at the moment when the minister's projected revolution was about to break out. A report was spread that Struensee had proposed to disarm the bürger guard, and that the colonel commanding it had replied, that if his men were deprived of their muskets they would defend the king with paving stones. Lastly, the disposition to envenom everything was so great, that Struensee, having set up his own carriage at this time, this novelty was also misinterpreted. It was declared to be the state coach, in which he would figure on the day of the revolution.†

In this earnest season, which afforded abundant scope for discouraging reflections, Struensee was, in some incomprehensible way, so busied with court fes-

---

* I give this anecdote on the authority of a pamphlet published in Amsterdam in 1773, under the title of " Die Struensee und Brandtische Kriminalsache," a translation of a pamphlet published on behalf of the British ministry in Copenhagen during the previous year.

† Reverdil, p. 307.

tivities, that he began to neglect those duties connected
with the government.   Business of importance was left
unsettled, and so rapidly accumulated, that the minister
decided everything without consideration.   It was evident that the blindness of this man, who trusted to his
luck, was increasing.   We have a confirmation of this
in the enterprise which he finally ventured, and which
deprived him of the last ray of his favour among the
populace, as well as the good opinion of the better
classes, and hence was precisely of a nature to hasten
his downfall.

A good deal of ill-blood had already been produced
by the disbandment of the Horse Guards, and all the
officers of the Guards being placed on a level with
those of the army and navy.   But now Struensee
resolved to disband the battalion of Foot Guards, under
the pretext that its existence had a deleterious effect
on the rest of the army.   Falckenskjold, at first, opposed this design, but at length gave way.

On December 21, Struensee issued a cabinet order
to the College of the Generalty, by which the five
companies of the battalion of Foot Guards were to be
changed into so many grenadier companies, and attached to five of the regiments composing the garrison
of Copenhagen.   The cabinet order was forwarded to
the college on the following day; and, though it was
Sunday, the members at once assembled in council,
but considered the affair of such consequence that
they requested to be supplied with the king's written

authority. Struensee then requested Falekenskjold to talk the matter over with General von Gähler; he told the latter that the minister would be offended if they refused to carry out the order, and urged the immediate despatch of the necessary commands to the commandant, General Gude, and to the colonel of the Guards, Count von Haxthausen.

Gähler, however, refused to give way, but, instead, joined his colleagues in drawing up a most submissive answer, in which they requested an order signed by the king in person, without which they must decline to execute the cabinet decree, which they considered extremely dangerous. Instead of being induced to reflect over this indirect good advice from experienced men as to the danger of his meditated enterprise, and wisely giving way before this first instance of a refusal to obey a cabinet decree signed by himself alone, the favourite at once obtained the required authority from the king, and forwarded it to the War Department, who immediately yielded.

On the next morning, December 24,—from which the ensuing quarrel was called the Christmas Eve fight,—the palace guard was relieved by the king's regiment, of which Falekenskjold was commander, and the whole battalion of Guards drawn up in line on the the Great King's Market: its effective strength only amounted to three hundred men. The king's order for their disbandment and incorporation with other regiments was read to them, and the officers were pre-

sent who would take them over. But when the
Guards saw that their colours were being taken from
them, they rushed forward in a body, and seized them
again by force, shouting:

"Those are our colours: we swore obedience upon
them! We will risk our lives for them!"

They also said that the agreement with them must
be kept, and that it was contrary to that agreement to
make them serve in other regiments. Hence, they
demanded their discharge, and formation into a fresh
corps. The Guards had always regarded themselves
as a corps quite distinct from the line: for they ranked
with non-commissioned officers of the army, and such
punishments as flogging and running the gauntlet
could not be inflicted on them.

All the representations of the officers were of no
effect. The majority of the mutineers proceeded with
the colours in front of the palace: a non-commissioned
officer assumed the command, as the officers had with-
drawn. Just as the insurgents were about to march
off, a courageous staff officer, Chamberlain Lersker,
drew his sword, in order to force them to go to their
barracks: but the mutineers fell on him and threw
him into the gutter. When the commandant also
tried to oppose them, they plucked off his peruke, and
on hearing him say to the officers of the Guards:
"Such fellows certainly deserve flogging," they
squeezed him against a wall. They seized Colonel
von Sames by the breast, when he also tried to draw

his sabre and assist the commandant. On arriving in front of the locked palace gate, they burst it open, drove the company of the king's regiment out of the corps de garde, occupied their posts, and closed the entrance gate of the palace.

In the meanwhile, the line troops attempted to arrest the Guardsmen who remained on the market-place, but the latter offered resistance: the picket stationed at the main guard, which was situated on the market-place, advanced, and there was a free fight. The majority of the Guards, however, cut their way through, and the pickets only succeeded in seizing a few loiterers, and carrying them to the main guard. But the escaped men no sooner saw this than they turned back and dashed at the main guard, in order to liberate their arrested comrades. Being received, however, by the pickets with levelled bayonets, they desisted, and fighting with the other soldiers, forced their way through the streets to the palace, in order to join their confederates. In the course of this disturbance, a Guardsman was killed, and several soldiers wounded.

During this period, Falckenskjold hastened with the news of the mutiny to Frederiksberg Palace, and alarmed the whole court. Count Brandt and Baron von Bülow hurried into the city and to the palace, and made every possible effort to appease the rebellious Guards, but with as little success as the two colonels. The Guards gave the categorical reply, " Remain Guards or our discharge."

After this, the Guards resolved that a party of them should proceed to Frederiksberg, and request an interview with the king. The party set out, found the western gate closed and held; but at the northern gate, the officer of the guard, who was a boy, allowed them to pass. As they were going along the fortifications they met Falckenskjold, to whom the disbandment of the corps was publicly imputed. They consulted together about killing him, but not being quite certain that it was he, they allowed him to pass. A moment after they met the king in his small English calèche, a postilion and an equerry forming his entire escort as usual, and Reverdil being alone with him in the carriage. The soldiers formed a line to let him pass: one of their officers, who had followed them so far, persuaded them to do so, and not to disturb the king, who might be frightened at their sudden appearance, and impute violent designs to them. Neither his Majesty nor Reverdil had received any news about what was going on, and the submissive air of this small company was far from occasioning any idea of a mutiny.[*]

When the Guards reached Frederiksberg, the alarm felt at the small body of mutineers was as great as that produced at Hirschholm by the Norwegian sailors, so that hurried preparations were made for flight. A detachment of dragoons had in the meanwhile arrived to reinforce the palace guard. The latter surrounded

<hr>

* Reverdil, p. 312.

the mutineers, but in no way terrified them, but were told by the latter that they wished to speak with the king.   One of their own officers, Major von Ahrenfeld, who was a favourite of the Guards, and had hurried to the palace, was sent out to the mutineers, to ask them in the king's name what they wanted.   They repeated their former answer, " Remain Guards, or our discharge;" and added, that in the latter case they wished to go wherever they thought proper.   The major assured them that he would report their demand to the king, and soon after returned from the palace with a reply that, as the king did not wish to keep any men in his service by force, they were at liberty to go where they pleased.

Satisfied with this answer, the Guards returned to the capital for the purpose of reporting it to their comrades, who were holding the royal palace.   But the latter refused to place any confidence in a merely verbal promise, and insisted on a regular discharge for each man before they surrendered the palace.   It produced no effect on them that this palace was surrounded by three regiments of infantry and three squadrons of dragoons; on the contrary, they only allowed their own officers to go in and out.   At length General von Gühler, fearing lest the scene might have a sanguinary issue, went to Frederiksberg, and brought back a discharge duly signed and sealed for the whole body.   But the soldiers, imagining that there was some deception, raised exceptions to the form of the order given them.   On hearing this, Struensee said to the Council of the Generalty, " You are soldiers, and must know the means of obtaining obedience; the king insists on the mutineers being removed from the *corps de garde* before midnight."*

How greatly the mutineers had public opinion with them, was seen by the fact that the citizens supplied them with provisions, wine, and spirits, of which a large stock had been laid in for the Christmas festivities.   These provisions were lavished on the insurgents, whose cause appeared to the lower classes, and even to three-fourths of the higher classes, that of the nation.   The sailors, another turbulent band, but who generally quarrelled with the soldiers, offered their help to the mutineers; and it was publicly reported that the gunners had let them know privately that they would receive them into the arsenal, and join them.

The reason for all this manifestation lay in the reports which had been maliciously spread.   It was alleged that the battalion was composed of Norwegians, whose well-known and invincible fidelity to the king would have been an obstacle to the minister's designs.   He was going to entrust the defence of the king and the palace to German mercenaries, and so on.

* Reverdil, p. 314.   During Struensee's trial much use was made of the form of this order and the absence of the king's signature.   The order in itself was most imprudent, for the queen dowager and her son were living in the palace which it was proposed to storm.

Even Reverdil is ready to acknowledge the absurdity of such rumours. Not more than one-half of these men were Norwegians; their service and duty had no connection with the king's personal safety; none of them had been on guard at Hirschholm during the summer, and the king was quite accessible to ill-disposed persons, if such existed. He was peculiarly at the mercy of those to whom evil designs were attributed. At Copenhagen the porters alone had orders to keep away suspicious persons; and if the pretended conspirators had been the ordinary inhabitants of the palace, the porters' guard was as useless as that of the soldiers. There were avenues which were not guarded, and the keys of which were held by the chief personages. The palace could be entered through the stables and the playhouse; lastly, any odious suspicion is destroyed by the fact, that the asserted disbandment of the Foot Guards never took place. They were to have been attached to the different regiments as light companies, but retain their officers and their high pay.* In that case they would have mounted guard in their turn.

The garrison remained under arms the whole night, and patrols marched through the streets until the requisite number of printed discharges, signed by the king, had been filled up, and one handed to every

* Reverdil, p. 309.

Guardsman, with a promise that three dollars should be paid him, and any advance he owed would be wiped off. In this way everybody was contented, and on the Christmas morning the disbanded Guards left the palace of Christiansborg, after holding it for twenty-four hours, and started for their homes. On the next day the Norwegians assembled in the streets, and took leave of the citizens, who collected in mobs round them, while the sailors and populace uttered angry cries for revenge.

When the commandant arrived with an escort of general officers and adjutants to order peace, he was dragged from his horse and hurled on the ground, while his suite were ridiculed, and some of them also maltreated. The discharged Guards, however, took no part in these fresh excesses, but the populace carried them on, and continued to keep the town in a state of excitement for some time after the departure of the Norwegians. How great was the terror at court is proved by the fact that no attempt was made to disarm the Guards, but they were allowed to depart with their arms and accoutrements.

At last tranquillity appeared to be restored in the capital. The king and queen attended divine service on this morning, which, under existing circumstances, appeared significant, as they rarely went to church; and on this Sunday evening, too, they were not present at the French play, as was usually the case.

For the third time, then, Struensee had proved himself a bold reformer at his desk, but a cowardly and undecided opponent of the embittered populace. To the prevalent hatred was now added a high degree of contempt for his capacity of resistance. This bitterness was not aimed against the person of the king, who was regarded as a prisoner in the hands of his minister. On the other hand, no one was disposed to say a word on behalf of the queen, for the most scandalous reports about an illicit connection between her and Struensee were spread about, which found most ready credence among the mob, who are always willing to ascribe their own bad conduct to the higher classes, and were even gladly listened to in better society, as affording an admirable scope for the most exciting scandal.

In this menacing state of affairs the English envoy, Colonel Keith, thought it dangerous to keep silence any longer. Although he held but an insignificant position at court, and slight attention was paid to his representations and proposals, he was determined to interfere, so that he might, at least, secure the safety of his monarch's sister, as he foresaw what was hanging over the detested minister unless he entirely altered his plans. Hence he went to Struensee, showed him the precipice on whose edge he was standing, and offered him a large sum of money if he would resign his office and leave the country. Struensee seemed affected by the minister's language, but considered that duty compelled him to remain at his post.*

Thus matters stood at court at the end of the year 1771. Black clouds were gathering over the heads of Caroline Matilda, Struensee, and Brandt, and ere long the storm would burst and crush them all three.

* That Sir R. M. Keith was strongly prejudiced against Struensee is seen in his Memoirs. After expressing his dissatisfaction at remaining at a post when he was prohibited from mixing himself up in the internal administration, he adds, "If I am ordered to grapple with these gentry, I already feel (thank God) the superiority which honesty has over low cunning. I am sure, if I had *carte blanche*, I could already have dismissed half a dozen of the most worthless fellows alive."

CHAPTER IV.

THE CONSPIRACY.

STRUENSEE'S BLINDNESS—DANGEROUS RUMOURS—WE ARE SEVEN—VON BERINGSKJOLD—A CONSPIRATOR—THE QUEEN DOWAGER'S ASSENT—SECRET MEETINGS—THE MASKED BALL —A FATALITY—RANTZAU'S VACILLATION—THE VISIT TO THE KING—THE ORDER TO ARREST CAROLINE MATILDA.

THE new year began, as the previous one had terminated, with a fruitless warning to Struensee. In spite of the anger which Rantzau-Ascheberg entertained against the minister, he had not given up all hope of inducing him to alter his mode of conduct. The Swedish envoy, Baron von Sprengtporten, who had no cause to be dissatisfied with Struensee's policy, and wished to effect a reconciliation between the cabinet minister and Rantzau, persuaded the latter to pay Struensee a visit.*

* In order to gain the confidence of the queen dowager and her party, Rantzau had taken formal leave of the royal family while at Hirschholm, and was living in *quasi* retirement. At the same time he quieted his creditors by assuring them that, so soon as Struensee was overthrown, he intended to pay off all his debts.—*Reverdil*, p. 328.

Shortly after new year's day Rantzau waited on the minister, turned the conversation to the events of the day, and represented the perils that menaced his old friend if he persisted in his present system. Struensee, who was by this time completely blinded by self-conceit, thanked his former attached partisan for his well-intended advice, but was of opinion that he could trust to the purity of his designs, and dismissed Rantzau with his expectations unfulfilled. Perhaps the interview would have been decisive had Rantzau had an honest intention of moving Struensee, and been a man who could imbue him with any degree of confidence.   But if the unhappy minister had calmly considered the circumstances of the remarkable visit, and the meaning of this unusual conversation, it is possible that Rantzau might still have been induced to stand off from his designs, especially as up to the last moment he was very doubtful of the result.[*]

Rantzau, however, made a second attempt.   At the next meeting of the College of Generalty he drew Falckenskjold on one side, imparted to him that a rumour of a conspiracy against Struensee was in circulation, and added, that in his opinion an investigation should be instituted.   He offered to help in it; but Falckenskjold heard the news coldly, because he considered Rantzau himself a suspicious character, and answered him, " In that case you should apply per-

* " Authentische Aufklärungen," p. 150.

sonally to Struensee."—"He will not listen to me," Rantzau retorted, and turned away.[*]

If we compare these repeated warnings, and the insurrectionary temper of the city with the last outbreaks, we cannot but accept it as a certain fact, that Struensee had grown blind to every danger that threatened him. He had not only the discharged ministers, officials, and courtiers, against him, but also the party of the king, the queen dowager, and Prince Frederick, the whole of the nobility, the clergy, and the bourgeoisie. It may fairly be said that he was an Ishmael, against whom every man's hand was raised, and he could rely on nobody but an imbecile king, ready to listen to the last speaker, and a young, inexperienced, and unfortunately deceived queen. Struensee must have built upon the almost inexplicable power which he had over the king, and that he would not be induced to injure his minister. Perhaps, too, he allowed himself to be persuaded by his pride sooner to venture everything than undergo the humiliation of resigning his authority.

As the reader will remember, from the anonymous letters sent to Brandt, secret designs were formed as early as the summer of 1771 to overthrow Struensee. But at that time it was not found possible to induce the queen dowager to take part in any plan for the removal of the favourite. It was supposed for a while that a suitable instrument had been found in Reverdil

* "Mémoires de Falckenskjold," p. 157.

to draw the king out of Struensee's hands; and Berger, the physician in ordinary, undertook to sound him. The honest Swiss, however, replied that, though he was not at all an admirer of Struensee, he had not sufficient influence over the king to induce him to discharge his minister. As, too, Reverdil was greatly attached to the queen, this was probably a further reason why he should feel disinclined to aid in the overthrow of her favourite.*

After seven months' absence, the court returned to Copenhagen on January 8, 1772, and the usual festivities began with a ball at the Christiansborg Palace on the following evening. At the end of the French performance at the palace theatre, which was given thrice a week, the ladies and gentlemen who had attended the theatre were allowed admission to the queen's ante-rooms. The first of the performances was on Saturday evening, January 11, and the queen paid a short visit to the company present; on the following Monday there was a *Cour.*

Arrangements for securing the safety of the royal family were also made in the capital. The palace

* When the well known Baron Grimm, some years after the palace revolution of 1772, requested Reverdil to give him a description of Struensee, he answered him, "Tacitus has drawn it for us," and read the baron the following passage from the ANNALS:—" Poor, unknown, and restless, he managed by secret machinations to satisfy the malicious temper of the prince, and ere long he brought every celebrated man into danger. Thus he attained power with one but hatred with all, and furnished an example how rich men are made poor, and despised men grand, by which he entailed first the ruin of others and then his own."

6 *

guard was doubled, a double cavalry post was drawn up at each entrance to the palace, and in front of the *corps de garde*, and day and night pickets of cavalry, with drawn sabres, patrolled the streets.

At the same time, the most fabulous reports were spread. It was declared that the garrison and the whole army, especially the artillery, had received private instructions, and had been supplied with many rounds of cartridge. Their hatred of the cabinet minister caused even sensible persons to credit the most absurd reports; among others, the invention that the king was going to abdicate, and the queen be declared regent during the minority of her son. Even the letter S, set in diamonds, affixed to the cap of Struensee's running footman, gave rise to the most disquieting explanations. In a word, such a violent and general fermentation prevailed in the capital, that it must lead to the worst, if a leader could only be found. For, though Struensee's enemies were so numerous, they as yet had no nucleus round which to gather. A fervent hatred of the minister filled all hearts, but fear kept the bitterness in check: they shouted and roared, but obeyed the authority, until the right leaders were found in the higher circles. These persons were Queen Juliana Maria, the hereditary Prince Frederick Guldberg, the prince's private secretary, Count Rantzau-Ascheberg, Colonels von Eickstedt and Von Köller, and the serviceable Beringskjold.

Juliana Maria and her son had long felt insulted by the seclusion in which they were kept, but the lady

had been very careful to keep her sentiments concealed.
She was described by her foes as an ambitious and blood-
thirsty woman: other writers, however, among them
the excellent Reverdil, declare that she was more sinned against than sinning.   Even the way employed to
draw her into the plot against the favourite, was of a
nature to deceive even a more sensible woman.   In
order to secure her adhesion, a paper was shown her containing a full account of the court plot: January 28
was the day fixed for the king's abdication, and the
appointment of Matilda as regent, and Struensee as protector.   The elder Struensee was said to have drawn
up the deed of abdication; and in order that no proof
might be wanting, a copy of this plan, *which never existed
in the original*, was allowed to fall into the hands of
Suhm, who was known to be a red-hot Dane.   This
copy he at once sent to Juliana Maria, and employed
the following argument to persuade her :—

" There was no time to be lost; for the man who
meditated usurping the regency ere long, would not
hesitate before a further crime.   The death of the
king assured him the couch of Queen Matilda, and the
prince royal, either immolated, or succumbing beneath
the rigours of his education, would make way for his
sister, the too manifest proof of their adulterine
amours.   For what other motive had Struensee revoked the law which prohibited a repudiated wife from
marrying the accomplice of her infidelity?" *

* Reverdil, p. 329.

Prince Frederick was not naturally bad hearted; but being as weak in mind as he was crippled in his person, he entirely depended on his mother's will. The annoyance of these two royal personages at their estrangement from court was notorious, and shared by many persons; but assuredly by no one so much as by Guldberg, who, as private secretary to Prince Frederick, was the confidant of both.

Owe Höeg Guldberg was born in 1731, at the town of Horsens in Jütland, where his father, who had failed in business, was sexton of the Town Church. The poor circumstances of his family rendered it necessary for him to obtain assistance while attending the Town Gymnasium, and he could not have continued his further studies, had not a well-to-do uncle helped him. After leaving school, he went to Copenhagen, but could not continue his studies for any length of time, for want of means. Hence he returned to Jütland, where he became a tutor, and employed his leisure hours in preparing himself for the university examination. In 1754 he passed the theological examination, and received a certificate of "haud illaudabilis;" after which he remained in Copenhagen, and turned author, although he devoted himself to religious subjects. The first book he published bore the title "Memoirs of a Converted Freethinker," and was an unmistakable allusion to such men as Struensee. Soon after he commenced a universal history of the world, which was not continued, however, as he be-

gun diligently studying the classics, which procured
him, in 1761, a professorship at the Sorö Academy, and
three years later the post of governor to the hereditary prince, who was then eleven years of age. Guldberg obtained the title of Etats-rath in 1770, about
the time when Struensee was appointed a councillor
of conference.

Guldberg was a man considerably below the middle
height. His forehead was lofty, and his nose aqui-
line: his eyes glistened sharply and expressively, and
round his lips there was a certain softness. The chief
expression of his face, however, was that earnestness
which is generally found in the countenances of piet-
ists. Another description of Guldberg* speaks more
decisively as to the true character of this leader of the
conspiracy against Struensee and Caroline Matilda.
According to this author, Guldberg's person was a
faithful copy of Fielding's Blifil, with the face of a
cat, and the glance of a fox. Twining and slippery
as an eel, crawling and submissive with higher persons, he was violent and coarse with subordinates.

Consequently, we may reasonably assume that it was
not so much Guldberg's devotion to his mistress as his
religious opinion of the mischief produced by Struensee's ministry and his national Danism, which urged
him to take a zealous but most cautious part in the conspiracy against the minister, for he was perfectly well

* By Jörgensen Jomton, a well-known literary man, and confidant of Christian VIII.

aware that his neck would be in danger if it failed. The most cautious of the coterie, and holding a high position, he had become the leader of the conspiracy, owing to his direct influence over the two royal participators in it.

As regards Rantzau-Ascheberg, whose character has already been depicted, we have only to say of him that he was now as angry with the Danish government, *i. e.*, Struensee, for his foiled expectations, as he had been with the Petersburg government. With extreme haughtiness he combined a permanent dissatisfaction with what existed, and a liking for extraordinary undertakings. In one respect he resembled Struensee: in decisive moments his courage broke down. Proud and ignorant, he appeared to believe that a noble descent and an arrogant manner must suffice to make him be regarded as a man of importance. He was utterly ignorant of the behaviour of an elegant and polished aristocrat. Naturally imperious and violent in everything he undertook, he seemed to regard reason and conscience as bugaboos to frighten children and weak-minded persons.

The fifth of the conspirators was VON KÖLLER, colonel of the Holstein infantry regiment. A partisan of Rantzau, he was one of the most important members of the conspiracy, because in his person he united all the qualities which are requisite to carry out revolutions coupled with high treason. A bold, though coarse soldier, urged by unbridled ambition, and

equally passionate in temper, he was at the same time
an impudent boaster, had an imposing person, and the
strength of an athlete.*

Brevet Major-General HANS HENRY VON EICKSTEDT
commanded the regiment of Seeland dragoons which
had taken the place of the disbanded Guards. Like
Köller, he was a native of Pomerania, whence his ancestors came to Denmark toward the end of the seven-
teenth century, and purchased several estates in Holstein. Eickstedt bought himself a regiment, which
was possible in the Danish army at that day, and, on
the accession of Christian VII., he was appointed colonel and chief of the above-mentioned dragoon regiment. He was considered a worthy man but of rather
limited intellect, which was probably the reason why
it was proposed to put him on half-pay in 1771; but
Falckenskjold, who knew his value in an administra-
tive capacity, prevented his dismissal. When the Seeland dragoons were ordered to Copenhagen, and to do
duty at the palace, Eickstedt believed he had a claim
for promotion, and as his request was not acceded to,
he joined the malcontents.

When the proposed conspiracy was hinted to him,
Eickstedt, who up to this time had been unknown by
the court and the nobles, and to whom this opportunity of playing a distinguished part appeared like a

* Struensee is reported to have said of Köller: "He looks as if he had no
mother, but was brought into the world by a man. Something innate in him
stamps him ruffian."

dream, was so raised above the sphere of his usual thoughts by the mere idea of being able to do a queen a service, that he was unable to reflect over the consequences of the commission entrusted to him. He blindly obeyed the queen dowager's will, and promised to do everything that was asked of him.[*]

The seventh in rank among the conspirators was the Commissary-General of War VON BERINGSKJOLD, who had been an acquaintance of Rantzau in Petersburg. His baptismal name was Magnus Bering; he was born in 1720, the son of a tradesman at Horsens, and was descended from Vitus Bering, the celebrated circumnavigator in the Russian service. The daughter of this seafarer, who was said to be married to Councillor of Chancery Lüxdorph, was raised to noble rank.

After Magnus Bering had studied for awhile at Copenhagen, he established himself as a colonial merchant, but soon became bankrupt, and cheated a poor student out of his entire fortune. As Bering was prosecuted for this, he escaped to Germany, entered the imperial service, and was ennobled, in 1753, by the Emperor Francis I. by the name of Beringskjold. He then proceeded to Petersburg, where he set up as a merchant again, and at the same time performed the part of a Danish spy. During his residence in the latter city the overthrow of Peter III. was decided on, and, as we have already seen, he and Rantzau took part in that sanguinary event. The emperor's murder

* "Authentische Aufklärungen," p. 152.

had been scarce accomplished ere Beringskjold set out at once for Copenhagen with the most agreeable news for the Danish court, and for his good tidings received a pension and the post of commissary-general.

Shortly after, Beringskjold purchased the royal domain of Nygaard, the present Marienborg, on the island of Möen, but, as he was unable to raise the sum of 10,000 dollars when the time arrived for a payment on account, he was dispossessed of the estate again. This fatality forced him to return to Copenhagen, where he renewed his old acquaintance with Rantzau, and willingly joined the conspiracy against Struensee, as he was always ready for intrigues and spying services.*

At the first glance, we might consider it an historical enigma that men like these five could succeed in carrying out in a few hours a thorough revolution, and that no other acts of violence should take place, save the immediate revolting ill-treatment of the three persons selected as victims. For us, however, it is no riddle. We are acquainted with Struensee's incaution: the hatred which the clerical party entertained for him: the detestation of the Danes: the numerous foes he had in the army and navy and the officials; in a word, his utter isolation. Struensee himself said, after his fall, that he had no other friends but the weak king and queen; and as, in spite of the numerous warnings that had been given him, he could not resolve to take

* " One Beringskjold, an infamous, abandoned wretch, capable of every crime or villany, and whom fame declares to be the man who put Peter, the late Emperor of Russia, to death."—*N. W. Wraxall's Private Journal.*

the necessary precautions for his ministry and his person, he positively offered the conspirators an opportunity for overthrowing him.

The greatest activity in this respect was displayed by the most notorious of the conspirators, Von Beringskjold. Well trained at Petersburg, he was fully aware that palace revolutions could not be carried out without military assistance. He it was that played the principal part in gaining over Von Eickstedt, and laid all the plans for inducing Maria Juliana to place herself at the head of the conspiracy. He found the proper person to effect this in Jacob Jessen, ex-valet of Frederick V., who was now living on a pension, but was at the same time purveyor of wines to the queen dowager. In October, 1771, Beringskjold went to this man, and mentioned, in the course of conversation, how opposed Struensee's government was to the *Lex Regia* and the laws of the country, that universal dissatisfaction prevailed in consequence, and that evil might be apprehended. When Jessen refused to believe the last statement, Beringskjold invited him to come to his house at ten o'clock the following morning, as Colonel von Eickstedt would then be with him. Jessen could remain hidden, and listen to the conversation with Eickstedt, by which he would most assuredly be convinced that a plan existed to overthrow Struensee.

Jessen appeared at the appointed hour, and heard that, beside Von Eickstedt, Colonel von Köller was

also present. The gentlemen expressed their deter-
mination to overthrow Struensee, and the two colonels
reckoned on the support of their regiments and of the
artillery in doing so. A few days after, Colonel Eickstedt sent the ex-valet a message, through Beringskjold,
to grant him an interview, which was to take place at
the rooms of the latter. Jessen went, and the colonel
proposed to him to go quietly to Fredensborg—where
the queen dowager and her son were residing at the
time—and inform them that an insurrection against
Struensee was being prepared, for which he (Eickstedt), Colonel Köller, and other gentlemen had drawn
up the plan. The queen and hereditary prince were
invited to place themselves at the head of the anti-
Struensee party, in order by their authority to prevent the excited populace from committing excesses
on innocent persons.

The queen dowager had already been fully prepared
for the event by the forged document shown her by
Suhm. She consulted with Guldberg, and declared her
willingness to accept the proposal made to her. The
party of the queen dowager was thus organized. Valet
Jessen conveyed the good news to Copenhagen, and
there performed from time to time the part of nego-
ciator between the conspirators at Fredensborg and
those in the capital. In order to avoid notice, he
made his reports in writing, and addressed his letters
sometimes to his mother-in-law, the waiting-woman,
Jacobi, at others to his little daughter, Juliana Maria

Jessen, who was afterwards a celebrated poetess, and at that time was living with her grandmother.

When the queen dowager returned to Copenhagen in November, the secret meetings of her party were held at the house of Abildgaard, chaplain of the Holmenschurch, close to the palace, whose wife was a relation of Beringskjold. The rectory had two entrances, from two different streets, and Jessen, who was thoroughly acquainted with the ins and outs of the Christiansborg Palace, offered the conspirators the most valuable aid at these secret meetings. He was also thoroughly conversant with the private staircases that led in the palace from the queen's apartments to those of the king and Struensee, so that it was eventually an easy matter for the conspirators to cut off all communication between the three parties most interested, at the moment when they carried out their enterprise.

The outbreak of the conspiracy was settled for the night between January 16 and 17, 1772. On Thursday, the 16th, a *bal paré en domino* was given in the palace theatre at Christiansborg, to which all nine rank-classes were admitted.

The French Opera House, as the theatre royal was called, was most gorgeously decorated. Innumerable chandeliers and lamps displayed the rich gilding of the boxes, with their hangings of violet and silk. The pit, appropriated on other occasions to the spectators, was raised to a level with the stage, so that the whole formed one large hall; while a numerous orchestra

occupied the sides of the stage, which represented
a grove. In the background, a large bower, dimly
lighted with variegated lamps, led to some small late-
ral cabinets, hung with red damask, the rich decora-
tions of which—splendid mirrors, sparkling chandeliers, and gilt sofas—plainly showed that they were
destined for royal personages. A semicircular saloon
at the back of all closed the grand perspective, which
was doubled by the mirrors against the walls, for it
was the dressing-room of the theatre. A series of
spacious and splendid saloons occupied the rest of the
wing.

In the boxes, card-tables were arranged; the king
played at quadrille with General von Gähler, Frau
von Gähler, and Justiz-rath Struensee. The young
queen, however, seemed to be remarkably cheerful on
this evening; danced continually; and looked very
beautiful. A circumstance occurred which ought to
have attracted attention. The king, queen, and court
entered the ball-room at ten o'clock; but Prince Frederick, contrary to his usual custom, and, in some
measure, contrary to the respect due from him to
their Majesties, did not arrive till more than an hour
later. His countenance was flushed, and his dis-
ordered looks revealed the agitation of his mind.
As soon as he came, the queen advanced to him, and
said playfully:

"Vous venez d'arriver bien tard, mon frère, qu'avez
vous?"

"C'est que j'ai eu des affaires, madame," he replied.

"Il me semble," the queen remarked, gaily, "que vous auriez mieux fait de penser à vos plaisirs qu'à vos affaires, pendant une soirée de bal."

The prince made little or no reply, and the conversation ended.

Köller was even more impudent. While playing at cards, Struensee went up to him and said: "Are you not going to dance?" To which Köller made answer: "No, I shall play a little longer; but my hour to dance will arrive presently."[*]

Courtiers and officials were still longing to read a kindly glance on the face of the omnipotent minister; and even the pious hypocrite, Guldberg, was present, for the first time in his life, at such an entertainment. Of the foreign envoys, Colonel Keith was the only one present. The king and queen and their nearest intimates supped together in a box, while Prince Frederick was left to get his supper at a buffet like the meanest of the guests. Curiously enough, Reverdil had interceded for the prince on the previous day, and begged Brandt to admit him to the king's table, but it was refused. Reverdil was much affected, for he was ignorant that the measure was full, and that one act of insolence more or less was of no consequence.

The king retired at midnight; but the queen continued dancing till nearly three o'clock. The company soon followed; and the two last persons who remained

---

[*] "Mémoires de mon Temps," p. 60.

in the ball-room were Brandt and the Countess von
Holstein, his mistress. They were engaged in conversation, when Le Texier, the master of the revels, went
up to Brandt, and said:

"Every one is gone, and I must order the lights to
be put out."

"I will give directions to that effect," Count Brandt
replied; "leave it to me."

A singular fatality seems to have attended the queen
and her friends. In order to seize so large a body of
men, many of whom it was unquestionable would
resist if they were not taken by surprise and sepa-
rately, it was necessary to attack them singly and
alone. The Countess von Holstein had invited a select party of ladies and gentlemen, among whom were
Struensee and Brandt, to drink tea in her apartments
after the conclusion of the ball. If this party had
taken place, it would have frustrated the plans of
the queen dowager and her son. They would, probably, have considered it too dangerous to attack
several of the first men in Denmark, collected together in one room, who were capable of resistance,
and might either have escaped or defended themselves
successfully. In such an attempt, the royal palace,
where the principal among them were lodged, must
have been rendered a scene of blood and horror. But
one of the ladies who was invited, Frau von Schimmelmann, having a violent headache, excused herself;
Frau von Büllow, unwilling to go without her friend,

made her excuses likewise; and the Countess von Holstein, being the only female remaining of the party, it was abandoned.

In the meanwhile, the preparations for carrying out the plan of the conspirators were being made very silently. The grenadier company of Colonel Köller's Holstein regiment had the guard, on this day, at the palace, together with a troop of the Seeland dragoons, commanded by Von Eickstedt. The military charge of the palace was, consequently, confided to two of the accomplices. At nine in the evening, Colonel Eickstedt entered the stables of the *corps de garde*, and inquired of the stable-sentry whether Lieutenant Schlemann, the officer of the day, was in his room.

" Yes," the dragoon answered; "does your excellency wish me to call him?"

" No," the colonel said at first, so as not to betray the fact that he had solely come to speak to this officer. But after pretending to remember something, he turned again to the sentry, with the remark:

"By the way, you can tell the lieutenant that I am here."

Soon after, the lieutenant came down into the stable from the officers' guard-room.

" I see," the colonel addressed him, "that all your horses are saddled. Have you received orders to that effect?"

" No, I did it on my own responsibility," the lieutenant replied. "I was afraid lest the mob might

employ this evening in making unpleasant riots, and
hence I wished to be in readiness to move at once.
Still, if you command it, I will give the order to un-
saddle."

As Eickstedt naturally did not desire this, but was
quite satisfied with the lieutenant's precaution, he ordered the latter to keep all the horses saddled throughout the night.   After the lieutenant had accompanied
his commanding officer to the gates, he was about to
retire, but Eickstedt gave him a nod, and whispered
to him to come to his apartments precisely at half-past
three in the morning; he would then find the door
open, but must not pass Colonel Falckenskjold's quarters, or drop a word to a single being of what he
(Eickstedt) had just intimated to him.

The entire plot, however, all but failed owing to
Rantzau's vacillation.   This man, upon whose courage,
fidelity, and secrecy no reliance could be placed, determined not only to withdraw his assistance from the
party in which he had enlisted, but to reveal the whole
conspiracy.   At eight o'clock on the evening before
the ball, he drove to the house of Justiz-rath Struensee.
When he was told here that the Justiz-rath had not
yet returned from a dinner party, he urged the servant
to inform his master directly he returned home that
Count Rantzau desired a visit from him as soon as
possible.   The count had hardly driven away, when
the Justiz-rath arrived, and the servant delivered the
message.

7 *

" The count is always in such a hurry about trifles," the minister's brother answered, " that the visit will safely keep till to-morrow morning."

He therefore deferred the visit, and dressed himself for the masquerade ball.

An apparently so insignificant occurrence decided the happiness and existence of numerous persons and the fate of the whole monarchy for twelve long years!

Rantzau went home, and sent to tell Colonel Köller that an attack of gout prevented him from keeping his appointment as agreed. In order to support the deception, he even had his feet wrapped up in flannel. The count resided in a royal mansion called the Palace, separated from Christiansborg by a ditch. The conspirators were in a state of great alarm, and sent off Beringskjold to the count. When Rantzau appealed to the state of his feet, the envoy suggested a sedan-chair, and on the count still persisting, he delivered the ultimatum from Köller that he would have him fetched by grenadiers if he did not come. This threat was effectual, and Rantzau appeared at the meeting-place, being conveyed to it by two grenadiers of the guard in a chair.

The ball was over at about half-past two, and profound silence prevailed in the palace. The conspirators alone did not sleep.

The two commandants, Eickstedt and Köller, took care that the garrison and palace guards should be held in readiness for any event. When Lieutenant

Schlemann kept his appointment with Colonel von Eickstedt, he found there Von Rönpstorff, the major of the regiment, who had several lieutenants awakened. When these officers arrived, Eickstedt lighted a candle, placed it under the table, and read to the meeting by this mystic illumination an order signed by the queen dowager and the hereditary prince.

This usurped order from persons who, in spite of their royal position, had not the slightest right to command the garrison troops, was to the effect that the king, having been hitherto surrounded by several bad people, the two exalted signers of the secret order commanded Colonels von Köller and Von Eickstedt to seize on the same night the Counts Struensee and Brandt, and several other persons named, and also to place the commandant, Major-General von Gude, under arrest. In this way the two chief actors secured the perfect fidelity of all the persons connected with them. After Eickstedt had read this precious document, which was drawn up by Guldberg, he warned the officers to be on the watch, and promised them to be himself at the spot where the greater danger was. He ordered the officer of the dragoon picket to have the horses bitted in the greatest secrecy, to advance at half-past three in the morning, to occupy all the entrances, and to allow no one to go in or out. He must try at first to keep them back politely, but if kindness did not avail, he must employ violence, if necessary, in effecting this.

About the same hour, Colonel Köller went the
rounds of the city guards, and took the officers of the
day with him to the captain's guard-room at the palace.
Here he stated to them that he had received orders to
arrest Counts Struensee and Brandt and several others,
and that he felt assured of having their aid in doing
so, if he required it; after which the officers returned
to their posts.

Everything was perfectly quiet in the palace, when,
at four o'clock A.M., the hereditary prince, Guldberg, Rantzau, Eickstedt, Köller, and the ex-valet
Jessen, assembled in the rooms of the queen dowager.   After Guldberg had shortly repeated here
all they had arranged, and offered up a prayer, the
conspirators, guided by Jessen, went along dark passages to the king's apartments, forced their way into
the bedroom of the valet Brieghil, aroused him, and
induced him to follow them.   As they found the right
entrance to the king's sleeping apartment locked, they
were obliged to go round by the secret staircase.
Brieghil went in front, and behind him came Guldberg,
carrying a candle in each hand.

When Juliana Maria, surrounded by her companions,
approached the king's bed, the latter woke, sprung up
with a start of terror, and asked, timidly, on seeing so
many persons assembled in his bedroom in the middle
of the night, what they wanted with him? The queen
dowager replied :

" My son, your Majesty, do not be frightened. You do not see us here as enemies, but as your true friends; and we have come——"

Here she began to shed abundant tears. Rantzau had agreed to be spokesman, but now held back, and Köller was obliged to thrust him forward. Thus forced, he at length said to the king that his Majesty's mother and brother had come to liberate him and the country.

After this, the stepmother went up to the bed, embraced the king, and repeated what Rantzau had just said. Almost fainting from terror, the poor weak king asked for a glass of water, and when he had drunk it, merely remarked that Rantzau had told him Eickstedt was there too. The latter stepped forward and confirmed Rantzau's statement, with the addition that the people were in a state of revolt, for a design was being carried on against his Majesty and his government, in which Struensee and the queen were the leaders.

When Christian heard the name of Matilda, he refused to place any credence in the affair, but Juliana Maria assured him of the truth, and Guldberg confirmed it. Rantzau then pulled out of his pocket the orders already drawn up, and laid them before the king to sign, upon which Christian exclaimed:

" My God! this will cost streams of blood!" Rantzau answered:

" Your Majesty may be of good cheer; with the help of the Almighty, I take everything upon myself, and will, as far as possible, prevent danger."

Pen and ink were produced, and the weak king was induced to sign two orders, whose contents his step-mother explained to him. By the first, Eickstedt was made a major-general and commandant of the city; by the second, Eickstedt and Köller received full powers to take all the measures necessary for the preservation of the king and the country.

After the king had signed these documents while still in bed, and the hereditary prince countersigned them, the former expressed a wish to get up. When he was dressed, the queen dowager, her son, and Guldberg led the king to the prince's apartments. Here he remained for some hours, and they were employed in inducing him to write a note to his consort, from Juliana Maria's dictation, which contained the following absurd words :—

" Comme vous n'avez pas voulu suivre les bons conseils, ce n'est pas ma faute, si je me trouve obligé de vous faire conduire à Kronenbourg."

After this, the king signed fifteen different orders, drawn up by Guldberg, which decided the fate of no less than seventeen persons. These were in turn: Count Struensee, Count Brandt, Professor Struensee, Lieutenant Struensee, Chamberlain Colonel von Falckenskjold, Lieutenant-General von Gähler, Frau von Gähler, Major-General Gude, Lieutenant-Colonel von

Hesselberg, Equerry Baron von Bülow, Rear-Admiral
Hansen, Etats-rath Willebrand, Lieutenant Abö, Cabinet Secretary von Zoëga, the Intendant Martini, and
Panning, Count Struensee's private secretary.   When
this was completed, the king, animated by the sweet
thought of doing injury, by the flattering idea of being
delivered from Brandt for ever, and by the remote
hope of shedding blood, spent the rest of the morning
in drawing up the requisite orders. Those which concerned the queen, such as the · order to Rantzau to
arrest her, another to the commandant of Kronborg,
where she was to be taken, and the order to the intendant of the court to provide the carriages, the king
copied himself from Guldberg's minutes; the others he
merely signed.*

While all this was going on in the royal apartments,
Eickstedt placed himself at the head of a troop of dragoons in order to inform all officers on duty of his
new dignity, strengthened the palace guard with forty
gunners, and then had all the gates of the fortress
closed.†

* Reverdil, p. 336.

† In giving the above account, I have principally followed the reports of the
party favourable to the queen dowager, except in those cases where a bias was
evident.   The fullest account will be found in the "Memoiren von Köller
Banner;" but I have also inserted numerous bits from pamphlets, though I
did not deem it necessary to quote my authority in each case.

CHAPTER V.

SHARING THE SPOIL

IMMEDIATELY after the signature of the orders, Köller delightedly offered his services in the odious task of arresting Count Struensee. Followed by Captain Malleville, Lieutenants von Eyben and Frank, and a number of soldiers, he proceeded to the rooms occupied by the favourite on the Mezzanine. Before he entered the bedroom, he made the captain promise to kill Struensee in the event of himself (Köller) being shot. But this precaution proved to be quite unnecessary.

On seeing the intruder, and hearing that he had orders to arrest him, Struensee asked him if he knew to whom he was speaking, and to whom he was intimating this command. The colonel replied:

"Yes; I know very well who you are. You are a

count and a cabinet minister; but now you are my prisoner."

Struensee requested to see the royal warrant, but as Köller did not possess this, he said:

"I cannot show you any written order; but I am answerable with my head that the order to arrest you was given me by the king."

Still, the count refused to surrender; so Köller placed his sword-point against his chest, and said very seriously: "I have orders to take you either dead or alive." Struensee sank back, fainting, on a sofa. When he recovered, he asked for a cup of chocolate, which was refused him. The colonel advised him to make haste and get out of the palace before daybreak, as otherwise he could not protect him against the infuriated populace.

Moved by these arguments, Struensee proceeded to dress himself, and was so unprepared for the event, that he only had the masquerade dress which he had so recently taken off. He was obliged, therefore, to put on the pink domino breeches, but was allowed to take his furs, as the weather was bitterly cold. Bound hand and foot, the late omnipotent minister was dragged to a coach, and conveyed, under a powerful escort, to the citadel. As he got into the coach, he groaned, "Great God, what crime have I committed?" When he got out of the coach again, he requested that a trifle might be given the driver, and Köller handed the latter a dollar. The driver expressed his thanks, but said, in good Danish, "I would have done it for nothing."

Struensee was then conducted to the commandant of the citadel, in whose presence he cursed terribly, till he was ordered to be silent. He was taken by the commandant's orders to the cell in which a notorious pirate of the name of Norcross had been confined for a long time. On entering it, he opened his eyes very wide, and said to the officer, "Where are my valets?" The answer was, "I did not see any of your valets following you." "But my secretary?"—"He is not here either." "I must have my furs; confound it, it is cold here, and I have no wish to be frozen to death." On seeing a wretched wooden chair, he exclaimed, "What is the meaning of this chair? bring me my sofa." The officer replied, with a frosty look, "There is nothing at your service here, sir, but a night commode." On receiving this answer the prisoner burst into an awful rage, and ran with his head against the wall to dash out his brains; but the watch prevented his design. On the commandant being informed of this, he ordered Struensee to be laid in chains, which hurt him more than all the other treatment, and he passionately cried, "I am treated *en canaille.*"[*]

The simultaneous arrest of Count Brandt was confided to a turncoat and now zealous accomplice of the

---

[*] These curious details are derived from a scarce pamphlet, "Leben, Begebenheiten und unglückliches Ende der beiden Grafen Struensee und Brandt, 1772" (no imprint).

conspirators, Colonel von Sames, ex-commandant of
Copenhagen.   Formerly an admirer of Struensee, he
had joined the minister's enemies after his own en-
forced retirement to make way for Major-General von
Gude, and was now anxious to regain the favour of
the new government.   Accompanied by a guard, he
crept to Brandt's apartments, but found the door
locked.   On Sames threatening to burst it open with
the butt-ends of muskets unless it were opened to
allow him to execute a royal order, Brandt at length
turned the key, but met the intruders with his drawn
sword.   When the guard, however, made preparations
to disarm him, he threw his sword away, remarking:

"This must be a mistake.   I am a minister of state,
and have committed no crime for which I can be arrested."

The officer observed that it was no error, and begged
him to yield.   He did so, with the words: "Eh bien,
monsieur, je vous suivrai tranquillement."

He was also conveyed to the citadel in a coach; and
on entering the quarters of the commandant, said to
him:

"Do not be angry, sir, at my disturbing you at so
early an hour."

"Not at all, sir," the commandant replied; "we
have been expecting you here for a long time."

After this, Count Brandt walked up and down the
room several times; looked about him; hummed an
Italian air; and at length said:

"On my soul, there are fine apartments in this castle;" to which the commandant replied, with very bloodthirsty humour:

"Yes, sir; but you will have an opportunity of seeing finer ones."

A few minutes after, Brandt's cell was shown him. It was very dark; and, on entering it, he said good-humouredly to his companions: "On my word, the commandant spoke the truth." Even though chained like Struensee, Brandt retained his firmness; amused himself with playing the flute; and generally showed a much sturdier character than the wretched Struensee.

After the new city commandant, Von Eickstedt, had provided for the safety of the king, and given his commands at the main guard, he rode, accompanied by Colonel von Arnsdorff and a lieutenant, at five o'clock in the morning, to the new barracks, for the purpose of arresting Colonel von Falckenskjold and his friend, Lieutenant-Colonel von Hesselberg, who were quartered there. After entering the colonel's room, Eickstedt awoke him, and expressed his regret at being forced to arrest a brother officer; then he read aloud his own appointment as commandant, and the warrant, and handed Falckenskjold the papers for his inspection. The prisoner carefully examined the order, and the king and prince's signatures, and believed he had discovered that both the order and the signatures were in Eickstedt's own handwriting.*

* "Mémoires de Falckenskjold," p. 238.

Still, we can hardly think that the conspirators would have ventured upon such audacity; but it may be fairly assumed that the signature of the king, who was frightened to death, was as illegible as that of the counter-signer with the uneasy conscience. After Eickstedt had expressed some alarm about the temper of the regiment, with which their colonel was a great favourite, and Falckenskjold had calmed him, he quitted the colonel, leaving a lieutenant and a sergeant to guard him.

On January 21, at eleven o'clock at night, a major and eight or ten subalterns rushed into Falckenskjold's bedroom, made him get up, and transferred him to the navy prison, intended for the vilest criminals. The cell was reached by a narrow flight of stairs, and the interior was not more than ten feet square. An officer constantly remained with the prisoner, who was compelled to sleep on the boards. As he was not allowed any knives, he was obliged to tear his food with his fingers. At first, he was allowed to keep his tooth-powder and some tea; but shortly after, he was deprived of them, as they might be poisoned.

Eight days after, Falckenskjold was transferred to a large room, which it was impossible to warm, and stopped here for weeks, till he was brought before the commission of investigation, and his unhappy fate eventually decided.

While Eickstedt was carrying out his task, Major von Rümpstorff rode to the deposed town commandant in order to put him under arrest, and take away the keys of the fortress, which were delivered to the first bürgermeister, Matthiesen, as the victorious party placed no confidence in the chief president, Von Holstein. From this house, the major went to Justiz-rath Struensee, whom he also arrested, and conveyed to the citadel. At the same time, Professor Berger was also arrested by Lieutenant von Eyben. The remainder were placed under house arrest, and had sentries posted over them, with the exception of Von Bülow, whose word of honour not to leave the house was considered sufficient.

Colonel von Köller undertook the task of arresting Lieutenant-General Gähler and his wife. The latter jumped out of bed in her night-dress, and tried to escape by the back-stairs; but she found them invested by two dragoons, and she was removed, with her husband, to the citadel. Councillor of Legation Sturtz also stood on the lists of proscription, as a partisan of Struensee, but was not arrested till some time later, when he fancied himself too secure. The domestics of Counts Struensee and Brandt were put into the Blue Tower, which was usually employed as a debtors' prison.

It was half-past eight o'clock A.M., when all these imprisonments had been carried out. But the most revolting scene in this palace revolution had been going on, in the meanwhile, at the Christiansborg.

Supplied with the note in the king's handwriting,

and backed up by three lieutenants, Beck, Oldenborg,
and Bay, Count zu Rantzau-Aschcberg proceeded to
the apartments of the reigning queen, Caroline Matilda, entered the ante-chamber, and tried to get into
the bedroom, but found the door locked. The queen
was aroused by the disturbance, and summoned her
women. They hurried to her; and the queen saw
fear and terror in their faces.

"What is the matter ?" she asked ; but the
women were silent. She repeated the question, and
received the reply that Rantzau was in the ante-
room with several officers, and was asking admission in the king's name. The queen sprang out of
bed in alarm, and threw on a few articles of
clothing.

" Make haste and summon Struensee, he must come
directly," she ordered her women; but they replied
that the count had already been removed.

"Betrayed! lost! eternally lost!" the queen exclaimed, with an outburst of despair. "Well," she
continued, after a little reflection, "let them come in,
the traitors, I am prepared for everything."

When the doors were opened by the women, the
queen walked boldly toward the persons entering, and
asked them what they wanted. Moved by the young
queen's decided behaviour, Rantzau gave her a low
bow, then said that he had come by the king's order,
read her her consort's note, and handed it to her.
She took it, and read it through without displaying

any alarm; but then threw it disdainfully on the ground, and trampled upon it.

"Ha!" she said, "in that I recognise the traitors and the king."

Rantzau implored her to submit to the king's orders.

"Orders!" she exclaimed, contemptuously; "orders about which he knows nothing, and which the most shameful treachery has extorted from his imbecility. No, a queen does not obey such commands."

Rantzau looked serious, and said that his duty admitted of no delay.

"I will obey no orders till I have seen the king," the queen answered him; "let me go to him: I must —I will speak to him."

And she advanced some steps toward the door: but Rantzau stepped before her with heightened anger, and his entreaties became menaces.

"Villain!" the impassioned queen cried to him, "is that the language of a servant to his monarch? Go, most contemptible of men. Go, you are loaded with shame and disgrace, but I am not afraid of you."

These words from the dauntless young queen infuriated the haughty Rantzau, but he did not dare to carry out his ruffianly orders by seizing the brave princess: hence he gave his comrades an imperious glance to interfere. The boldest of the three advanced and seized the queen round the waist, but she tore herself away from him, shrieked for assistance as loudly as she could, and hastened along the passage to the

secret stairs; but her women held her back, and
said :

" Your Majesty cannot pass out, for all the doors
are guarded by sentries, and no one will listen to your
cry for help."

Left alone with four armed soldiers, and rendered
desperate by anger and shame, the unfortunate princess rushed to a window, tore it open, and was about
to hurl herself out, but an officer seized her round the
waist and held her back by force. Beside herself
with passion, she seized the impudent man by the hair,
and struggled with him alone, when another of the
officers had to assist his comrade against a defenceless
woman. She resisted him as well, and, though half
naked, continued the struggle with the courage of
despair, till she at length fell back in a fainting state.
Rantzau watched this scene with great gusto, and
when the women brought their mistress round again,
he ordered them to conduct her into an adjoining
room, and dress her, while he sent for Count von der
Osten, who might induce her to yield.

Although this practised diplomatist was acquainted
with all the facts of the conspiracy, he had refrained
from taking any active part in it. Now, however,
that he knew Struensee and Brandt were safe in the
citadel, he accepted Rantzau's invitation the more
willingly, because he at once saw that the revolution
could only be carried through by the queen's overthrow. By his quiet and sensible representations he

8 *

at length succeeded in persuading the now weeping queen to yield compliance.

Je n'ai rien fait : le roi sera juste," she said quietly, in the consciousness of her innocence; but then she became more impetuous, and declared to the count that she would not move a step from the spot unless she were allowed to take her children with her.   The diplomatist, however, succeeded in making her comprehend that the prince royal must not be removed, and the poor mother at length agreed that she would only take with her the little princess, whom she was herself suckling.*

At length the preparations for departure were completed, and Fräulein von Mösting, one of the ladies-in-waiting, came in to accompany the queen.   Rantzau and two officers followed their prisoner to the

* There are as many variations in the account of Caroline Matilda's arrest as there are writers on it, but I have mainly followed that of Prince Charles of Hesse, even passing over the " Private Journal" in its favour, for the following reasons :—First, Prince Charles was a friend of the queen dowager, and continued in the Danish service; hence he had every opportunity of bearing the correct details from some of the principal actors. On the other hand, Mr. Wraxall's informants were friends of the queen, and both already under arrest, so they could only repeat the affair at second-hand : and even though Mr. Wraxall was in Copenhagen so shortly after the occurrence, all Englishmen were regarded as spies, and I do not think he found any opportunity of hearing the exact facts from the chief conspirators. The two narratives, however, differ very slightly, and this is a confirmation of the correctness of the Landgrave's story, because Mr. Wraxall was informed by the queen herself of the whole details. Unfortunately, he delivered to George III. all the confidential papers and letters connected with the affair, and from this cause I am unable to say with certainty whether the " Private Journal" is based on the story of Caroline Matilda herself. Still, my grandfather was not the man to give up important papers and keep a copy of them, and I therefore believe that the narrative I have before me is drawn up from the statements of Bulow and Le Texier.

coaches held in readiness for her in the back yard of the palace. On the stairs, Rantzau offered her his hand to conduct her down, but she repulsed it with disgust, and exclaimed: "*Loin avec vous, traître! Je vous déteste!*" She then walked alone to the carriage, and entered it. Fräulein von Mösting seated herself by her side, and a bed-chamber woman opposite to her, but the fourth seat was occupied by Major von Carstenskjold,* of Eickstedt's dragoons, with his drawn sabre. In the second coach followed the nurse with the little Princess Louisa Augusta, and two of the queen's attendants. The carriages were guarded by thirty dragoons, and Queen Caroline Matilda bade an eternal farewell to her capital and her palace.

During the tedious journey to the fortress, the queen remained in profound sorrow, and did not utter a word: but when the coach drove through the gloomy archway into the yard of the fortress of Kronborg, she started up, and said in a lamentable voice: "Great God! it is all over with me. The king has deserted me!"

When she left the carriage and attempted to ascend the stairs, the unhappy queen's strength failed her, and she was carried up to a sleeping apartment, in order to be laid on a bed. On seeing the couch, however, she shrieked: "Away! away from here! There is no rest for the miserable, no rest for me any more!"

* A descendant of this officer accompanied the Princess Alexandra in her triumphal entrance into London. But this is only a further proof of the well-established fact that the whirligigs of time bring strange revenges.

She was seated in an easy-chair; heavy sighs burst from her oppressed bosom; her whole body seemed bowed down by the weight of sorrow, till at length she found tears to relieve her.

"Thanks, Heaven, thanks!" she fervently exclaimed; "that consolation comes from Thee, and it is the only one of which my enemies cannot rob me."

She heard her daughter's voice and flew to her.

"You, too, here! dear, innocent creature! Oh, in that case your poor mother is not utterly wretched."

And the queen clasped the child to her breast, and then seated it in her lap. Two days elapsed ere the unfortunate queen could be induced to take any food, and lie down on a bed; then, she gradually regained her calmness, and accepted her fate more patiently.

It seemed as if the victorious queen dowager studied every occasion by which she could humiliate her victim. Caroline Matilda was not even allowed to have the necessary clothes to appear with decency, and to prepare herself against the severity of the weather; she was conveyed to Kronborg not like a state prisoner, but with all the marks of contempt shown to the worst offenders. A queen, whose personal charms would have melted the heart of a ruffian, was scarcely allowed in this inhospitable fortress what is requisite to support nature, and not indulged with more conveniences in her apartments than those granted to the lowest criminals. She was treated, during the earlier part of her captivity, with great indignity by her unfeeling keepers

and an insolent soldiery, and confined in rooms which
would have hardly been allotted to her favourite dogs
in the days of her prosperity.*

After the queen dowager had been informed by
Von der Osten of the successful removal of Caroline
Matilda, the conspirators at once set to work com-
pleting the affair they had begun. In the first place,
it was considered necessary to make the king go
through a scene, which would convince him that everything that had been as yet effected, met with the
approval of the multitude.

The constant driving, and the galloping of dragoons
through the streets at an early hour, aroused attention
and apprehension among the townspeople: for the
conspirators had taken care that in the last days the
most dangerous rumours of attempts on the king's life
should be propagated. At length, the terrible events
of the last hours oozed out. The town captain, Treld,
appeared in the streets, and when he was asked what
was to be done, he answered: "What else, but shout

* The latest traveller in Denmark, De Flaux, gives us the following account
of Caroline Matilda's apartments at Kronborg:—"In a tower is a small oval
room, the windows of which are still lined with iron bars. It was here that
the queen was confined. I was shown the prie-dieu used by this unfortunate
princess. It was on the faded velvet that covered it that she rested her beautiful head. Who knows whether the spots on it were not produced by the
tears of despair she shed. Was it not while kneeling on this chair that she
heard the terrible sentence that sent her two friends to the scaffold, and herself
dishonoured to the Castle of Aalborg?" Mr. N. W. Wraxall, describing his
visit to Kronborg, says that the rooms which the commandant had the mercy
to give his prisoner were vast, unfurnished, hideous, bare walls; never warm
in July.

huzzah that everything has succeeded!"   The mob
now burst into an universal shout of "Long live
King Christian VII.;" and several voices were heard
applauding the queen dowager and Prince Frederick.
After this, the masses flocked to the palace, and at
10 A.M. the king, followed by his brother, stepped out
on the balcony, while the old queen showed herself at
the window in *négligée*.   The king waved his pocket-
handkerchief, and when the populace responded to
this salute by a deafening shout, he joined in, and
hurrahed to his dear people, who were offering him
such enthusiastic thanks for the heroic deed he had
just carried out.

A few hours later, the king, splendidly dressed, and
accompanied by his brother, entered a state-coach
drawn by eight white horses, and drove through the
city, to show himself to his people.   The throng was
so great, that the carriage could hardly pass, and many,
in their delight, proposed to take out the horses and
drag the king themselves.   They drove slowly through
all the principal streets: Prince Frederick had let
down the window on his side, seemed greatly delighted,
and bowed incessantly to the surging crowd, and the
windows crowded with ladies and gentlemen.   The
king, however, as usual, kept his window up, and
stared indifferently at the crowd: loud shouts of joy
were raised in all the houses which the royal procession
passed.   The ladies expressed their delight by waving
their handkerchiefs; some of them even pulled off

their caps and shook them in the air, in order to testify their enthusiasm at the incomparable felicity of seeing their beloved sovereign, who had escaped from the mighty peril with which he had been menaced by Struensee and Queen Caroline Matilda.

When the drive was over, and the king and prince returned to the Christiansborg, the whole victorious party had assembled at court, to offer their congratulations to the three royal personages on the successful overthrow of the " Cabal," as they deigned to christen the defeated party.   But the king only made his appearance in company for a moment.

After dinner the king, the old queen and the prince, went to the French play, where they all sat in the royal box, and were received with universal rejoicings when they entered.   The whole city was illuminated, the townspeople nearly all turned out in their Sunday clothes, salvoes were fired from the ramparts, rockets were discharged, and the whole population seemed drunk with joy.

But the people, once unchained, were not satisfied with mere rejoicings, and hence soon turned the seamy side of their character outwards.   The public regarded Esther Gabel, one of the queen's waiting-women, as Struensee's mistress.   This girl's father had purchased Count Schulin's house, situated in one of the most frequented streets, and by the cabinet minister's orders, and partly at his expense, it was said, had converted it into a public establishment for balls,

concerts, and assemblies, with a splendour hitherto
unknown in Denmark. Struensee's enemies, however,
spread a report that the minister had engaged fifteen
pretty English girls to wait on the guests, and the
portraits of these girls were hung up to attract the
visitors. Toward evening, when the streets were
crowded, a man, wearing a gold-laced hat, stopped in
front of this house, drew his sword, and shouted to
the people as he smashed the lamps: "This house,
the English b——, is given up." Scarce had this
man—it was Beringskjold—given these instructions,
when the mob rushed into the house, destroyed or
carried off all the furniture and valuables in it, and
smashed every pane of glass. In the upper floor of
the large building there still remained a portion of
Count Schulin's library, which was afterwards valued
at 8,000 dollars, and this now perished, or was stolen.
In the cellar was a large stock of spirits; the furious
mob naturally forced their way into it, drank what
they pleased, and then staved all the wine and rum
casks, so that they waded up to the ankles in liquor,
and afterwards it took a day and a half to pump the
cellar dry.

After these desperadoes had finished their barbarous
job, and had done damage to the amount of 40,000
species dollars, though without finding the fifteen English beauties, they attacked the "Jungfern Comptoire,"
which were scattered over the city, and employed for
improper purposes: in a few hours only the bare walls

remained of these houses, which were sixty in number. The unfortunate girls found in them were dragged into the streets by the hair or legs, and treated with the most cruel brutality.*

In order to check the mischief, the head of the police at once asked Eickstedt for dragoons to drive out the ruffians. But the court were of a different opinion. They were afraid that the interference of the military might entail loss of life, and they did not wish to overcloud so glorious a day as January 17 had been. Therefore, instead of the dragoons, a Herr von Bülow, page of Prince Frederick, was sent to the mob, with instructions to offer them the king's thanks for the devotion displayed toward his house upon the abolition of Struensee's despotism, and to promise that the king would henceforth reign to the general satisfaction, and especially remember the sailors. The king, however, ordered that every one should now go quietly home. But the envoy had scarce ended the first part of his address to the people, when Beringskjold shouted in a stentorian voice: "There, you hear, the king thanks you for destroying this —— house. So to work again!"

An attempt of the mob to get hold of Struensee's state-coach, which was valued at 6,000 dollars, was

* Reverdil adds to this fearful picture: "There was another house let to the Italian actress, and doubtless more impure than the others; but the people behaved more civilly here, and, wishing to treat it like the rest, ordered the girls to leave it first, *respecting in their persons the amusements of the king.*"

prevented by the palace guard.   The intention of destroying the house of the chief of the police was also foiled.   They had set to work about it, when a respected dockyard official forced his way into the mob and induced them to desist, by making himself responsible for this man's right sentiments.   It was not till the crowd made preparations to plunder the Mont de Piété that Eickstedt's dragoons dispersed them.   On the next day, patrols of the line, the bürger guard and the marines, paraded the streets, in order to prevent further excesses; and in the afternoon royal heralds rode about the city, announcing that the king thanked his people for the fidelity they had displayed, but had learned, to his displeasure, that their zeal had gone too far.   Hence he forbad any further excesses, and any one caught in the act might expect exemplary punishment.   With this the plundering certainly ceased, but the patrolling had to be continued for a whole week, before persons and property could again enjoy perfect security.   On January 23 a police order was issued that all those persons who held stolen property by purchase, or in any other way, must, under penalty of heavy fines, deliver the articles to the police officers, so that they might be returned to their rightful owners.

In the meanwhile the principal participators in the conspiracy had received their reward. Count von Rantzau-Ascheberg was requited for the brutality he had displayed toward Caroline Matilda, by his nomi-

nation as General-in-Chief of the Infantry and Knight
of the Elephant.   At the same time he was told that
the government undertook to pay his debts.

Major-General von Eickstedt and his Pomeranian
landsman, Von Köller, were promoted lieutenant-
generals, and decorated with the star of the Danne-
brog.   Köller was also offered naturalization, with the
name of an extinct illustrious noble family.   He replied that, being a Pomeranian gentleman, he esteemed
his own name as much as any other; but that, as he
intended to devote his life to Denmark, he consented
to adopt a name belonging to that country.   He was,
therefore, known henceforth as Köller-Banner.   He
was also created first aide-de-camp, with apartments in
the palace, and inspector of the king's chamber.*

Commissary-General von Beringskjold, who, in addition to his other services, had given the signal for
plundering, was rewarded with a chamberlain's key,
received a pension of 2,000 dollars, and was let off a
sum of nearly 40,000 species dollars, which he had
been unable to pay for the crown estate he had purchased in the island of Moën.   Of his two sons, the
elder was appointed page, with a salary of 1,000
dollars, while the younger was promised a captaincy
in the army.

All the officers of Eickstedt's and Köller's regiments, even Captain von Falckenskjold, the colonel's
brother, although he had been asleep during the arrest,

* Reverdil, p. 343.

gained one or two steps. Jessen, the ex-valet, who had played the go-between, received a gratification of 2,000 dollars, and was honoured shortly after by the title of councillor of justice. Major von Carstens-kjold, who with his drawn sabre had prevented any possible attempt at flight on the part of Caroline Matilda, from a coach surrounded by thirty dragoons, was made a lieutenant-colonel for his gallant conduct. Colonel von Sames, as he was overhead and ears in debt, received, as a reward for his altered sentiments, 10,000 dollars in cash. Lastly, Major von Rünp-storff, of the prince royal's regiment, was given his lieutenant-colonelcy for commanding the escort re-quired for the arrests.

It is not quite clear why at the same time the well-known artillery-general, Von Huth, was appointed a general of infantry. When, at the time of the Russian war, General St. Germain was summoned to Denmark as commander-in-chief of the army, he effected the retirement of Huth, because he was afraid of so scien-tific a rival. Huth, consequently, retired with a pen-sion of 2,000 dollars, and went home to Hesse. Under Struensee's government St. Germain had been recalled, but no satisfactory arrangement was made: the French general returned to Paris, and was there appointed minister of war. Immediately after, General von Huth was recalled to active service by the advice of the Landgrave Charles, with whom he was on very intimate terms; but he kept aloof from Struensee.

Guldberg, the chief councillor of the conspirators, was the only man who received no reward. But as this ostensible modesty was certainly purposed, it serves to throw light on the man who from this time governed Denmark for twelve years. He was certain of his influence, and consequently was in no hurry about personal distinctions. His clear understanding also told him, that an apparent disinterestedness would be of great advantage to him with the public.

CHAPTER VI.

THE NEW GOVERNMENT.

THE next care of the new government was the amusement of the weak-minded king, who was now a helpless tool in all matters connected with the administration. Juliana Maria proposed to him, in turn, various persons to take Brandt's place; but he continually answered " No " to all the names mentioned, until the queen dowager at last came to Von der Osten, the minister of foreign affairs. At this name the king exclaimed with pleasure, " Yes: I will have him." As this gentleman, however, did not feel at all disposed to exchange his pleasant post for the dignity of a companion to a half-childish monarch, but preferred the comforts of his own palace, Lieut.-General von Köller, Queen Juliana Maria's declared favourite, was ap-

appointed to the office. We do not know how the poor king liked this coarse soldier in the place of the polished Brandt, so intimate as he was with all the details of court life.

In order to acquire the best men of business for the new government, one of the nocturnal accomplices, Major Malleville, was sent to Privy Councillor Count Thott to invite him to take part once more in the business of the state, and a similar invitation was forwarded to Privy Councillor Schack-Rathlau and the Stifts-amtmann Scheel, who had both been removed by Struensee. The ex-premier, Count John Hartwig von Bernstorff, was also thought of: Carstens and Schumacher spoke in his favour, but Von der Osten and Rantzau were opposed to it, because both hated him. The matter was disposed of, however, by the two royal personages, who did not particularly like the count, and by Guldberg, who feared a dangerous rival in the practised statesman. Hence, neither Bernstorff nor Moltke was recalled; although among all the remaining candidates for office there was not one who possessed Bernstorff's experience in affairs of state. Conferenz-rath Shumacher was also reappointed private secretary to the king, while retaining his post as deputy in the Chancery.

On January 19, the first Sunday after Struensee's downfall, thanks were offered to Heaven from all the pulpits in Copenhagen and the vicinity for what had happened; and, of course, the sermons were filled with

all kinds of allusions to the overthrown godless government. On the following Sunday, the third after
Epiphany, there was, in obedience to a royal circular,
a general Te Deum in the churches of the capital, and
this afforded another excellent opportunity for again
insulting the fallen. Instead of offering up a prayer
of love and charity for the sinner, the clergymen only
spoke of the "fearful vengeance of the Lord upon the
godless people, as a cause for rejoicing and thanksgiving." Nor did they even spare her Majesty, who
was still reigning, but poured out the vials of their
wrath upon her, and were not ashamed to urge their
congregations "to hate and execrate the queen."

How great the bitterness of the clergy at the freedom
of religion granted in the hitherto strictly Lutheran
country by Struensee must have been, is proved more
clearly by the fact, that even the celebrated theologian
and converter, Dr. Münter, joined in their cry. "Godless men ruled over us," he said from the pulpit of the
palace chapel, "and openly defied God. They, to
whom nothing was sacred, either in heaven or on earth,
despised, ridiculed, and mocked the creed to which we
belong. They, doubtless, were meditating violent
measures, in order to secure themselves for ever. But
thanks be to God, that He did not yield us up as a
prey to their teeth: that He overthrew their faithless
and blood-thirsty schemes (for they could not have
been otherwise), and gave us tranquillity and peace
again, at the moment when murder and rebellion were

close at hand.   Our king, to whom access was entirely
precluded; for whose sacred person we often felt
anxious, because we knew in what hands he was; our
king is once more ours: we are again his people." *

It was in all probability this sermon which caused
Münter to be selected to hear Struensee's last confessions and attempt his conversion.

Still, almost immediately after the catastrophe, there
were respectable authors who dared unhesitatingly to
oppose the zealotry of the clergy, although this was
accompanied by double danger at the time. " Religion," so wrote one of them, " is employed as a cloak,
for the purpose of deceiving the nation about the events
that have occurred.   The bought voices of clergymen
who deserve punishment, mix up with praises of the
Supreme Being the evident lies of calumny.   Struensee
was to be held up as a regicide, and the deluded people
were expected to thank Heaven for saving the king
from a peril which had never existed."

But what could these isolated protests effect against
the fanatical fury of the priests in a time of universal
excitement, when not only the new governing party
gave their protection to the worst zealotry, but even
other respected men took the part of the revolution in
word and writing? Among all these men, none carried
matters so far as the well-known historian, Suhm, who

---

* This grand sermon was duly printed, and is lying before me, but I mercifully spare the reader further extracts. I may mention, however, that the
text was taken from St. Matthew, chap. viii. 1—13.

was chamberlain to the queen dowager. He published an open letter to the king, whose contents are an everlasting brand on the name of an otherwise esteemed literary man :—

"Long enough," we read in the beginning of this pamphlet, "have religion and virtue been trampled under foot among us; long enough have honesty and integrity been turned away from our frontiers. A disgraceful mob of low people had seized on the person of the king and rendered access to him impossible for every honourable man. He only saw and heard with their eyes and ears—while the country swam in tears, while the Danish land had become a name of shame, and men, when abroad, did not dare express that they belonged to it; while the rich were plundered, the sun of the royal house turned pale, and everything was given up to ignominious robbers, blasphemers, and enemies of humanity. And while all this was going on the king was cheerful and happy, in the belief that the welfare of his subjects was being promoted."

After a fulsome panegyric of the queen dowager and her son (of whom Suhm says in a foot-note: "Theologians will decide whether these names designate glorified angels or angels still living on earth"), the writer proceeds to thank all the patriots "who with firm intention helped to tear the bandage from the king's eyes which prevented him from seeing, who raised up the king and country again, risked their lives to save the land, and restored the king his true and legitimate power." After which effusion of gratitude the zealous chamberlain burst into fresh assertions: that it was the highest time for the work of salvation to be carried out, for the capital would perhaps have become within a few days the prey of the flames—one immense ruin; while Denmark and Norway might have been happy under a king who entertained the most fervent wishes for their welfare.

This famous rubbish terminated with a warning appeal to the king, " to let the blood of so many kings that flowed in his veins warm his heart, and make him look at his people himself. Thus Christian IV. and Frederick IV. had acted. But he must not allow himself to be persuaded by flatterers that he was already what those kings had been, but strive to become as they." Then came a tremendous flourish. " From God and your nation you have received the autocracy: you are, therefore, also responsible to God and the nation for the use you have made of this power. You must set bounds on your own might, by regarding God as possessing a higher authority than your own, and by choosing the worthiest man for your government: the most worthy you have in your brother.* You must mercifully chastise those who have some claim to be treated graciously, but punish justly and without mercy the men who have dishonoured the

* This lad was but seventeen years of age, and nothing was known as yet of his capacity.

king and the country. . . . You ought to fear God, love your people, take the government into your own hands, and believe your brother."

One more passage, and I will close this pamphlet.

"Who would not praise and esteem that dangerous but honourable night! Future Homers and Virgils will sing its praises, and so long as there are any Danish and Norwegian heroes left, the glory of Juliana Maria and Frederick will endure, but cannot be augmented, as that is impossible. Sooner shall the world fall into nothingness than their glory pass away."

In such a fashion as this, an otherwise honourable and educated man ventured to address his monarch, to heap up the heaviest charges and most manifest insults on men who were imprisoned but not yet sentenced, and even went so far as to urge on the sovereign who would decide their fate the inhuman request that he should mercilessly punish them. For all that, this public letter was praised by the majority as a proof of patriotic zeal, and of worthy liberality; and Counts Bernstorff and Von Reventlow even thanked the author in writing for his patriotic deed.

Probably encouraged by praise from such high quarters, the same author issued shortly after a second pamphlet, bearing the title, "To my Countrymen: Danes, Norwegians, and Holsteiners." In it he declared that it was only a reasonable feeling "if everybody hated Struensee and desired vengeance upon him; for all the nations of Europe would regard a people that allowed itself to be governed by a Struensee, as a vile and cowardly people, and not call the man a barbarian who removed such a monster."

Justiz-rath Langebeck, keeper of the archives, a well-known historian, also accused Struensee in a pamphlet, "Liberal Thoughts on the Day of Requital," of the most scandalous things, and at the same time abused the fallen party in a truly Danish fashion, selecting his complimentary titles from the infernal regions and the entire animal kingdom, calling them sometimes murder-fiends and firebrands of hell; at others, goats, apes, brute beasts, wolves, tigers, &c. "But Julianna Maria's renown would last to the end of time, and far, far surpass that of Semiramis."

A third sample of the literary cynicism prevailing at that time in Denmark was supplied by Etats-rath Tyge Rothe, ex-tutor of the hereditary prince, whom Struensee had appointed, in the first place, burgomaster, and then deputy of the finances. In a poem, bearing the title of "On the Day of January 17, 1772," which was published by order of the government, we read: "In later times the fury against divinity had been truly Pharaonic, and persons wallowed in Caprean pleasure;" but "those men of fine mind and cool courage, possessed of strength and fiery souls—they, O people, prepared this festival for you." By such flattering terms the writer alluded to men like Rantzau, Eickstedt, Köller, and Beringskjold.

A multitude of anonymous pamphlets flooded town and country, such as "Thanksgiving of the twin Kingdoms," "Evening Thoughts upon the 17th of January—a Day so memorable for both Kingdoms," "The Hymn of Victory of the Copenhagen Citizens," "The Joy of the Israelites at their Liberation from the Claws of Haman," &c. In all these miserable pamphlets Struensee was represented as "the great northern thief," "Apollyon, or the great dragon," "the ex-barber and traitor," whose crimes and misdeeds were so horrible that they "could not be sufficiently punished by blows, or by sulphur, tar, or the executioner's sword."*

The amusements of the court were in no way interrupted by the events that had occurred, although the previous behaviour had been discovered to be so godless. Accompanied by his brother, or, speaking correctly, under his charge, the weak-minded king took frequent drives through the streets of the capital to Frederiksberg, and to the island of Amack; and as a great deal of snow had just fallen, sleighing parties were got up. The queen dowager, also, often drove

* Among other insults to Struensee, may be mentioned his portrait being placed in the shops, with the following couplet, containing a reference to his name, beneath it :—

"Sic regi mala multa Struensee an perdidit ipse,
Jam victus claustris, qui modo victor erat."

Which, for the benefit of the ladies, may be translated: "Thus the man who prepared much evil for the king destroyed himself; and he now lies in prison, who was shortly ago lord of all."

to Frederiksberg, in order to enjoy her authority in the apartments of her overthrown rival.

As early as January 23, there was a state dinner and ball at the Christiansborg, and a *Cour* on the following day. These festivals were numerously attended, but especially that on January 29, the anniversary of the king's twenty-third birthday. In addition to the three royal personages, only twelve selected guests sat down to the banquet in the Rittersaal. After dinner the king proceeded with his suite to the palace theatre, where two new French vaudevilles* and a ballet were performed. At night there was a grand supper of seventy-five covers in the Rittersaal, to which the foreign envoys and the most distinguished of the nobility were invited. On the following day there was a masked ball at the palace, and three days after a *bal paré*. The royal party did not stay away from any festivity, and it was evident that they wished, by these uninterrupted revelries, to convince the king of the universal feeling of joy at what had happened. For not only did the newspapers contain frequent accounts of the amusements at court, but the king appeared at the great city theatre to witness Danish performances, which was a most unusual event.

The two boys and the young negro girl, who had formerly constituted the domestic amusements of his most gracious Majesty, were, however, removed from

---

* The titles were *L'Ambitieux* and *L'Indiscret*, either by accident or through a vile eagerness on the part of the comedians.

the palace immediately after the downfall of Struensee and Brandt. Even the king's favourite dog, Gourmand, who had a carriage for his sole use when the king travelled and a lackey to attend him; who was served with food from the king's table, and was often fed by his royal master's hand—even this dog shared the fate of the favourites, and was returned to the nobleman who had presented him to the king.

Although there was an attempt at court to lead to the belief that nothing had happened, a certain uneasy apprehension began to be felt, when it was rumoured that the lower classes were beginning to grow dissatisfied, and an almost ludicrous occurrence at the royal theatre revealed to the public the fact, that at times a guilty conscience can induce even great personages to lose their countenance.

A few evenings after the eventful January 17, while the whole court were at the French play, there was a disturbance in the upper boxes, which continually increased, and was only augmented by those who tried to restore peace. One rumour followed the other, and in the end it was even stated that the convicts had broken prison and joined their friends and the sailors, for the purpose of creating a riot and an opportunity for plundering. This news ran like wildfire from box to box, through the pit and gallery, and all the audience, royal personages and court included, were in a fearful state of excitement. All began running to the doors, in order to get out and save

themselves.   The king, too, rushed from his box with
wild looks, the hereditary prince followed his example,
and the queen-mother tried in vain to keep them back,
until she, overcome by terror, fell in a fainting fit.
Similar scenes took place in the other boxes, and
fainting ladies might be seen everywhere.   The news
of the affair had reached the city by this time, and
curious persons collected round the theatre and tried
to force their way in against those who were pouring
out, until some cooler men discovered the origin of
the whole business.   A woman had taken her child
with her into the gallery, and the latter disturbed the
more immediate spectators by crying.   They began
quarrelling in consequence with the nurse, and in this
way a general disturbance was brought about in the
upper part of the playhouse.*

The confusion produced by this interlude caused
Bililke, the marshal of the court, to issue an order
on January 23, by which, in future, children would not
be allowed to be present at performances in the royal
theatre, and grown-up persons would only be admitted
on showing their tickets, to the amphitheatre, the pit-
boxes, and the second tier.   At the same time, he
warned all those who wished to visit the theatre to
behave themselves in the way which the presence of
the royal family dictated, and not to disturb the performances by loud talking or noise.   Any one who did

* " Authentische Aufklärungen," p. 271.

so must expect to be refused admission to the theatre
in future.

The alarm displayed by the three royal personages
and their intimate adherents in the theatre, had, however, been too great and too public for them to be satisfied with the above order.   Hence, police regulations
were made to prevent mobs and street riots.   The
masters were ordered to keep their apprentices at home
at night, or otherwise be responsible that no street
disturbance was produced by them.   Further, it was
prohibited to illuminate the houses henceforth on the
birthdays of the king and the prince royal.   The
order against sitting in pot-houses after ten o'clock,
which Struensee had revoked, was again established,
and everybody was warned against letting off guns and
pistols in the streets, shooting rockets, or throwing
crackers.   The city gates, which had been left open,
were now again locked at night, and this order was soon
after extended to the hours of divine service.   Lastly,
it was ordered that the passports of all persons leaving
the city must be issued by the Danish Chancery, and
all house owners were requested to give immediate
notice to the police of the arrival of strangers and
travellers.

The persecution of Struensee's adherents, and the
distribution of rewards among near and distant participators in the *coup d'état* were not interrupted by all
these matters, and several of the deposed officials were
again placed on active service.

On the days immediately following January 17th, arrests, reprimands, and dismissals occurred in rapid succession. On the 18th, Lersner, the master of the hounds, was arrested, and although he was released again soon after, it was with orders to quit Copenhagen and Danish territory within thrice twenty-four hours. He had hardly reached Roeskilde, when a government courier caught him up with orders to hurry his departure from the king's territory as much as he could.

The minister's younger brother, Lieutenant Struensee, was ordered to leave the Danish states with the same speed. As his name was his sole proven crime, and he was poor, he was given 200 dollars for his travelling expenses, and a pass as a law student, and he quitted Copenhagen at the same time as the master of the hounds. Five years after, he was permitted to reside with his parents at Schleswig, but on the condition that he must not show himself in the Danish portion of the kingdom. He afterwards received an appointment in Prussia, through the interest of his brother, the Justiz-rath, who eventually became the Prussian Minister of Finances.

Captain Charles Düval, of the Norwegian king's regiment stationed in Copenhagen, met with the same fate. As, however, he was able to prove his perfect innocence, he was recalled and given a company in the Borncholm regiment. As we have seen, Brandt employed him to engage actors in Paris for the king's playhouse; and he had been recommended to the cabinet minister as a trustworthy man. By what means the captain succeeded in cleansing himself from the stigma of trustworthiness to his late employer, is not known.

It excited attention that about the same time one of the conspirators received orders from the king to quit Copenhagen. This was the amply rewarded Beringskjold, who was commanded to select as his residence the little town of Wordingborg, at the southern extremity of Seeland, and was told that he must not leave it under the king's most serious displeasure. Ilis offence is stated to have consisted in calling the minister of foreign affairs, Von der Osten, a rogue, because he had intrigued against Chamberlain Kragh being removed from his office of governor of Laaland, so that Beringskjold might take his place. It is probable, however, that a motive of greater weight led to his banishment from the capital. As the reward he received in cash did not satisfy him, he spread a report that he had foiled the plan of excluding the king's children from the succession to the throne, and this statement of his was repeated to the people in authority. For the fact that the queen dowager at first entertained such plans in order to elevate her beloved son to the throne, is as certain as that Guldberg opposed them, for he was sensible enough to see that such a daring scheme would be immediately followed by a protest from the nation and the foreign powers, England at their head.

Of the other arrested persons, General Gude, and the three cabinet clerks, Von Zoëga, Martini, and Panning, were soon after set at liberty, and no further measures were taken against them. Frau von Gähler, who had numerous friends, was removed from the citadel to her own house as state prisoner, while her husband remained in prison. The servants of the two counts, Struensee and Brandt, were set at liberty, as innocent creatures beneath revenge.

On the other hand, the Chief Equerry Baron von Bülow, whose pretty wife was regarded as an intriguing lady, received peremptory orders to quit the capital at once, and as the couple were compelled to stay on the road in Seeland, in order that the lady might get over her accouchement, a second order was sent after them to hurry their journey to Holstein. Herr von Bülow had drawn the hatred of the hereditary prince on himself, by giving the prince's horses a stall separated from the royal stables.

Queen Matilda's two maids of honour, Von Kalkreuth and Von Thienen, who were so devoted to their mistress, were sent off to the German duchies, and even the queen's hairdresser was compelled to quit the capital. Chamberlain von Warnstedt voluntarily went out of the way of the storm; returned to Schleswig, and was eventually appointed chief forester there.

The next man who fell under proscription was excellent Reverdil, who has supplied so much curious information about the court of Christian VII. If he had

not believed in the guilt of Caroline Matilda, I should
have liked him better; but as it is, I will not let him
drop out of this history without giving some account
of his overthrow.

At six o'clock on the morning of January 17, Reverdil heard a knocking at his door, and a voice
exclaiming, "Do not be frightened; no harm will be
done you; it is I, your friend, Colonel Köller." When
Reverdil let him in, he handed him a note from the
king to the following effect: "I shall not see you for
the next few days; circumstances oblige me to this."
Reverdil spent the day among his friends, picking up
information, and went that night to the French play,
where the royal family were present. The next morning, Köller came from the king to arrest him for dis-
obedience of orders. The conversation between the
two was capital.

"May I know what procures this arrest?"

"I do not know. How do you stand with Count
Osten?"

"Neither well nor ill."

"It was he who gave me this message, as he came
out of the king's cabinet."

"But what have I done since yesterday morning?"

"You went to the play; and the king, who wrote
to you that he did not wish to see you, saw you there,
———— or might have seen you."

"Oh, come, that is impossible; he is too short-
sighted; and then I was under his box; besides, I

could not give that meaning to the order you brought me."

It was all of no use.; Reverdil remained under arrest, in his rooms, till the 23rd, when the cabinet secretary, Shumacher, set him at liberty, and said that the king, presuming he would prefer living in his own country, was willing to pay him 1,000 dollars for his travelling expenses.   Shortly after, the queen dowager requested an audience of Reverdil.   When he entered the room, she said:

"I cannot tell by what mistake you were arrested. I only heard of it yesterday.   I had given orders that you should not be; and last Friday, when you came to see me, I said to myself, 'At any rate, he will not be disturbed.'   I only wish I could have spared the rest.   But the queen had forgotten everything that she owed to her sex, birth, and rank.   Still, my son and I should have refrained, had not these irregularities affected the state.   The kingdom was in trouble, and going to ruin. ,God supported me; I felt neither alarm nor terror."

The queen dowager then spoke with some detail about her son's grievances; the insolence the favourites displayed toward him; the impenetrable secrecy he kept before the 17th; and the courage he showed in the execution.   Reverdil heard from the queen one of the instances of harsh behaviour toward her son. He was fond of riding on horseback, and this exercise was necessary for his health.   In rainy and snowy weather he could only satisfy this taste in the riding school. The palace one was an academy three days in the week; on the other three days it was reserved for the royal family. Queen Matilda and Struensee, since their return to Copenhagen, occupied it on these three days, and had the entrance closed against the king's brother.

Still Reverdil's liberty caused Osten and Rantzau some alarm. They both feared lest, by regaining his intimacy with the king, he might employ his credit on behalf of the prisoners. Count von der Osten, whose principal talent was espionage in the palace and intriguing with the pages and valets, was informed of Reverdil's interview with the queen dowager, and was afraid that he might re-suggest the plan of recalling to court Count von Bernstorff or Prince Charles of Hesse, with whom he maintained a correspondence. Hence Von der Osten advised Reverdil to leave "for his own sake;" and the Swiss, who was only too glad to shake off the dust of a palace, left Copenhagen about a week after.

For a while, Reverdil resided at Nyon, but eventually entered the service of the Helvetic Republic, and died in 1808, the same year when Christian VII., driven by the English out of his capital, ended his wretched existence in Rendsburg. After Reverdil's dismissal, Jacobi, whose mother was bed-chamber woman to the queen dowager, was appointed reader to the king, and Nielsen director of the king's private library.

The number of prisoners was augmented by a few other disagreeable persons, who, however, were nearly all set at liberty again. Among the latter were Gabel, the owner of the destroyed hotel, and his step-daughter. The brother of Chamberlain Falckenskjold, though he had been asleep during the revolution, and was promoted like his comrades, was obliged to put up with several days' arrest at the main guard, because he ventured to make some harsh remarks about his brother's treatment. However, he was soon after set at liberty again, and eventually rose to the rank of colonel in the army.

Legations-rath Sturtz was at first left untroubled. He had lately drawn away from Struensee, and written the latter, shortly before his arrest, a letter, in which he reproached the minister for meditating the recall of Bernstorff's pension, and pointed at the great services of the discharged minister. That Sturtz felt no apprehension on his own account upon Struensee's fall, is proved by the fact that he arranged for his marriage with the daughter of Major Mazar de la Garde to take place on January 24, and placed none of his papers in safety. But as he ventured to suggest the recall of Bernstorff to the new holders of power, he had ere long to pay dearly for this want of caution. On January 20 he was dismissed from his post with a pension of 500 dollars, and ordered to live in a small town of Seeland.

Unfortunately for Sturtz, one of the officers watching

Falckenskjold happened to mention his name to the prisoner. The latter asked eagerly, had he been arrested too? No more was required: the question was reported, and armed men were at once sent to Sturtz's house. His door was burst open, his papers were sealed up, and he was himself removed to the main guard, in default of another prison, on the very day of his intended marriage. His father-in-law having been seen under the windows of his prison, bars were placed on it so brutally that Sturtz was attacked by convulsive fits, and became dangerously ill.*

I have already mentioned the removal of Colonel von Falckenskjold from the barracks to the Navy prison, only intended for vulgar criminals. This was but a counterpart of the inhuman treatment of the two chief culprits, and a further proof of the revengeful sentiments of the party in power.

On the evening of January 17 the fetters were brought from the forge with which Counts Struensee and Brandt and Justiz-rath Struensee were to be chained. The fetters of the two counts weighed eighteen pounds apiece, ran from a manacle on the right hand to a similar one on the left leg, and thence with a length of three yards to the wall, in which they were fixed. The furniture of the close, gloomy cells consisted of a night-stool and a settle; but afterwards a chair and a small table were added. After the pri-

* Reverdil, p. 363. Sturtz wrote to him afterwards that this affair had seriously injured his health; and, in fact, he died at the early age of forty years.

soners had been deprived of everything that might
be considered dangerous, strait-waistcoats were put on
them. They were not entrusted with knives and forks
to eat with, but the turnkeys were ordered to cut up
their food and carry it to their mouths. They were
not allowed to be shaved, even when they offered to
let their hands be held. At first only half a dollar per
diem was allowed them for food; but it was afterwards
increased to one dollar.

A curious circumstance, which I find only in one
pamphlet,* is, that the smith at the citadel was a slave
whom, about a year before, Struensee had seen in the
streets of the capital chained. This man had asked
him for alms, and begged him to intercede with the
king to procure his liberty. At that time the minister
gave him alms, and said to him, "You do not wear
this chain on account of your virtue." When this
fellow put the chain on his prisoner, he remarked:
" Your excellency, I do not put this chain on you on
account of your virtue."

Shut up in this awful dungeon, Struensee, who had
so suddenly been hurled from power into the lowest
state of misery, and was unable to endure the contrast
between the past and present, revolved means for put-
ting an end to his existence. Pretending to be suffering from toothache, he begged the turnkey to send

* " Gespräch im Reiche der Todten," a very virulent Danish pamphlet, with
the motto,

     " Aude aliquid brevibus gyaris et carcere dignum,
      Si vis esse aliquid ; probitas laudatur et alget."

some one to his cabinet, where he would find some tooth-powder in paper, which would lull the pain. This powder, on being examined by Von Berger the physician, proved to be a dangerous poison, and hence it was not given to the prisoner.

Struensee then resolved to starve himself to death; for three days he was allowed to do as he pleased; but on the fourth the commandant gave orders that he was to eat and drink, and unless he did so of his own accord, he was to be thrashed until his appetite returned. Certainly, a very Danish mode of creating an appetite; but this desperate conduct on the part of the prisoner was a natural result of his insupportable arrest; for had it been rendered more humane, it would not have been necessary to threaten him with such barbarity.

After awhile, Struensee promised to behave himself better, and a bed was given him on which he could lie down. But all the buttons were cut off his clothes, because he had twisted off and swallowed a couple of them. His shoe and knee buckles were also removed, and he was made to wear an iron cap, so that he could not dash his brains out against the wall. At last the hope of saving his life gained the victory over the prisoner's desperation; he began to occupy himself with reading, and thus calmed his outraged feelings.

Count Brandt endured his terrible fate with a perfectly different temper. He was always cheerful, and almost merry, played the flute, his favourite air being one from the "Déserteur," beginning "Mourir c'est notre dernier ressort," and saved six schillings out of the twenty-four he received daily, which he intended as a present for his future executioner. One of his favourite expressions was, "A small mind may allow itself to be depressed by trifles, but a great one raises its head high above fate." Brandt also had a chain three yards long given him, so that he might lie down on a bed.*

Justiz-rath Struensee was also laid in fetters in his cell, but was not fastened to the wall. Luckily for Professor Berger, there were no more chains ready, and so he was allowed to walk about his cell at liberty till they were made. But neither of these prisoners was allowed the use of knives and forks, or of his own bed, although the barber was permitted to shave them, their hands being held the while.

On January 21, a Commission of Inquisition, consisting of eight high officials, was appointed, to whom a ninth member was eventually added, whose duty it was to conduct the investigation of the twelve prisoners, and pass sentence upon them. Still, five weeks passed ere the examination of witnesses was commenced. All Europe looked with horror on these unheard-of events at Copenhagen, and anxiously awaited the end of a state trial which had begun with the imprisonment of a young queen.

The members of the commission had the reputation

* " Die Struensee und Brandtische Kriminalsache.

of being enlightened and honourable men, but were not selected on that account to try the prisoners, but, because their sentiments, as regarded Struensee and his adherents, were perfectly well known.   At the same time as this commission was established, Lieut.-General von Köller-Banner, Councillor of Conference Schumacher, Chamberlain Suhm and Guldberg, received orders to examine the papers of the prisoners, and send them to the proper quarter, but to pay over all moneys found to the Royal Exchequer.   A proclamation of January 27, ordered all persons who were in possession of money, papers, and other matters belonging to the persons arrested on January 17, and the following days, to deliver up such within eight days to the Commission of Inquisition, which sat daily from 9 A.M. till 4 P.M., at the Christiansborg Palace.

During the five weeks that passed ere the Commission had made all the requisite preparations for examining the prisoners of state, the new rulers appointed the officers who would henceforth constitute the government.   Immediately after Struensee's removal, a Privy Cabinet Council was instituted under the presidency of Prince Frederick.   The other members of it were Count Thott, Privy Councillor Schack Rathlau, Admiral Römeling, and Lieutenant-Generals von Eickstedt and Von Köller-Banner.   On January 23, this cabinet council met for the first time, but its installation was not made generally known by public proclamation.   The chief president, Von Holstein,

who was disliked, resigned his post, and left the capital
with his wife, in order to resume his former office
of bailiff.

On February 13, however, public notice was given
that the king had thought proper to establish a
government college under the title of the Privy Council of State.   It was the king's will—so the proclamation ran—that in future all matters should be first laid
before the college, which would examine them, and
then have them decided by men who were well acquainted with the laws and constitution of the country.
In consequence of this, he had resolved on establishing
a Privy Council of State, and giving it the proper
instructions.   In addition to Prince Frederick, the
council of state would consist of the following members: Count Thott, General Count zu Rantzau-Ascheberg, Privy Councillor Schack Rathlau, Admiral Römeling, Lieutenant-General von Eickstedt, and the Minister of Foreign Affairs Count von der Osten, who
would wait on the king upon certain days of the week.
No other member of the council but the Minister of
Foreign Affairs was allowed to be head of a department.   Should the king think proper to issue resolutions otherwise than through the council of state, to
prevent the confusion which would result from the colleges interested being unacquainted with the contents
of such resolutions, the holder of such a resolution
would be expected, ere he made use of it, to inform the
college interested of it, so that a most submissive

report might be drawn up by the latter, and the formal expedition take place through the Secretary of State's office.   All requests, representations and reports, with the exception of those relating to the German lands, were in future to be drawn up in the Danish language, and all reports handed in by the colleges be discussed in the privy council of state, where they would receive the royal sanction.

By this restoration of the privy council of state, the at first intended institution of a cabinet council, which too much resembled Struensee's hated government, was avoided; and as the overthrown minister had drawn such odium on himself by despising the language of the country, the new ministers certainly acted prudently and wisely in restoring it.   Ere long, they made a further improvement by introducing Danish instead of German in the army drill.   The members of the new council of state were also all natives of the monarchy, which would not have been the case had Bernstorff and Moltke been introduced into it.

By the last regulation of the instructions for the future course of business in the council of state, the king's signature was deprived of all force and validity, except in council.   It is true that this restriction might be regarded as emanating from the king himself, and be used to avoid any possible forgery of his signature.   Still, it was quite certain that, henceforth, the king could undertake no affair of state that had not previously received the sanction of the council. And yet it was regarded as a crime worthy of death in Struensee, that he issued instructions to the colleges in his Majesty's name, and his enemies appealed to paragraphs three and twenty-six of the *Lex Regia*. These may be as well quoted, once for all, as frequent reference will be made to them :—

Sec. III.—Hence the king shall have alone the highest power and authority, both to issue and explain laws and regulations according to his will, to make them invalid, to pass others in their place, and even to abrogate laws passed by himself or his ancestors (always excepting this royal law, which must always remain immutable and uninjured as the right foundation of the royal authority and a fundamental law). The king can also liberate and exempt any person he pleases from the general law.

Sec. XXVI.—. . . . And as both daily experience, as well as the lamentable examples of other kingdoms, sufficiently prove how injurious and ruinous it is if the clemency and kindness of kings are so misused, that their power and authority are cut away from them almost invisibly by one or the other, and, at times, even by their most privy ministers; and, through this, both the commonwealth and the kings themselves suffer the greatest detriment . . . . . . We therefore wish to recommend this earnestly to our successors, the hereditary rulers in Denmark and Norway, that they should take special care to protect their

hereditary right and sovereign rule; that is to say,
preserve the supreme monarchical power perfect and
unlessened, as we have left it to them for an eternal
inheritance in this our royal law.   And hence we
order and decree, for its further confirmation, that if
any one, no matter who, should venture to desire or
appropriate anything which could be injurious to the
sovereign rule and monarchical power in any way,
everything obtained in this manner shall be declared
null and void, and those who have got possession of
such things shall be punished as insulters of majesty,
because they have impudently committed the greatest
crime against the supremacy of the royal monarchical
power.

According to these paragraphs, the writers of the
instructions for the new council of state who had extorted the king's signature, and the members of the
council who obeyed the instructions, must indubitably
be regarded as guilty of high treason, while the instructions, even after the king's signature had been obtained,
must be considered null and void, according to the letter
of the *Lex Regia*.

The members of the privy council received in their
patents the title of Ministers of State and Excellencies.
Count Thott became reporter for the two Chanceries;
Privy Councillor Schack Rathlau for the Treasury;
Count von der Osten for Foreign Affairs; Count
Rantzau-Ascheberg for the Army; and Admiral
Römeling for the Navy.   Count Thott, as president

during the king's absence, had a salary of 6,000 dollars; the other members 5,000.   The question was long discussed whether a secretary should not be attached to the council in the person of Chamberlain Suhm, the writer of the famous open letter to the king; but they altered their mind at the eleventh hour, and resolved not to keep any report of the proceedings of the council.

Köller was not taken into the council, because two representatives of the army could not sit in it.   On the day when the council was established, however, he was made a Danish nobleman, and an unfurled banner was given him as his coat of arms.

Guldberg, who drew up the instructions, still contented himself with the mere title of Etats-rath, but, for all that, was the most influential man in the government, and esteemed Eickstedt.   Rantzau, on the other hand, soon remarked that his authority was departing.

CHAPTER VII.

WHAT THEY SAID IN ENGLAND.

COLONEL KEITH—BAD NEWS FROM COPENHAGEN—DEATH OF
THE PRINCESS OF WALES—THE PUBLIC PRESS—JUNIUS'S
LETTER—ATTICUS—A FOUL LIBEL—THE EARL OF BUTE DE-
NOUNCED—ANOTHER APPEAL FOR THE QUEEN—THE STATE
OF PUBLIC OPINION—THE APPROACHING TRIAL.

So soon as the *coup d'état* was an accomplished fact,
Colonel Keith, the British envoy, lost not a moment
in acting on behalf of the sister of his monarch. Dark
rumours were afloat that a family council had been
held to decide the fate of the queen; and it was even
said that proposals to execute her at once were entertained. Colonel Keith, under these circumstances,
forced his way into the Christiansborg, and de-
nounced war against Denmark if a hair of her head
were touched. This done, he despatched a messenger
forthwith to England, and immediately locked himself
and his household up until the answer should arrive.

What the nature of Keith's despatch was it is impossible to tell till the Foreign Office shall give up its

dead, by repealing the absurd regulation that no state
papers may be inspected after the year 1760.   For the
present, therefore, I am only able to inform my readers
of what the public journals of the day said, and that is
naturally rather in the shape of surmise than fact.

As early as January 23, the *General Evening Post*
spread an uneasy feeling by the following portentous
paragraph :—" It is affirmed by letters from the Continent that a royal princess is certainly detained in a
tower inaccessible to every creature except such as are
appointed to attend her, but that an absolute silence
is imposed throughout the kingdom on this subject."
On January 26, the journalist being unable to offer
more precise information, and yet unwilling to let the
subject drop, keeps it alive by a paragraph to the following effect :—

" So exceedingly cautious are foreign states when
they marry a daughter of England not to let an English woman attend the princess into their territories,
for fear of her having too much influence over the
mind of her royal mistress, that when the Queen of
Denmark was sent over to her illustrious consort, she
had only one bed-chamber woman in her suite as far as
Altona, and even this one was sent back on her arrival
at that place, that the Danish ladies only might have
the ear of her Majesty."

On January 29, just as the king was about to hold
a levee, an express arrived from Copenhagen, bearing
the news.   It threw the royal family, we are told, into

the profoundest affliction; his Majesty seemed deeply
affected by the news; and the queen and the Princess
of Brunswick were observed to shed tears.   But there
was another member of the royal family whom the
news would afflict even more: the mother of Caroline
Matilda, who, as we have seen, felt persuaded that her
daughter had been guilty of gross indiscretion, and
who, in the previous year, had attempted to turn her
from a course which her own experience of court intrigues told her must end in ruin.

The Princess Dowager of Wales was at this time
dangerously ill with a throat complaint, and it was
therefore proposed to George III. that this new misfortune should be concealed from her.   But the king
answered, incautiously, "My mother *will* know everything, and, therefore, it is better that I should break
it to her by degrees."   He therefore went to her
directly, suddenly forbidding his levee just half an
hour before it was going to begin, and thus was the
first to publish the disgrace of his sister.   Walpole,
who is our authority for the above,* adds, in a strain
of reflection unusual with him :—

"Such an accumulated succession of mortifications
has rarely fallen on a royal family in so short a space.
They seemed to have inherited the unpropitious star
of the Stuarts, from whom they are descended, as well
as their crown.   The marriage of the Duke of Cum-
berland with Colonel Luttrell's sister, the dangerous
illness of the Princess of Wales and the Duke of Glou-

* Walpole's "Journal of the Reign of George III."

cester, and the dishonour of the Queen of Denmark:
all happening within three months."

We are told—though let us hope that it was only
the floating gossip of the day—that the princess dowager, on receiving the fatal news from the Continent,
prayed most fervently for her speedy dissolution; de-
claring that the world could not be more weary
of her than she was of the world, and desiring her attendants never to mention the name of a "certain
princess" in her presence.

For the next few days the newspapers necessarily
contained only what information could be picked up
at the coffee-houses.   Thus we find that it was generally believed that the worst part of the news from
Denmark was not yet published, and, therefore, all
was suspense, doubt, and anxiety, among the constant
visitors at St. James's.   The politicians at the new
Lloyd's Coffee-house very busily engaged in specula-
tive bets upon a war with Denmark; but considerate
people imagined that Lord North was much too wise
to engage offensively against any power merely on
account of a family *faux-pas*, especially when the
conduct of the person to be supported was inde-
fensible.

The natural inclination to think ill of one's neighbour was only heightened at this time through the
profound secrecy maintained by the government.
Still, it is gratifying to find some writers at this early
period calling for the assistance of a fleet to vindicate,

rather than the voice of the British nation to condemn, the Queen of Denmark; and further on in the same article Caroline Matilda is spoken of as the "Royal Innocent."

Early in February, a long letter appeared in the *General Evening Post*, calling attention to the whole affair in very powerful language. The writer, after urging the nation not to decide on *ex parte* statements, proceeds to defend Caroline Matilda in the following warm terms :—

"Recollect the manner in which that lady was educated, and that, when delivered into the hands of her husband, she was in full possession of every virtue. All the graces were in her: she knew nothing but what was good. Can it then, with any degree of reason, be concluded that in so short a time the lady could forget every virtuous precept, and abandon herself to infamy? My dear countrymen, it cannot be; and until we have a certainty of guilt, believe it not, though an angel from Copenhagen should affirm it. It was but the other day we were told of certain regulations which had taken place, and are for the advantage of that kingdom, and which were wholly attributed to the counsel of that lady. Alas! there is too much reason to fear that her exalted character, justly acquired with the populace, has produced in those of rank—envy, hatred, confusion, and ruin."

The writer, who like most of his countrymen appears to have been in a state of blessed ignorance

about the affairs of foreign courts, then bursts into a
furious and quite irrelevant diatribe on poor Baron
Schimmelmann, whom he supposes to be the prime
minister of Denmark.   After giving a concise account
of that gentleman's chequered career, and displaying
an amount of malice in raking up dirty things which
makes one believe that C. P. owed Schimmelmann a
grudge, he vents his bile in the following words, which
certainly contain some truth:—

"It is wickedly asserted that the monarch's (Christian VII.) illness is attributed to some medicines
given him by his physician, &c.   The truth is, that
you ought rather to wonder that his Majesty is now
alive, than that he is afflicted with nervous and paralytic disorders.   My eyes were witness to the manner
and excess of his living when he was at Altona.   I
could say a great deal, but it does not become me.
I shall only say this one thing, which is an indisputable truth: that many who then saw his Majesty,
concluded from his delicate constitution that it could
not hold long, and execrated our baron for his introducing him to, and encouraging him in, the most destructive vices.   Therefore, if any disorder affects the
head of his Majesty, may it not be more justly attributed to such excess than to the queen, who was educated in the fear of God?"

The illness of the princess dowager prevented
George III. from taking any decided action on behalf
of his sister.   On the morning of February 8 the

11 *

princess departed this life.   On the previous evening
her physician felt her pulse, and told her it was more
regular than it had been for some time; her Highness
answered, "Yes, and I think I shall have a good
night's rest."   She then embraced the king, and he
observed nothing particular in her except that she
kissed him with greater warmth and affection than
usual.   The king afterwards retired to a private room
with the physician, who told him that her Highness
could not outlive the morning, which determined his
Majesty on staying at Carlton House all night.   He
did not see his royal mother any more till she was
dead, for she remained very quiet all the night, and
gave no token of death, till a few minutes before she
expired, when she laid her hand upon her heart and
went off without a groan.   His Majesty was then informed, and he came in and took his mother's hand,
kissed it, and burst into tears; a short time after which
he returned to St. James's.*

There is but little to add to the character of this
princess than that communicated in the opening chapter.   When she was gone to a state far superior to mortal
praise or blame, where the lying voice of calumny and
faction could not reach her, people began to discover
that "never was a more amiable, a more innocent, or
a more benevolent princess."   It was publicly denied
that she had interfered in the politics of the country,
or influenced the king in affairs of state.   She dis-

* "Annual Register, 1772."

charged, to the utmost of her power and out of her
own income, the large private debts of her husband.
Her charity was extensive; and it was stated that she
gave away upwards of £10,000 a year, and that so
secretly, that the recipients of her bounty would only
learn who their benefactress was through the cessation
of her charities. Hence it is not surprising that she
made no will, for she had nothing to leave.

Though the Princess of Wales constantly read all
the public papers till within a few weeks of her death,
the unmerited abuse with which they teemed never
excited in her the least emotion of anger or resent-
ment; nor was she ever heard to speak disparagingly
of any individual. She was steady in her friendships,
and so indulgent a mistress to her servants, that she
was ever anxious to give them as little trouble as possible. Her understanding was clear and solid; her
temper even, serene, and placid, and her religion real
and unaffected, which enabled her to meet death with
a truly Christian resignation. To the very last minute
of her life she was sensible and composed, and gave
apparent signs of satisfaction at the truly filial concern
which the royal pair displayed, and the great attention
they paid her in her last extremity. A writer in the
Gentleman's Magazine sums up the character of the
Princess of Wales so fairly, that I am tempted to extract the concluding passage:—

" In her royal highness we have a striking instance
of the instability of human happiness. Many now alive

can remember her the happiest of wives and mothers, and universally beloved, as our good queen now is. She was for many years the very idol of the people of England; and, without any blame on her part, she has been publicly and repeatedly traduced beyond all example.   She has long been bereaved of the best of husbands: (?) has outlived several of her children, and has had the recent mortification of seeing one marry indiscreetly, another languishing under a dangerous illness, and a third a prisoner in a distant kingdom. Overwhelmed with these accumulated misfortunes, and struggling with bodily distempers, Heaven, as a reward for her pure and virtuous conduct in every relation in life, has graciously and seasonably delivered her from the sorrows of this mortal state to the mansions of endless felicity, where the wicked cease from troubling, and the weary are at rest."

One of the most unfortunate results of the death of the Princess of Wales in this crisis of affairs was, that the crafty Von der Osten had time to persuade the King of England that this affair was not one of those which ought to be treated by ministers as between nations; that it was personal; that his brother, the King of Denmark, would write to him in his own hand, and that his Britannic Majesty should reply in the same way.   George III., who was so honest as to believe everybody, fell into the trap so artfully laid for him.

On February 28, Lord Suffolk, the foreign secretary, sent despatches to Colonel Keith, adding to them a personal letter, in which he expressed the king's satisfaction at the ability, spirit, and dignity the envoy had displayed, and enclosing the Order of the Bath as a reward.   From Danish accounts I learn that George III. replied to Christian's letter, that what had happened grieved him deeply, but he hoped that justice would be observed, and every possible indulgence shown.

With this letter Sir R. M. Keith proceeded to demand a private audience of the King of Denmark, and a day being appointed for the purpose, the envoy, on entering the ante-chamber, was much surprised at seeing, instead of the king, some members of the council of state, who intimated to him that his Majesty, not being very well, had charged them to receive what the envoy had to communicate, and they would inform him of it. Sir R. Keith replied, that the orders he had received from his master were to speak to the king in person, and not to his ministers; and that he was not a little surprised that after his Danish Majesty had consented to give him the audience he requested, he should refer him to his ministers.   He then added, that he should not fail to inform his royal master of what had occurred, and retired extremely dissatisfied. As he went, Sir Robert fired a parting shot, to the effect that if the Queen of Denmark was not treated with the respect due to her birth and rank, the king, his master, would not fail to resent it.

Keith, doubtless, informed George III. of the results

of this interview, and opened his eyes as to the jugglery that had been practised. Consequently, subsequent despatches from England assumed a more earnest character, and, finally, even contained menaces. At the same time, however, George III. remained true to his word, and said that he would not interfere in the matter, so far as it affected the marriage of Christian VII. with his sister. Hence he consented to the arrest of the queen and her long imprisonment during the trial, but refused to sanction any further or life imprisonment of the accused princess.

There is but little to be learnt from the English papers as to the progress of the negociations. It would appear as if Baron Dieden, the Danish envoy at St. James's, was left without instructions for a time, as he shut himself up in his house till he received commands as to his future conduct. Perhaps fear had something to do in the matter, for Reverdil, who was then in London, states that an anonymous letter was sent the envoy, to the effect that he must answer personally for the safety of the queen. When Dieden finally made his appearance at court, George III. would not speak to him, and the minister took his revenge by standing out of the circle, and laughing impertinently at the king to the Prussian minister.*

* Walpole's "Journal of the Reign of George III.," to which we are indebted for another anecdote. About a week after the account came, Count Maltzahn, the Prussian envoy, asked Mr. Dayrolles, with a sneer, "Qu'est devenu votre Reine de Danemarc?" Dayrolles replied, with spirit, "Apparement qu'elle

In the absence of settled news, the gentry, who occupied themselves with writing letters to the papers, had a splendid time of it. The ball was opened by that three-decker Junius, who discharged a double-shotted battery into Lord North. After the usual denunciations of the minister, which the latter probably regarded with his usual pachydermatous indifference, Junius proceeds as follows :—

"An insignificant northern potentate is honoured by a matrimonial alliance with the King of England's sister. A confused rumour prevails that she has been false to his bed : the tale spreads, a particular man is pointed at as the object of her licentious affections. Our hopeful ministry, however, are quite silent : despatches, indeed, are sent off to Copenhagen, but the contents of those despatches are so profound a secret, that with me it almost amounts to a question, whether you yourself know anything of the matter."

After giving a far from flattering description of the remaining members of the cabinet, Junius adds an argument, which certainly is forcible :—

"In private life the honour of a sister is deemed an affair of infinite consequence to a brother. A man of sentiment is anxious to convince his friends and neighbours that the breath of slander has traduced her virtue : and he seizes with avidity every extenuating circumstance that can contribute to alleviate her offence

est à Spandau avec votre Princesse de Prusse,"—who had been divorced for adultery.

or demonstrate her innocence, beyond the possibility
of cavil.

"Is our pious Majesty cast in a different mould
from one of his people? or is he taught to believe that
the opinion of his subjects has no manner of relation
to his own felicity? Are you, my lord, quite devoid
of feeling? Have you no warm blood that flows round
your heart, that gives your frame a thrilling soft sen-
sation, and makes your bosom flow with affections or-
namental to man as a social creation? For shame, my
lord, however wrong you act, you must know better;
you must be conscious that the people have a right to
be informed of every transaction which concerns the
welfare of the state. They are part of a mighty em-
pire, which flourishes only as their happiness is promoted ; they have a kind of claim in every person
belonging to the royal lineage. How, then, can they
possibly remain neuter, and see their princess imprisoned by a banditti of northern Vandals?"

After an historical survey of Denmark, not particularly pertinent, Junius informs us that:—

"There is a barbarous ferocity which still clings to
the inhabitants of the north, and renders their government subject to perpetual convulsions; but the Danes,
I fancy, will be found the only people in our times
who have dared to proceed to extremities that alarm
all Europe, nay, dared to imprison an English princess,
without giving even the shadow of a public reason for
their conduct."

After an allusion to the conduct of the Empress Catharine in justifying the murder of her husband, Junius concludes with one of his most impassioned declamations against the sluggish minister, who is so careless of British honour:—

" The present Machiavellian Dowager Julia may send the young queen's soul to Heaven in a night, and through the shameful remissness of you, Lord North, as prime minister of this unhappy country, the public may remain ignorant of every circumstance relative to the murder. Be not, however, deceived: the blood of our sovereign's sister shall not be suffered to cry in vain for vengeance: it *shall* be heard; it *shall* be revenged; and what is still more, it shall besprinkle Lord North, and thus affix a stigma on his forehead, which shall make him wander like another Cain, accursed through the world." *

This vigorous appeal for Caroline Matilda was followed shortly after by a temperate letter in the *Public Advertiser*, signed Q. Q. ·This writer has the merit of seeing further through a millstone than his fellows. He was of opinion that the Danish revolution, far from being general, was merely the effect of a court faction, and that a squadron of British ships

---

* It is amusing to notice the transparent cloak employed by public writers even when bespattering their political foes the most fiercely. Thus Junius invariably addresses Lord N—, alludes to his M—y, and tells the premier, not that he shall be accursed, but a—d. It reminds me of the rule that only allows boxing matches in France with the gloves on, though the latter may be made of the thinnest silk.

sent to Copenhagen would "inspire the queen's friends
with confidence and courage, and will check and dis-
pirit those who are her opponents, so that she may
either expect to have her conduct cleared up by a fair
and impartial trial, or, if it is thought an indignity
to submit to that, she may at once be restored to
that rank and authority which I am well persuaded
she never deserved to lose."

It must not be supposed, however, that Caroline
Matilda's defenders were allowed to have it all their
own way. A fellow, writing under the name of
ATTICUS, befouled the columns of the *Public Advertiser*
with one of the most scandalous libels on an unoffend-
ing woman which ever appeared in those unhappy
days, when liberty was confounded with licence of the
press.

According to this worthy, the Earl of Bute advised
the war with Denmark, and Lord Sandwich seconded
him in the hope of increasing his income at the Admi-
ralty. Lord North, "perplexed lest he may on the
one hand be deserted by a perfidious master in the
midst of the tempest, or, on the other hand, lose the
favourite's influence, therefore, temporises, flatters,
and procrastinates."

After defending the queen dowager from the charges
brought against her and alleging the notorious intimacy of the queen and Struensee, Atticus draws the
following inference :—

"I will refer the conclusion (of the intimacy) to

those best acquainted with women, whether it ever so happens that they surrender power, confer honours, and resign up all reputation to any man who had not made a *deep impression?* I am a married man, have a very good kind of dame at my table, and am not at present disturbed with jealousy: but were I to see my wife fond of another man's company, solicitous to do him partial honours, and impatient for his increasing glory, happiness, and renown, and prefer his interest to mine, it would to me be a more certain proof of her criminality than is commonly produced in cases of divorce."

After a lengthened account of Struensee's elevation and fall, not more incorrect than the majority of the fables current at the time, Atticus takes up the common but generally successful radical trick of imputing motives to political opponents.

"The day was fixed, *a favourite fell.* Methinks I hear the Earl of Bute whisper to his poor affrighted soul, and every corner of his hiding-places murmur with these expressions: God bless us! a known and established favourite ruined in a single night, by a near neighbour—the frenzy may reach this country and I am undone. Englishmen, too, are haters of favourites and Scotchmen; these old, rascally, Whig families, whose power and virtue seem almost lost, may re-unite. In the meantime I must do something—a lucky thought occurs to me: I'll fill the minds of the people with prejudices against those haughty Danes.

Bradshaw and Dyson shall bribe the printers to suppress any contradictory reports; Englishmen are always
ready to vindicate injured virtue at any expense.
Therefore, nothing shall be heard *but the honour of the
king's sister.* I know the queen-mother was ignorant
of the matter till the deed was done; but I will have
her represented as an intriguing old Brimstone. It
will go down, because the late dowager here must have
prejudiced them against all queen-mothers. By the
ghost of Charles, I'll make war against those rascally
burghers, which will completely answer my purpose.
I will divert the ministers of the two people, weaken
the two Protestant states, make room for my name-
sake, and restore favouritism."

Such were the arguments of a member of the peace-
at-any-price-party in 1772. They certainly display a
coarse cleverness befitting a demagogue, and doubtless
represented the feelings of a considerable section of
deluded Englishmen at the time. Let us hope that
none of his readers, however, shared the sentiments
expressed in the following odious passage:—

" Be assured, my dear countrymen, the queen's supposed inconstancy was in no part the cause of the late
revolution in Denmark. Had she committed adultery
in the streets, but preserved decency in matters of
state, she might now be at liberty, and in that round
of amusements. The patriots of Denmark do not make
adultery an article of grievances; and if they did, she
has been the betrothal of a sovereign prince; she is

his lawful wife, subject to the laws of that country. Her brother made no settlement of exclusive power—either for her as a wife or a queen; at least, his pious nature must have forbidden the declared right of —— dom. I wish George III. had entertained the same ideas as did his grandfather, with respect to the slippery tricks of his family; who, in his letter to the Prince Ferdinand, near the close of the late war, concludes with these words: 'Let me advise you to be more careful of your person—your reputation is established, for though our family has produced many ——s, it never produced a poltroon.' "*

An anonymous writer in the *Gentleman's Magazine* stepped forward at once to meet the doughty ATTICUS in the field, and it is to be regretted that his armour was not stronger. He pleads *in misericordiam* for Caroline Matilda, appealing to her birth, education, and former behaviour, and concludes with the opinion that a squadron will be the best way of cutting the legal knot. Atticus speedily returned to the charge, but without his former vigour, except, perhaps, when he argues that persons who accept crowns must put up with the inconveniences connected with them. When George III. gave his sister to Christian VII. in marriage, both were aware that Caroline Matilda was

---

* I have allowed this revolting passage to stand, as it exemplifies the language which a subject dared to use about the reigning family in those days. It is not surprising that a nation, which could tolerate language of this nature in the public press, should be ready to credit the Queen of Denmark's guilt.

to become obedient to the will of an almost unlimited
monarch. " The event should teach them both the
superior excellency of a limited monarchy and the in-
estimable value of its laws." Atticus winds up by
saying, that if the vengeance and power of England
were to be exerted against any prince who married into
the British royal family, no matter what his wife's
conduct might be, the princesses would soon go beg-
ging for husbands.

Such were the arguments employed by our grand-
fathers when they talked over the fate of the Queen
of Denmark. I fear, though, that the tide gradually
turned against her, and that this was, in a great
measure, owing to the mystery kept up about the
affair. Lord North, when pressed in his parliamen-
tary intrenchments, contented himself with answering,
"with his natural air of frankness," says Reverdil,
who was in London at the time, "that unless expressly ordered to do so by the House, he would not
reveal so delicate an affair; that time would discover
everything and justify the ministry." Ninety years
have since elapsed, but the justification has not been
published. All we know for certain is, that an innocent
woman's character was blackened by the unwise conduct of those to whom she had a natural right to look
for protection. We know, too, that she was allowed to
remain in prison for upwards of four months, await-
ing the result of a trial which ought never to have
taken place.

These considerations, however, should be deferred

until I have given all the details connected with this extraordinary trial. In doing so, I shall, fortunately, be enabled to produce documents which have not hitherto been laid before the English public. Whether I shall be able to prove the perfect innocence of Caroline Matilda by their aid, it does not become me to say; that I must leave to the verdict of my readers. But one thing I can with certainty affirm: the treatment of the unfortunate Queen of Denmark was equally fiendish, cruel, and, in every respect, revolting, whether she were guilty or not. Not the slightest evidence could be brought against her: all the statements of the witnesses, which extend to matters rarely produced in a court of law (except, perhaps, in the case of Caroline of Brunswick), will prove themselves to be supposititious, or simple calumnies. It is for this reason that I attach such value to the evidence which has so recently been obtained from the secret archives of Denmark, and which enables me to lay the whole affair, for the first time in full, before the impartial judgment of the English reader.

CHAPTER VIII.

STRUENSEE IN PRISON.

So soon as the privy council of state had been established and commenced its governmental functions, the examination of the state prisoners was proceeded with at the quarters of the commandant of the citadel, Lieutenant-General von Hobe. The two gates of the fortress were closed during the whole day against every one who did not reside in it; and, in the city, the garrison and bürger guard were held in readiness for any eventuality. At ten o'clock A.M. on February 20, Count Struensee was taken in the commandant's coach, and under the guard of the officer of the watch and six men, to the place of examination. He was dressed in a fur coat, which had been granted him on account of the cold; and before he was introduced to the commission, his chains were removed, and an armchair placed for him. Although very firm, generally, he was seized with a tremor when his fetters were removed, and afterwards when they were put on again at the end of each sitting.

The first examination lasted till two o'clock; it was resumed at half-past four, and continued till seven o'clock. Neither on this day nor on the next morning did Struensee make the slightest confession. He explained all the orders he had given during the last portion of his government as precautions against a popular *émeute*. He even denied having given any special order; he had merely recommended General Gude to provide effectually for the public safety. On this head, his judges had the strongest proof of his innocence in the fact that all the other prisoners, when they were arrested, believed that it was done by his orders.

As regarded the accusation of gallantry, the prisoner constantly denied it during these first three sittings, with a calmness that astonished his judges. One of them, Councillor Braëm, having used abusive language to him, Struensee exhorted him to imitate his tranquillity, adding, that the affair concerned himself more than anybody. It is stated that this same Braëm menaced him with a certain apparatus, which was ready in another room, and by means of which the truth was torn from obstinate criminals. Struensee replied, that nothing could be drawn from him by torture, seeing that he had nothing to confess or reproach himself with. If he were threatened with torture, which appears very doubtful, it was only on one occasion, for Braëm was not authorised to do so; and it is not true that the instruments were prepared.[*]

Struensee's firmness, there is little doubt, was based on an opinion which for some time past had formed his sole security; he had persuaded himself that no one would dare to attack the person of the queen, and that the closer he connected his fate with that of Caroline Matilda, the less risk he would himself run. When he learnt that his protectress was herself arrested, his firmness abandoned him: he was troubled, and burst into tears: he deplored his misfortune in attracting insults and disgrace on the persons to whom he was most attached, and, conscious of his weakness, he implored his judges to allow him to return to his prison, that he might regain his calmness, and stanch his tears. The judges were careful not to let this moment of victory slip: they pressed him more than ever; and what neither their questions nor threats could draw from the prisoner, they obtained from his weakness and emotion. He confessed that his familiarity with the queen had been carried to the fullest extent.[†]

It is more than possible that Struensee, in his terror

* Reverdil, p. 898.

† A French petit maître, who protested against this weakness of Struensee, and in whose presence the discretion of his own countrymen in such matters was called in question, retorted: " Un Français l'aurait dit à tout le monde, et ne l'aurait avoué à personne."

and confusion, hoped to save his life by dragging the queen into the matter, falsely expecting thus to prevent an examination that must lead to scandal, and to escape with banishment. It is also probable that his crafty judges led him into this belief, and by insinuations induced him to betray the honour of a woman. But what man to whom honour was `dear would have made such shameful confessions about a woman, which must not only dishonour her in the sight of all Europe, but infallibly cost her the throne? Whether, therefore, we should consider Struensee guilty or innocent of the crimes he confessed, his head from this moment belonged to the executioner, and by his own act he destroyed public sympathy with his fate.[*]

But Struensee degraded himself even more, if possible, by his ensuing confessions. When he had taken the first step, further avowals cost him nothing, and the whole story poured from his lips without restriction or reservation. His interrogatory affords details too precise and circumstantial to be reproduced here.[†]

---

[*] That Struensee's contemporaries were of the same opinion, will be seen from what Baron von Bülow said to Mr. Wraxall on the subject:—"Had Struensee persisted pertinaciously in disclaiming any sort of criminal intimacy with the queen, should a contrary declaration have afterwards been made by him under torture, all the world would have said that such a confession was worth nothing, as having been extorted by the rack—as being the mere effect of pain. He would probably have then been put out of the way in prison, but to latest ages he would have been called a great man; nor could they then have touched Queen Matilda. She denied everything till she was shown Struensee's confession."

[†] This confession still exists: indeed, I have a copy of it. But, however anxious I may feel to arrive at the truth, it is simply impossible to republish

It results from it that the criminal relations between the queen and Struensee began in the spring of 1770, shortly before the Holstein tour.

It was important to know whether the king had kept entirely aloof from the queen, and what opinion should be formed about the legitimacy of the little princess, whom it was at first proposed to disinherit, and whom the courtiers called familiarly in January and February the "Mamselle." But the king had acknowledged her, and openly announced her birth to all the foreign courts. For this reason it was considered advisable not to stir the matter up.

When Struensee was asked who had helped the queen and him in carrying on their illicit connexion, and what confidants they had had, he replied that no one had served them in this matter, and that neither the queen nor he had confided it to any one : it was probable that he had spoken about it to Count Brandt; but he did not remember having confessed to him the exact state of affairs, as he was very cautious on this point.*

it. The few general hints I give in the text, and further on in the indictment of the queen, will suffice to indicate its disgusting character.

* Reverdil makes a remark on this, which would have weight if we could believe a word that Brandt said. He observes:—"I learnt from Brandt such peculiar details, which at the same time agreed with all the rest, that I could neither doubt their truth nor their origin. Brandt was so petulant in his curiosity about matters of gallantry, that it was necessary either to deny as impudently as he questioned, or to confess everything. And as he spared nobody, and took a pride in dispensing with those reservations most commanded by decency. I do not doubt that by showing himself thoroughly acquainted with the affair, he forced the queen to speak to him as clearly as his friend did. In his examination he confessed to having been a confidant."

The truth was, that the queen had first given him
marks of her tenderness at a masked bàll, but that
their intimacy commenced at the Christiansborg Palace.
To these confessions, which he attested by his signature, Struensee added :—

" He was forced to confess that through his conduct
he had compromised the queen's reputation : that he
was maintained in the same habits by circumstances,
although he had often desired and sought means to
prevent this inconvenience : that the conduct of the
king and queen frequently had the effect of renewing
appearances, from the fact of the queen ordering him
to take steps which looked suspicious : that the king
sent him to the queen at all hours, and with all sorts
of messages : that the queen frequently asked for him
and seized upon him, as he had already stated, proposing to him to go out with her, *tête-à-tête*, on foot,
on horseback, or in a carriage : that he frequently proposed to her to take some one with them, especially
females, and that for this object he encouraged several
of the latter to mount their horses : that the queen
had the custom of refusing everything : that he had
been obliged to yield, lest he should lose her confidence : that he was thus placed in the alternative of
ruining his fortunes, or succumbing to the will of the
queen.   In other respects he referred to the confession of the queen, as facts spoke so loudly against him,
that even if he had not had culpable relations with
her, appearances would condemn him."

Count Brandt was examined for the first time on February 22. He was perfectly calm, and answered the questions asked with a coolness which evidently showed that he considered himself entirely innocent. The chief charge against him naturally consisted of his assault on the sacred person of his Majesty, about which he spoke quite unreservedly, and penitently begged pardon for the insulting expressions with which he had challenged the king to wrestle.

As a reward for the explanations they had given, the two counts were allowed, on February 26, to have their six-weeks-old beards removed, which Brandt had previously attempted to do with a pair of snuffers. During this operation, the following precautions were used: the prisoner sat as far away from the wall as his chain admitted, so that he could not move one hand, while a turnkey held the other.

Struensee seems either to have made up his mind to the inevitable, or else to have accommodated himself to circumstances with remarkable easiness. He began to take his meals with something of an appetite. He breakfasted about nine, on coffee, rolls, and biscuits; at one he dined, took a glass of light wine, and a cup of coffee; drank tea about five or six, and perhaps ate a biscuit or two; he took no supper, but drank a glass of port wine and water. He was always very abstemious as to wines and spirits, at least after he was placed about the king. Everything furnished by the restaurateur for his use was carefully examined;

even the bread was cut open, and the napkins shaken
and held up to the light; and his meat was cut for
him, as he was not allowed a knife, lest he might
commit suicide.

It seems as if some remarks that were dropped
during the examination soon reduced Brandt's hopes,
for almost immediately after, he, by the advice of the
commandant, requested the aid of a clergyman. On
February 24, Hee, provost of the Navy church, was
selected by the commission, and he paid the unhappy
prisoner frequent visits. His exertions to convert the
free-thinking count proved successful. Still the conversion did not seem to extend beyond Deism, for he
would not listen to anything about the fall of man,
original sin, and some other matters concerning religion.

Brandt had received an excellent education. He saw
none but good examples in the house of his parents, who
had chosen the best tutors to form his young heart for
the fear of God. He himself was sensible of this in
his prison, and assured Dean Hee that he very often
had felt the power of the converting grace of God in
his soul. He recollected more particularly the time
when he was first admitted to the sacrament of the
Lord's Supper, and added, that he could never forget the words of the clergyman, which made a great
impression on his mind: "Hold that fast which thou
hast, that no man take thy crown." That he possessed
an easily moved mind is proved by the fact that, in his

conversations with the clergyman, he frequently burst
into tears when the latter reproved him for his "former
life and the depravity of his heart," and expounded to
him the greatness of God's mercy. Hee was greatly
troubled on hearing that so soon as his back was
turned, Brandt used to relapse into his old levity. On
upbraiding the prisoner with this, the latter said, humbly enough, that "it was possible such words might
have escaped him, on account of the levity of his heart,
but he hinted that some person or other, who wanted
to bring such reports among the people, had given
occasion for it, of which he made use while his heart
was not upon its guard." Dr. Hee thought the best
way of preventing this was by giving his penitent religious books to read, but the choice does not appear to
have been very wise, for among them was "Hervey's
Meditations." The tendency of this work was to
render Brandt quite quiet, and the commandant spoke
in the highest terms of his behaviour, which was most
edifying. Still, I cannot help thinking that there was
a certain amount of hypocrisy in the affair; at any rate,
so long as Brandt thought there was a chance of saving
his life. For instance, it seems rather *outré* to find
the prisoner frequently taking up his chains and kissing
them, to which he would say, " When I believed myself
to be free, I was a miserable slave to my passions; and
now that I am a prisoner, truth and grace have set me
at liberty." Nor should much faith be placed in his
denunciations of Voltaire, with which old advocate of

Shaitan he had spent four days on his travels, and had
heard nothing from him (as he said) save what could
corrupt the heart and sound morals. Another curious bit Dr. Hee shall tell us in his own quaint
language :—

"He spoke of Struensee, and said he was a man
without any religion, who, from his infancy, according
to his own confession, never had any impression or
feelings of it. As to himself, he assured me that,
though he had been far from being virtuous, yet he
always entertained a secret reverence for religion, and
had spoken several times about it to Struensee, in
hopes of leading him to better sentiments, but he never
would hear him.   It appeared to me a little odd that
the blind should thus have led the blind; I therefore
made no answer, thinking it might, perhaps, be his
self-conceit that made him speak so, or that he wanted
me to entertain a better opinion of his errors than I
had reason for: hence I would not tempt him to support an untruth by defending what he had told me."

Attention was also paid to the state of Struensee's
soul.   At first he declined to see any clergyman, but
when the confession that decided his fate had been
drawn from him, his persecutors resolved to send him
ghostly counsel even against his will. The choice fell,
as has been stated, on Dr. Münter, at that time provost of the German Peter's church in Copenhagen.

This worthy divine has left us an account of Struensee's conversion, which everybody used to read in

the last century, but is utterly forgotten now. It is invaluable, however, for a proper comprehension of Struensee's character. In every page we seem to have before us a weak, sensual man, incapable of resisting any persevering pressure; incredulous through levity, purified by misfortune, sincerely converted, feeling the same contempt for the judgment of posterity as for that of his contemporaries; badly guided at the outset by too strict a father, but possessing excellent quali- ties, full of forgiveness for his pitiless enemies, and perfectly resigned.   Over such a character a man like Münter soon gained the upper hand: he was a theolo- gian, but would have made a first-rate lawyer, and at the same time a passionate Christian, who, while he believed that he was only labouring to save a wretch's soul, aided his implacable foes to consummate his ruin.

On March 1, Dr. Münter paid his first visit to Stru- ensee's prison.   When the count was informed of the clergyman's arrival, he inquired whether it was or- dered, and on being answered in the affirmative, he endured the presence of the doctor.   He welcomed him with a sour and gloomy countenance, in the atti- tude of a man who was prepared to receive many severe reproaches, and with a silence that showed con- tempt.   But so soon as the clever Münter had told him that he was well aware of his obligations toward an unhappy man, and sincerely wished to make the visits he was ordered to pay him agreeable and useful, Struensee quitted his constrained attitude, and his

countenance grew more serene.   He offered the doctor
his hand, and thanked him for the sympathy he took
in his fate.   The latter, in return, gave Struensee the
assurance that he would say nothing that could offend
him, and begged that if accidentally in the course of
conversation a word might slip from him that appeared
offensive, Struensee would overlook it.

"Oh, you may say what you please," the prisoner
answered.

Münter repeated his assurance that he had no other
design but that of being useful to his hearer, and for
that reason requested his confidence, which he (Münter) would return with the most thankful friendship,
even though Struensee in the beginning might take
him for a weak and prejudiced man.

Struensee was moved by this assurance, and Münter
continued :—

"If you desire to receive comfort from me, who am
your only friend on earth, do not cherish that unhappy
thought of dying like a philosophical hero."

To which the count replied :—

"In all my adversities, I have shown firmness of
mind, and, agreeably to this character I hope I shall
not die like a hypocrite."

"Hypocrisy," Münter said, "in such moments would
be even worse than an affected firmness, though even
this would be a kind of hypocrisy.   In case of death,
do not trust to your old resolution and compare your
former adversities, which were, perhaps, nothing but

sickness and distress, with that fate which is now
ready to fall on you. But, perhaps, you entertain
some hopes of saving your life?"

" No," Struensee said, " I flatter myself with no
hopes at all."

" But you do not see death near you," the doctor
urged; "you do not know the time when you shall
leave this world. Suppose I were to tell you that you
were to die to-day or to-morrow, would not your
courage fail you?"

Struensee was silent, and Milnter implored him to
turn his entire attention to the important intent of
their conversation, which was to prepare him for eternity. Then he added—

" But I must expect that we are not both of the
same opinion in regard to the state of man after death;
yet, though you might have persuaded yourself that
there is no life to come, and, consequently, neither
rewards nor punishments, I cannot help thinking that
there was a time when you were fully convinced of it.
Your inward feelings have frequently contradicted you.
The thought of eternity frightened you, though, unfortunately, you had art enough to stifle it in the birth.
However, it will always be out of your power to prove
that there is no eternity."

Struensee listened attentively, but would not own
that he ever had any inward impressions of immor-
tality, or had been afraid of it. Perhaps he might
have been, but he did not recollect. He owned that

the thought that he should soon entirely cease to be,
was disagreeable to him: it frightened him: he wished
to live, even though it were with less happiness than
he now enjoyed in his prison. But he did not find
the thought of total annihilation so terrible, as he
had noticed it was to many who entertained the
same principles as himself. In conclusion, he remarked:—

"My opinion, which is opposed to yours, is so
strongly woven into my sentiments: I have so many
arguments in favour of it: I have made so many ob-
servations from anatomy and physic which confirm it:
that I think it will be impossible for me to renounce
my principles. This, however, I promise: that I will
not wilfully oppose your efforts to enlighten me, but
rather wish, as far as it lies in my power, to concur
with you. I will not dissemble, but honestly tell you
of what I am convinced, and of what I am not. I
will deal with you openly: for such is my character,
and my friends can bear witness to it."

At Münter's request Struensee then explained to
him his religious principles, of which an account has
already been given.

On this first visit, Münter did not press his penitent
home, but as he observed that he was really very
uneasy about some of his actions, he thought it proper
to increase this uneasiness. With this view, he told
the prisoner, as he took leave of him, that Count
Bernstorff had died at Hamburg on February 18.

Struensee exclaimed, with great emotion, "What! is he dead?" and seemed to shudder.

"Yes," Münter answered, "he is. His wisdom, religion, and piety have preserved to him the character of a great man to the last; and it is generally believed that the grief of his latter years has hastened his death."

As Münter said this, he looked at the prisoner with an air which the latter seemed to understand, for he blushed.

On his second visit, Dr. Münter strove to convince the count of the falsity of his system, that man was a mere machine. Struensee answered, that in his present situation his mind was neither composed nor serene enough to examine into the nature of his principles. Münter, however, would not allow himself to be foiled in this manner, but earnestly warned the prisoner that it was his ambition alone which prevented him from doing justice to truth.

"Oh!" said Struensee, "this inclination is gone, and I am now very little in my own eyes; and how could I be ambitious in this place?"

Münter speedily discovered the tender side in his opponent. The thought of having dragged his friends and adherents into ruin with him grieved him most, and hence he found his only comfort in repentance. The doctor, consequently, had hardly touched on this topic, ere Struensee confessed to him with tears in his eyes, that he felt guilty in this respect. Münter confirmed him in his sorrow, hoping thus to induce him to speak about his other actions. He told him that, in order to qualify himself for God's mercy, it was necessary to search his former life, and to acknowledge his errors and crimes.   Then, in order to hold up to him the necessity of repentance, Münter delineated to him the outlines of his character, as he had reason for thinking it to be.

"God," the doctor said, "has given you an uncommon understanding, and, as I believe, a good natural disposition of heart; but, through voluptuousness, ambition, and levity, you have corrupted yourself."

Struensee confirmed Münter's conjectures, and admitted that voluptuousness had been his chief passion, and had contributed most to his moral depravity.

At the seventh conference Dr. Münter thought it advisable to hand Struensee a letter from his parents, which he had kept in his pocket for several days.   This letter is curious, as showing how far the idolatry of royalty was carried at that time.   Struensee's crime was considered so horrible, that no one imagined that it could be pardoned.   Even his parents, the letter shows, writing to him in his wretched dungeon, do not once testify a desire that his sufferings should be alleviated, or that he should be spared the death which he so justly merited.   The body was surrendered to man, who must be inexorable; the only thing to be effected was the salvation of the soul. The letter was to the following effect :—

My second Son!

I could wish that these lines, if possible, may reach you, that you may read and consider. The melancholy, grief, and anxiety of your parents on account of their sons, I am not able to express. Our eyes swim in tears day and night. Our souls cry for mercy to God without ceasing. But I will speak no more of this. There is but one thing that lies heavy on my mind, and that of your much afflicted mother. You know our sentiments. You know our intentions when we educated you. You remember how often and how seriously we inculcated this great truth, that godliness is profitable unto all things.

As often as I had occasion to speak to you, even then when you were in a public character, I reminded you of the omnipresent God, and exhorted you to be careful in preserving a good conscience. Your own heart will tell you how far you have lived up to the exhortations of your father.

Your parents have been in great anxiety about you for a long while. As we lead a retired life, and have very few acquaintances, and as you yourself have written nothing about your circumstances, the prayers and sighs of our straitened hearts have ascended to God in secret, and in our anxiety we cried that your soul might not be lost. Three different times, at Halle, Gedern, Altona, you were looked upon as a dead man by those who stood about your sick bed.

God saved you, and preserved your life; certainly with the sole intention of preparing you, in this time of grace, for a happy eternity. The same is now the chief intention of your gracious Redeemer in your prison. You are His creature. He loves you. You are redeemed by the blood of Jesus. God is a reconciled Father. You are baptized in the name of the Trinity. He will make an everlasting covenant with you, and will not desist from doing good to you. Return to your God, my son. He will not hide His face of grace from you. Mind the voice of your conscience, and the conviction which the spirit of God produces in your soul. Pray to God that He may disclose to you the true inward state of your soul, that you, enlightened by God, may see how much you are corrupted. Employ the solitude you are now in to search your whole life in the sight of the omniscient God, that you may see how great and detestable your sins are. Do not flatter yourself. Be rigorous with yourself. Accuse yourself, and judge yourself before the tribunal of God, whilst you are still enjoying this time of grace.

When you shall feel your sins to be a heavy burden, your heart then will humiliate itself before God, you will pray for mercy, and you will seriously detest and abhor your transgressions. You will then see the just importance and necessity of the redemption of Christ. You then will take refuge in Him who receives sinners, who was made to be sin for us, who has paid the debts of our sins, and suffered their punishment, that we might be made the righteousness of God in Him, and might have redemption through His blood, the forgiveness of sins, according to the riches of His grace.   Still the blood of Christ speaks for you. He that is merciful still stretches forth His hands. Without Jesus there is no salvation.   He is the cause of it.   Even for your sake He has received gifts.   You may have in Him righteousness for your peace of mind, and for your sanctification.   Oh that Jesus might be glorified in your heart!   In Him we have happiness while we live, while we suffer, while we die, and after death.

Your mother sends her love to you.   She weeps, she prays with me for our unfortunate sons.   My son, my son, how deeply do you afflict us!   Oh! could we but have this only comfort, that our sons turned with all their heart unto the Lord, and that we might with joy find them again in eternity before the throne of the Lamb!

Your crimes which brought you into prison are not properly and sufficiently known to us.   What is talked of and read in public about you is of such a nature that your parents condemn and detest it.   Oh! would to God that you had remained a physician!   Of your rise to honours we were informed by the newspapers; but it was no matter of joy to us; we read it with grief.   Oh! that you had kept, in all your transactions, a clear conscience, with much wisdom, piety, and humility, for the good of Denmark, and that you might have submitted with due subjection to all the commands of your sovereign. We cannot altogether judge of this matter for want of information. But know that, though we love our children, we nevertheless do not approve of their crimes, nor will we excuse or palliate them, or call them good; we rather hate all sins; detest, condemn, and abhor them; and praise God when He manifests His just wrath over the wicked, and shows His mercy to the penitent and the faithful. The Lord our God be your physician in your imprisonment, and cure thoroughly the wounds of your soul!

We, your parents, recommend you to the love of the Lord, who has mercy on you. May Jesus, who is a compassionate High Priest, remember you for good at the right hand of God, that you may receive mercy before the throne of grace, and be pardoned unto everlasting salvation. Yea, Jesus! Thou great friend of mankind, who wilt in nowise cast out him that comes to Thee, help parents and children to life everlasting.

I am, your heartily afflicted father,

ADAM STRUENSEE.

Rendsburg, March 4, 1772.

Struensee took this letter with eagerness, and began reading it; but it is not surprising to find that he had not half finished it when he laid it down, weeping bitterly. Shortly after, he received a letter from his mother, written precisely in the same Calvinistic strain as that from his father, and not containing one single trait of that maternal affection so necessary under such trying circumstances.

At length, after twenty-one days' exertions, Struensee was so far converted, partly by reading the New Testament, Jerusalem and Gellert's works, and partly, also, by Münter's earnest exhortations, that he burst into the following penitent words :—

"I should be guilty of the greatest folly if I would not embrace Christianity with joy, when its arguments are so overbalancing, and when it breathes such general benevolence. Its effects upon my heart are too strong. Oftentimes I cannot help crying when I read the history of Christ. Even now I think with hope on my death. I have acquainted myself with its most terrifying circumstances. I do not know how I shall be when the awful hour arrives. At present, I am not uneasy about it; I find nothing that makes me anxiously wish for life. I will confidently expect forgiveness of my sins through Christ. And to you, my dear friend, I am infinitely obliged that you have brought me so far."

Struensee then expressed a wish that those friends of his who entertained the same sentiments as he had done on religious matters might also be brought to a sense of their errors; and he felt an especial interest in Brandt's fate. It was consequently arranged that

Münter should bring Dean Hee to Struensee; and, when this took place a few days afterwards, the prisoner begged the latter to inform Brandt of his conversion. Shortly after, the dean delivered Brandt's answer, to the effect, "that he greatly rejoiced to hear of Struensee's conversion. For his own part, he found his only comfort in religion, and from his heart forgave Struensee for all that he had done to draw him into his misfortunes." Struensee was pleased to hear this, and from this period seemed to have his mind relieved of a great burden. Of the sincerity of his conversion the following passage seems to offer a convincing proof:—

"The Christian religion," Struensee said on one occasion, "is so engaging, that it must certainly please every one who is properly acquainted with it. We should see the best effects of it among the common people in reforming the world, if it were properly re-presented and rendered intelligible to the capacity of different sorts of people. They should be made sensible that in this life they could never be happier than by following the precepts of Christianity. Every one then would be convinced that, supposing even this religion to be a mistake, it must be such a one as contradicts entirely the nature of error and delusion, because it is the best and truest way of happiness. Every one would think it worth his while to maintain this opinion, and to propagate it.

"I wish you and other divines," he continued to

Münter, "would write small pamphlets, to acquaint the people with the advantages of Christianity, which might be of greater service than preaching. In this manner Voltaire has written, as you are aware, innumerable little pieces against religion, which contain the same ideas over again under different titles, and in a different dress. Rational friends of Christianity should learn of him this method, by which he does much mischief, and apply it to better purposes. Voltaire boasts of having found out this method, as he says, to enlighten the world. I remember, that when I conversed with d'Alembert in Paris, he spoke in high terms of praise of this method, and admired Voltaire's wisdom on this point. However, I do not believe him to be the inventor of it. Perhaps he borrowed this way of spreading his principles from Christ himself, who taught truth, sometimes in parables, sometimes in questions and answers, sometimes in sermons."

When Struensee at length received permission to write, he drew up, after consulting with Münter, a description of his conversion, which, however, was in some passages quite confused, and far from clear. It is a further proof how greatly the mind of this naturally talented man was thrown off the balance by the awful position in which he found himself.

The examination of the other prisoners, and the hearing of the witnesses, took place alternately in the citadel and in the Christiansborg Palace.   Professor Berger appeared at the bar on February 22, and so soon as he returned to prison he was allowed to be shaved and to eat with a knife and a fork.   He was also granted a better room, was permitted to sleep in his own bed, was allowed tobacco, and to read books from his own library.

Justiz-rath Struensee passed his time in prison in playing at chess with the officers of the watch.   After he had undergone an examination on March 7, the favour was also granted him of smoking a pipe, and drinking wine from his own cellar.

At last, on March 18, or two months after their arrest, came the turn of Colonel von Falckenskjold and Lieutenant-Colonel von Hesselberg to be examined. It has already been stated how scandalously these two gentlemen had been treated during their imprisonment at the main guard of the royal docks.   Permission had been asked of Prince Frederick to have Falckenskjold removed to a more wholesome cell, but he refused it, and answered, with a jeering laugh, "A man who has fought with the Turks must be able to endure such a punishment."   On the day of examination, the two prisoners were conveyed in litters to the citadel, but when they returned to prison they were allowed knives and forks, and freed from the constant presence of the officers of the guard in their room.

On March 25, Major-General Gude and Count

Struensee were confronted. On the following day, Admiral Hansen and Lieutenant Aboe made their statements, and as Etats-rath Willebrandt had been taken ill, he was examined in his house by a special commission.

The investigation gradually assumed such immense proportions, that the sittings to examine the prisoners and witnesses could not be closed till the end of March, or for nearly two months and a half.

CHAPTER IX.

THE QUEEN'S TRIAL.

THE QUEEN'S LETTERS—AN EXTORTED CONFESSION—THE HIGH
COURT OF INQUIRY—THE INDICTMENT— STATEMENT OF WIT-
NESSES—REVOLTING DETAILS—AMATEUR DETECTIVES—THE
MAIDS-IN-WAITING—FRAULEIN VON EYBEN—SENTIMENTS—
PRESENTS—THE VERDICT DEMANDED.

WHEN the new power was established in Copenhagen,
a species of suite was appointed to wait on the unhappy Caroline Matilda, less in the quality of attendants than of spies and gaolers.   The persons selected
were Fräuleins von Sperling and Von Schmettau,
Count Holstein zu Ledreborg, and Gentleman of the
Bedchamber Von Raben, all persons who were disagreeable to her.   Juliana Maria, who was nothing if
not bigoted, at once set to work to provide spiritual
assistance for her prisoner, and one Chemnitz, garrison
preacher at Elsinore, with incredible ferocity insulted,
in the name of Heaven, a princess who was already so
unhappy.   He chose as his text the following verses
from Isaiah, chapter xiv. :—

" And the people shall take them, and bring them
to their place: and the house of Israel shall possess
them in the land of the LORD for servants and hand-
maids: and they shall take them captives, whose captives they were; and they shall rule over their oppressors.

" And it shall come to pass in the day that the
LORD shall give thee rest from thy sorrow, and from
thy fear, and from the hard bondage wherein thou
wast made to serve.

" That thou shalt take up this proverb against the
king of Babylon, and say, How hath the oppressors
ceased! the golden city ceased!"

Another preacher, Hansen, who was appointed to
the same duty on alternate days with Chemnitz, derived, from chapter lxiii. of the same prophet, the
subject of an even more cruel insult:—

" Wherefore art thou red in thine apparel, and thy
garments like him that treadeth in the winefat?

" I have trodden the winepress alone; and of the
people there was none with me: for I will tread them
in mine anger, and trample them in my fury; and their
blood shall be sprinkled upon my garments, and I will
stain all my raiment.

" For the day of vengeance is in mine heart, and the
year of my redeemed is come."

Neither of these clerical ruffians was either punished
or even reprimanded for his shameless audacity.

At first, the royal prisoner was confined on the

ground floor of the castle, the windows being lined with iron bars; she was strictly guarded, none but her watchers being allowed to have access to her. In February, she received another heavy blow on hearing of the death of her beloved mother, and, in her agony, wrote the two following letters, which she contrived by some means to send out of the castle:—

To Sir RODERT KEITH, *Envoy of Great Britain.*

From the first day of my iniquitous arrest and severe captivity, I foresaw that the rage of my enemies would insist on the loss of my liberty and life. I am perfectly resigned to my fate either way; but the thought of my reputation being tarnished and my dear children abandoned to the mercy of a people unjustly prejudiced against the legitimacy of their birth, overwhelms me with the most pungent grief. Has the king, my brother, then abandoned me? Great God! will no one, then, avenge my innocence and my memory? I doubt whether my merciless Arguses will suffer this letter to reach you; in case you receive it, contrive to do me all the good offices in your power. I shall never forget the zeal which you have testified in the cause of innocence; and if ever Heaven should restore me to the rank and pre-eminence from which I have been so unjustly degraded, you shall have more convincing proofs of my gratitude. Oh! were I in England, my dear country, where the meanest criminal

has the privilege of being tried by his peers! Am I
forgot by the whole universe?   I am greatly fallen
away, and my health is much impaired since I have
been immured within these walls.   There is not a
single person about me whom I do not suspect; and
I despair of ever recovering my liberty.   For the love
of God, endeavour to visit me.   The time approaches
when my trial will take place; but I am apprehensive
my sentence is already determined.   I pray God that
He will take you under his holy protection.*

MATILDA.

The queen wrote about the same time another letter
to the king, which, of course, never reached its desti-
nation, though a copy of it was fortunately preserved :—

SIRE,

If justice and humanity still dwell in your royal
breast, I have an undoubted right, as your most injured wife, to claim your Majesty's protection from
this vale of misery. Your honour is impeached as
well as my virtue; if the sense of both cannot inspire
you with tender feelings for my inexpressible woes
and the indignities offered to supreme authority by
the most flagitious combination of all the engines the
blackest calumnies could play to blast my innocence
and reputation, I appeal to your Majesty's own conviction of my spotless and inviolable fidelity. I do

* This letter was first published in the English papers early in April, 1772.

not entreat mercy, but I demand justice.   Were your
heart callous to my inexpressible sufferings, sure what
you owe to yourself and the dear pledges of conjugal
affection should call for the utmost exertion of your
power to maintain your prerogative, which has been
so daringly encroached upon, and to avenge the out-
rages I have been forced to submit to, by an unparal-
leled confederacy of traitors determined to snatch the
sceptre from your hands, and to sacrifice your guiltless
consort and your progeny to their wicked ambition.
I wish for a fair trial, and that I may face and confound my accusers.   To the Supreme Judge, who
knows all hearts and all motives, I submit the justice
of my cause.

MATILDA.

On March 8, 1772, the commission appointed by
the new authorities, acting in the name of a king
without a will, arrived at the fortress of Kronborg for
the purpose of examining the queen.   It consisted of
two members of the lately-established privy council,
Count Thott and Schack Rathlau, and two members
of the committee of investigation, Actuary of the Supreme Court Baron Juel-Wind, and Stampe, Attorney-
General of the Danish Chancery; that is to say, of
opponents of the fallen minister, and zealous participators in the conspiracy.

This composition of the commission justifies the
supposition that it was solely intended to extort from

the unhappy queen a confirmation of the confession made by Struensee on February 21, of improper intercourse with her, and thus afford an excuse to the English court for the way in which she had been treated.

According to Reverdil, Colonel Keith had contrived to warn Caroline Matilda beforehand of the impending arrival of the commission, and to advise her conduct. She would receive these pretended judges with kindness and dignity, like subjects who had come to pay their court to their sovereign. If they afterwards attempted to interrogate her, she would act wisely in merely saying that she had no answer to give them, and that she recognised no superior, or judge, but her husband.

Thus forewarned, the queen, whose heroic soul had not been bowed down by a succession of agonising days spent in the most miserable solitude and the most torturing suspense, received the commissioners with a calm dignity, in which her strength of mind was fully displayed. The complicated and crafty questions asked her had no power to confuse her senses; her answers were noble, short, and accurate; she declared that she had nothing to reproach herself with, and caused the commissioners the utmost embarrassment by her steady and unexpected behaviour. When the crafty Schack lost all hope of overcoming the queen's mind, he fancied that her heart would not have the strength to withstand a similar attack. In order, therefore, to obtain the confession which was required for the predetermined condemnation of the queen, he employed a villanous device which will brand his name for ever. He was no longer the noble-minded man who, once on a time, preferred to sacrifice rank, prestige, and fortune, sooner than remain in a council whose traditional authority had been degraded; he was now a crawling courtier, who allowed himself to be used for anything, so long as favour, power, or money was promised him; who had lost all his strength of mind, and no longer possessed any marked character, but could only flatter the powerful, defy the weak, and deceive the good hearted. A long and painful illness had weakened his intellect; the vexations of a hampered fortune had rendered him selfish, and deprived him of all respect from those of noble mind; and, on this occasion, he put the final touch to his character.*

Schack Rathlau hastened to inform the queen that their next proceeding would be to lay before her Majesty Struensee's confessions, and to request her confirmation of them; after which he read to her the original document signed by the unfortunate man.

Blushing with anger at the accusation it contained, the queen indignantly denied everything, and declared the impossibility of Struensee having made such statements, as they were utterly false!

Schack Rathlau presented the damning paper, so that the queen might herself read it, and be convinced of Struensee's autograph. She rejected it with scorn,

* "Authentische Aufklärungen," pp. 223, 224.

but took a searching glance at the signature, and to
her horror recognised the well-known hand.   Schack,
noticing the betrayed queen's embarrassment, thought
the moment favourable to complete her temptation.
With a reverential bow he advanced a step nearer, and
said, as if disgusted by the false charge:

"Si l'aveu de M. Struensee n'est point vrai, Madame,
alors il n'y a pas de mort assez cruelle pour ce monstre
qui a osé vous compromettre à ce point."

Caroline Matilda, who had been kept in utter ignorance of all that was taking place in Copenhagen, and
probably had formed no idea of the deadly peril impending over her ex-cabinet secretary, fell back into
her chair on hearing Schack Rathlau's fearful menace:
honour and feeling contended powerfully in her breast,
while the inquisitor eagerly tried to read the effect of
these words of terror on the queen's countenance.   At
length, she regained some slight composure, and looking Schack firmly in the face, asked:

" Mais si j'avouais les mots de Struensee, pourrais-je
sauver sa vie par là?"

· Schack Rathlau—it is hard to say whether he believed in the probability of such a rescue, or merely in
his legal arrogance triumphed at the palpable result of
his menace—answered, with brazen brow:

" Surement, Madame, cela pourrait adoucir son sort
de toute manière."

Saying this, he spread out the prepared document,
containing the confirmation of Struensee's confession
for the queen to sign.

" Eh bien, je signerai," the unfortunate lady said, as she seized the pen eagerly offered by Schack Rathlau, and appended her signature.   She had hardly done so, however, when the consciousness of her want of caution and precipitation so affected her, that she sank back on the sofa in a fainting state.*   The commissioners, however, hastened back to Copenhagen in great delight with the decisive document.

After ninety-two years posterity gazes with compassion on the historical picture of the royal martyr who, in the first bloom of youth, fettered through political motives to a husband, from whom all eyes were averted with feelings of anger and disgust, certainly committed no other crime than that of taking pleasure in the society of the only man who seemed her sincere friend, a man who had a heart for her connubial sufferings, who ever tried to alleviate them, and to whom alone she dared impart her wrongs.   The confirmation of this truth must be left to the poor betrayed martyr herself.   Still, for a proper comprehension of the cabal against her, one fact, speaking decidedly for the queen's innocence, may be quoted, in which a plausible explanation of Struensee's otherwise inexplicable conduct can be found :

" On avait dit à Struensee qu'il se sauverait en

* According to another version of the story, given by Falckenskjold and the "Authentische Aufklärungen," the queen fainted after writing the first syllable, CAROL——.   Schack Rathlau seized the queen's hand, forced the fallen pen into it, and guiding it, added the missing syllables INE MATILDA.   This statement, however, is highly improbable, and nowhere confirmed by the queen.

compromettant la reine, dont la conduite ne pouvait
être l'objet d'une condamnation juridique, ou même
d'un procès criminal, et on avoit ajouté à ce motif le
menace de la torture."*

The twofold treachery explained by this passage
hardly requires comment. To overthrow Struensee
was not sufficient, as the queen might have regained
her authority over her husband. Hence, Caroline
Matilda must be destroyed, and though the *Lex Regia*
expressly prohibited the judges from trying matters of
high treason, the new authorities did not care for that.

Immediately after the return of the commissioners
from their successful expedition, a General Commission,
consisting of no less than thirty-four members, was
appointed as a Supreme Court to pass sentence in the
cause of the king against the queen. The court was
composed of—the Bishop of Seeland and four other
clerical councillors: the four ministers, Counts von
Thott and Osten, Baron von Schack Rathlau and
Admiral Römeling: the members of the commission,
to whom the trial of the other prisoners had up to the
present been entrusted: the other members of the
Supreme Court not belonging to the commission:
two officers of the army and two of the navy: several
councillors of state and one of the civic authorities.

The court opened its session on March 16, in the
audience hall of the Exchequer. A royal order appointed Bang, lawyer in the Court of Exchequer, to

* Falkenskjold's " Memoirs," p. 222.

undertake the king's cause, and Uldall, of the Supreme Court, that of the queen. Both the judges and the lawyers were released from their oath of allegiance during the trial.

In his indictment of March 24, Bang demanded that her Majesty Queen Caroline Matilda, by virtue of par. v. of the xvi. cap. of section 3 of the code of Christian V. should be condemned as guilty of having broken her marriage vows with his Majesty King Christian VII., and that the latter might be at liberty to form another alliance.[*]

Bang's Indictment of Queen Caroline Matilda.

After a short introduction, the accuser proceeds in the following terms:—

The command of my king alone could induce me to write against her Majesty the Queen, and it is with a feeling of the deepest submission, with horror and grief, that I here investigate the conduct of Queen Caroline Matilda, and the proof that she has broken her marriage vow.

[*] The indictment and defence of the queen have never before been published—with the exception of a few fragments in Höst's "Grev Struensee og hans Ministerium." They are given here in full, save some passages which decency forbids being rendered public. Höst, who wrote his history in the reign of Frederick VI., was compelled to omit the passages which might compromise the memory of the queen. But historic truth urges me to publish everything that may serve to clear up this matter and enable a correct opinion to be formed.

I am emboldened to indict her Majesty, because the king's marriage bed must be kept pure and unsullied before that of all others. This the king can demand as a husband, and he must assert it for the honour of his house and the welfare of his nation.

As husband, he has the right of the compact on his side; as the first of his house, he is bound to guard the antiquity, supremacy, respect, honour, and purity of the Danish royal family. Who is there that is ignorant of the virtues of this exalted royal family! But, if a foreign race were grafted on the royal stem, and the descendants of lackeys were to bear the name and supremacy of the king, would not its antiquity cease, its supremacy disappear, its respect be lost, its honour be insulted, and its purity sullied?*

For the sake of his nation the king must demand this. The inhabitants of Denmark and Norway have sworn fidelity, obedience, and allegiance to the descendants of Frederick III., and all our progeny will do so after us. But would we or our posterity so submissively subject ourselves to descendants of Queen Caroline Matilda, who are not at the same time scions of Christian VII.? What a source of troubles! Hence, his Majesty, as husband in his house, as first of his sex, and as king in his land, has appointed this com-

* No objection can be raised against this assertion generally. But the Danish code forbade the courts from hearing charges against the domestic honour of royal persons, and decreed that the king must be sole judge in such affairs. The constitution of the commission was therefore illegal from the outset.

mission.   His personal right, the honour of his house, and the security of the nation, simultaneously demand that the justice and strictest loyalty, which alone animate this commission, should, in accordance with the laws of God, of nature, and of this country, dissolve the marriage tie which bound her Majesty Caroline Matilda to our Christian VII.

I will not speak in this affair, but allow her Majesty herself to speak: I will let the person speak, who, by her Majesty's confession has uttered the truth; I will let facts, and lastly witnesses, speak.

On March 9 last, her Majesty at Kronborg Castle, replied to the three questions submitted to her by the plenipotentiaries appointed by her lord the king. To question 2, her Majesty acknowledged that she had broken the marriage vow which she made to his Majesty; and to question 3, her Majesty acknowledged that she had thus forfeited her marriage rights.

Count Struensee, on February 21 last, replied, after long reflection and with great agitation, to question 239 laid before him by the commission, whether the intimacy between Queen Caroline Matilda and himself had gone as far as it can go between two persons of different sexes—

" As all the circumstances are so incriminating that even if the greatest intimacy had not existed, still appearances would prove it, he confessed that it was difficult to resist opportunity and the natural weakness of women, but he begged the commission, in consideration of his mental emotion, to spare him more detailed reminiscences."

Count Struensee repeated this confession on February 25 with more ample details, and then signed it with his own hand.

Count Struensee's full confession was laid before her Majesty on March 9, and its truth acknowledged by her.

These confessions, so ample and concordant, made in the presence of the royal commissioners, might in themselves be regarded as sufficient proof in accordance with the article of the law that "it is not sufficient that the accused person herself should confess her guilt, because it is often found that many persons make false statements, in order that the one may get away from the other, and injure him or her, with whom he or she confesses to have sinned."

The quoted presumption, that the one might wish to get rid of the other, cannot be applied to her Majesty, and the same is the case with the second part of the article, "in order to injure the person with whom the sin has been committed;" therefore, the entire supposition of the law, that the accused might bear false witness against him, or her, self, is not applicable. As, moreover, all the circumstances which were in this case stated in Count Struensee's confession, and acknowledged by the queen, have been proved by clear evidence and numerous other data, which are always the precedents, companions, and results of such an illicit intercourse, it is my most humble duty to lay all these things before the commission.

Thus, the answers of Count Struensee to questions 3, 4, and 5, relating to the time and way in which he entered the queen's apartments, the ensuing warnings and short abstinence are proved by the evidence of witnesses. The wives of Councillors Blechinberg and Schiötte, who were at that time maids of honour to her Majesty, and bed-chamber woman, Anna Petersen, declare that in the winter of 1769 and the beginning of 1770 they formed suspicions from Struensee's repeated and long visits to the queen, and maid Petersen more especially noticed that the door of the dark passage, which leads from the queen's bed-chamber to the hermitage (Mezzanine floor), was opened on some nights and merely left ajar; and the deceased lackey Hansen also remarked how he had heard this door opened at night. After talking together, and consulting Councillor Blechinberg and the deceased Hansen, they sought to acquire a certainty in the matter, more especially as they knew that no one but the queen could open this door, as none else except a bed-chamber woman had a key to it. With this object they put wax in the keyhole, and bits of paper between the hinges, and at the same time placed wax in the wards of the key, which lay on the queen's toilette table. They then found on each occasion next morning that the wax had fallen both out of the keyhole and the wards, and the paper slipped out of the hinges

on to the floor, and thus acquired a certainty that the
door had been opened during the night.   The waiting
maid also strewed powder on the boards of the dark
passage in the evening, and on the next morning all
the witnesses saw marks of large feet in the powder
up to the door of the queen's bedroom, and thence to
the bed.   In the morning, when such footsteps were
found in front of the bed, maid Petersen and maid
Bruhn, now Councilloress Blechinberg, came in to
make the queen's bed, and called in maid Horn, now
Councilloress Schiötte.*

Grieved for her Majesty's beloved name and reputation, and terrified by the awful consequences of
this daring deed, in which they feared they might be
innocently entangled, they resolved, after due reflection and with masculine resolution, to lay their sorrows
and most devoted submission at her Majesty's feet.†
Hence the two maids, Bruhn and Horn, one day
with quaking hearts and tear-laden eyes approached
her Majesty, who ever then as now had a heart full
of kindness, and asked them, with emotion, what was
the matter with them, and if she, the queen, had done
anything to grieve them ?   This gracious reception
still more aroused in these faithful servants all the
feelings of reverence and devotion, with which they

* The queen's women respected nothing, and even made their mistress's bed
and linen the object of their examination.

† It should be mentioned that the original indictment is written in such a
barbarous and illogical style that it is very difficult to make it endurable by
the reader, without injuring the legal meaning.

were filled at that time.　　Maid Horn, who was so affected that she was unable to speak, left the execution of their mutual design to maid Bruhn, upon which the queen leaped from her seat, threw her arms round maid Bruhn's neck, and said, "Tell me, dear Bruhn, what is the matter with you?"　This command of her Majesty loosened maid Bruhn's tongue. "There is a report," she said, "that Struensee spends the night with your Majesty.　We feel so grieved at it, because it is stated that the two queens dowager and the council are aware of it, and purpose interfering."　The maids then hinted that they were acquainted with the story of the door leading to the Mezzanine, and wished that the whole rumour might be unfounded.　The queen asked them whether they believed it; requested to speak with Struensee at once, who, as she said, would soon find a remedy; and, in conclusion, asked, " Do you think that the rumour will die out, if I do not let him come so often?　I cannot entirely abandon him, as that would arouse too much attention."

Her Majesty's confessions dispense me from making any reflections on this head.

After the queen had consulted with Struensee on the same day, she said to her waiting-women, " Do you know that any one who speaks in such a way about her queen can be punished by the loss of her tongue?"

After this incident, the intercourse between the

queen and Struensee ceased for about a fortnight; but then became worse than before. Still from this time the witnesses noticed no nocturnal passage through the corridor to the Mezzanine, while the familiar and gracious intercourse of the queen with these her maids ceased from this day; so that she only addressed them in the tone of a mistress.

That which her Majesty wished to deny to her maids she confessed, however, to her lady-in-waiting, Von Eyben; for when the latter found the queen one day weeping and in grief, she asked what was the matter with her Majesty; and the queen told her of the conversation with the maids, but confessed that the affair was unfortunately true, and said that Struensee had advised her to bribe her women, which she refused to do; nor would her Majesty follow the advice of her women, and "displace" Struensee.

Among the things which are inseparable from such actions is rumour, which follows them as their shadow. And who is unacquainted with these rumours?

As regards the queen's intercourse with Count Struensee, Professor Berger, now under arrest, declares, that it had appeared to him most suspicious, and Struensee's lodgings highly improper. Struensee had always behaved to her with impropriety, and ventured on excessive familiarity. This improper conduct began first in the city in 1770, was continued in the same year on the Holstein tour, and afterwards on the return of the royal family to Denmark.

Count Brandt declares that in the summer of 1770, while the royal party were in Holstein, the queen was alone one morning early with Count Struensee, and that the latter drove out with her alone in a carriole. The intercourse between them proved in every way that they loved each other; they sought one another, were delighted to meet; in a word, love was revealed in that manner which can be perceived but not described. If at times they quarrelled, Struensee said that the queen was jealous of him, and accused him of not being so amiable as usual, and hence Struensee was always obliged to dance with the oldest ladies at balls. Brandt also declares that Struensee made him a "confidence" of this amourette, and said that he could make love to the queen best at the masquerade.

Fräulein von Eyben, and the sixth, fourth, and twenty-ninth witnesses about Struensee's suspicious intimacy with the queen, assert: "While the court was residing in Holstein in 1770, the queen drove out alone with Struensee, remained away a couple of hours, and did not return till seven o'clock." Furthermore, the two first witnesses declare that once, when they were about to enter the queen's cabinet, they found Struensee seated by her side on the sofa, and that the queen ran toward them and sent them away. Afterwards, the queen told them that the king was so frightened when they, the witnesses, came to the door, that he tried to run out of the room, and that was the reason why she hurried toward them.

Furthermore, they state: In Schleswig, there was a flight of stairs in Gottorp Castle, leading from the queen's retiring-room to Struensee's apartments, which her Majesty frequently made use of. The queen went once, at Frederiksberg, at a late hour of the night, into Struensee's room, which was next to the apartment of the prince royal, where Madame Petersen and Madame Schönberg were.* At Frederiksberg, too, Struensee one evening, after he was undressed, put on an overcoat, and in that state went up to the queen's cabinet. —(*Cfr.* the statements of witnesses, 18, 19, 20.)

Witnesses 2 and 17 have also given very incriminating evidence about Struensee's visits to the queen at a late hour of the night. Thus, during the whole of the summer of 1770, Struensee continually, and generally at unusual hours, visited the queen in his surtout and dirty boots, and frequently sat down on her bed: he drank tea and coffee with her every forenoon; often remained with her till one in the morning on evenings when there was no ball or masquerade, and on the latter evenings even later. He frequently went up the secret stairs to her bedroom unannounced, and on such occasions ordered the waiting-women, contrary to the rule, to retire from the rooms next to the queen's chamber.—(*Cfr.* statements of witnesses 2, 5, 6, 12, 13, and 18.)†

* It was a scoundrel deed to bring forward this charge, as everybody knew that this took place at the time when the prince royal was attacked by the small-pox, and the anxious mother watched every night at his bedside.

† At the period specified, Struensee was physician in ordinary to both their

Struensee acknowledges these facts, though with a certain apology, that he was obliged to hand medicines to the queen, and that he did not remain with her till a late hour of the night. Against this we have the later confession of February 25.

Her Majesty's conversations with her bed-chamber people seem to prove that her heart felt more warmly for another man than for the king her lord. Thus her Majesty, for instance, asked her maids whether they entertained love or sentiments for any man? for if they had such, they ought to follow their object to the gallows or the wheel, or, if it must be, even to Hell. On the maids objecting, but suppose such a person were to prove unfaithful, her Majesty replied: In such a case she would lose her senses, or take her own life. She next praised the good fortune of the maids, who could marry as they pleased, and added, that if ever she became a widow, she would marry a private person whom she loved, even if she were obliged to leave the country and the throne in consequence. On this occasion she showed the witnesses a garnet cross, which she always wore on her bosom, and remarked that there were sentiments connected with it, for she had it from a very dear friend; and when the witness said it must be the king, she answered jeeringly, "Of course, the king."

Majesties. As it is well known that at the time Caroline Matilda was suffering from an odious disease communicated to her by the king, it is not surprising that her physician should remain with her till a late hour.

I do not know in which class to reckon the following fact, whether as forgetfulness of self, or as a fruit of the intercourse with Struensee. Her Majesty often displayed herself perfectly undressed to her chamber women, walking in broad daylight in a room which had windows on both sides, and at a time when the guard mounting was taking place, and then asked the maids whether they had ever seen Eve or Christ? I quote this fact here, because it appears as if this trait originated in the above-mentioned sentiments.—(*Cfr.* statements of witnesses 2, 4, 5, and 6.)

To these strange sentiments, which were probably poisoned by Count Struensee, is attributable the fact, that her Majesty remarked to witness 6, that she was well aware what people said about her, but did not care for it; and further, that there was no harm in a wife being unfaithful to her husband, if he became old, or she had been compelled to marry him. The queen also stated to witness 10, that although she knew what people said of her she would not alter her conduct. About this time, in order to facilitate this improper intercourse, Struensee asked for a *passe partout* to the palace, which did not belong to his office, as he has confessed.

With the same object the queen's sleeping cabinets at Christiansborg, Frederiksborg, and Hirschholm, were at this time so arranged that people could go from her rooms to Struensee's unnoticed. This was especially the case in the autumn of 1771 at Christiansborg, when the queen's bedroom was removed to the chapel corridor, which could be reached by a private flight of stairs from the Mezzanine. It also deserves mention, that after this bedroom and two other rooms had been prepared, in 1770, for her Majesty's use, by her own orders, a privy passage and stairs, which had always been closed, were opened, and lamps were burning in the passage from three P.M. till eight in the morning, though during the whole period the valets were not allowed to look after the lamps. It was in one of these cabinets over the chapel corridor that her Majesty drank tea and coffee with Struensee in the morning. —(*Cfr.* the survey of the commissioners.)

The peculiar presents which her Majesty made to Struensee, and received from him in return, are of importance when connected with what the queen has acknowledged. Her Majesty received from Struensee a pair of red-striped garters, which she always insisted on wearing, whether she required them or not, (!) assuring her maids that they were " sentiments' garters." The count confesses that the queen received these garters from him. He alleges .that he purchased them in Hamburg, and the queen, seeing them once, kept them, because they were perfumed; but he was paid for them.

Her Majesty also always carried about her person a green case, in which was Struensee's portrait in Indian ink, and allowed no one to see it. When she was delivered at Hirschholm, during the last summer, she asked for this portrait, and gazed at it. .On her departure for

Kronborg, on January 17, her Majesty took it with
her, and when she arrived at the castle she fastened
it on her naked body, from which Madame Schönberg
dissuaded her. She now keeps it at night under her
pillow, for fear lest any one might take it from her.
—(*Cfr.* statements of witnesses 5, 6, 10, 12, 13;
Maid Arnsberg's answers to question 29, and Struensee's to question 227.)

Among the presents accepted by the queen there
was probably a gold cross set with garnets, which her
Majesty wore for a long time, and concealed in her
bosom, took it out frequently and kissed it, remarking,
that it was a present from a dear friend, and that sentiments were attached to it, although Struensee denies
ever having seen this cross.[*]

Among Struensee's effects the following valuables
were found, which, as he says, the queen gave him:—
I. A case containing a concealed miniature of the
queen. II. A pin with a large brilliant. III. A ring
with an antique. IV. A large brilliant ring. V. A
sapphire. And VI. Another large sapphire. Of the
last Struensee says that it belongs to the king, but
witness 6 declares that it belonged to the queen, who
consequently gave it to Struensee. VII. A blue en-
amelled golden heart, which, as Struensee confesses,
the queen gave him once when she was talking about
friendship. Of this valuable, witnesses 2 and 4 state
that the queen wore it on a watch, which she brought

---

[*] An annulet given to the queen in England before her marriage.

with her from England.   Various other data confirm
the correctness of the confessions made.

On one occasion the queen had a blue mark on her
bosom, which she carefully concealed from the king.
At the same time she asked her waiting-women how
they supposed the mark was produced?   Maid Horn
answered, that it looked as if it had come from suck-
ing. The queen laughed, and held her tongue. Modesty
and the queen's confession save me from saying anything further on this point.

In the same way the queen once felt a pain in her
side, under the breast.   Struensee came daily to rub
the spot, and the queen would not allow her maids or
any one else to be present.   When the lady of the
bed-chamber spoke with the queen about this, her
Majesty became angry, and afterwards said to the
maids, that the lady of the bed-chamber treated her
like a child, who must not be allowed to be alone with
the doctor.—(See the evidence of witness 2.)

It appears to denote an exaggerated intimacy, that
Struensee, in the summer of 1771, was present at
Hirschholm when the queen was delivered, although
it was not his duty, and afterwards dined alone with
her, and drank tea on her bed.—(*Cfr.* evidence of
witnesses 6, 7, 10, 12 and 15.)

During the last summer, when the sailors marched
to Hirschholm, or at the time when the ox was given
—for the witnesses cannot state positively on which
of these occasions it was—the queen intended to ride

15 *

away with Struensee, and ordered her riding-habit to be brought into her room for the night. After she had undressed, and gone to bed in great confusion without a nightcap, she rose again and collected her jewels in a coffer, while orders were sent to the stables to hold her saddle-horse in readiness. (See statements of witnesses 12, 13, and 20, and of Count Brandt.)

Before the queen commenced her journey on January 17 to Kronborg, the first thing she said, when maid Arnsberg announced to her that Count Rantzau was there with several officers, was: " Where is the count?" After this, her most Gracious Majesty ran in her night-dress down the privy stairs to Struensee's rooms, in order to seek the count. As, however, she only found his valet, who was under arrest, she said to the guards that they must fetch the count for her on peril of their heads.

At Kronborg, where her Majesty is now residing,(!) she one night asked maid Arnsberg where the count was; and when the latter answered, " In the citadel," the queen said: " Is he in chains, or does he have anything to eat? does he know that I am at Kronborg?" Hence, then, her Majesty's memory is still burdened with a tender memory of the count.

Such are the confessions and proofs on which this question, unique in its way, is founded. In my indictment I have contented myself with merely writing down and quoting the words of her Majesty, Count

Struensee, and the witnesses, in order not to venture reflections of my own, and thus insult the illustrious person against whom my instructions compel me to plead.

I venture to hope that I have written in accordance with the commands given me, without encroaching on the reverence and deep respect which I owe to her Majesty.

And as the witnesses, to whose statements on oath I have appealed, were not examined in her Majesty's exalted presence, owing to the most submissive respect entertained for her Majesty's exalted rank and birth, although by the law this should be done, I expect that her Majesty's advocate, Herr Uldall, will make a declaration to the commission that he has no objections to raise to the credibility of the witnesses; and, as both her Majesty's own acknowledgment, and Count Struensee's confession, have been in every way confirmed by the evidence of the witnesses, there is no reason for believing the confession to be untrue. I, therefore, in the name of his royal Majesty, demand a verdict :—

"That by virtue of the fifth paragraph of the sixteenth section of the third book of the Code, her Majesty Caroline Matilda, shall be declared guilty of having broken her marriage vow, and that it be dissolved, so as not to prevent his royal Majesty, the king, from contracting a new alliance."   O. L. Bang.

Copenhagen, March 24, 1772.

Every effort was made to procure evidence against the queen, and yet the result was the wretched *potpourri* which Advocate Bang brought forward. Among others whom it was attempted to suborn was Sarti the composer, who had been music-master to Caroline Matilda.   So far, however, from having any such evidence to give as it was sought to extort from him, Sarti declared that the queen's conduct, of which he had numerous opportunities of judging, was marked by the most perfect propriety and decorum, and he utterly repudiated the idea of her guilt.

But the judges had not been appointed to execute justice, but to crush the vanquished, and hence it is not surprising to find that no objection was raised to the utter perversion of the law which Bang displayed throughout his atrocious indictment—an indictment, be it remembered, made in writing, and not publicly announced, because hundreds of respectable citizens would have voluntarily come forward to assert their confidence in the queen's innocence.

CHAPTER X.

THE QUEEN'S DEFENCE.

CAROLINE MATILDA'S FEELINGS—ADVOCATE ULDALL—THE DEFENCE—THE QUEEN'S INNOCENCE—A FAIR TRIAL DEMANDED—CHARACTER OF THE EVIDENCE—THE LAW OF ADULTERY—VALUE OF EVIDENCE—STRUENSEE'S FAVOUR—FRAULEIN VON EYBEN—TRIFLES LIGHT AS AIR—THE QUEEN'S ATTENDANTS—A FLAW IN THE ARGUMENT—REVERDIL'S APPEAL—THE SENTENCE.

So soon as Advocate Bang had concluded his indictment, the queen's advocate, Uldall, requested an adjournment of the court for eight or ten days, so that he might have sufficient time to consult with his exalted client about the defence to be offered. This being granted, Uldall proceeded to Kronborg, where he had a long, important, and affecting consultation with the queen. The unfortunate princess was standing, at a tender age, and adorned with all the gifts which could have ensured permanent felicity, on the verge of an abyss, in which her honour, her dignity, her peace, would be swallowed up for ever. A single

day might tear from her her husband, children, and
throne: and she would survive this loss! what fearful
reflections!   The queen felt them in their full extent:
her whole feeling was poured into the expressions in
which she depicted to Uldall the terrible images that
occupied her mind.

" I should be inconsolable," she said to him, " if
the least of my actions could inflict injury on the
king, or his monarchy.   I was, perhaps, incautious,
but never wicked: my sex, my age, the circumstances
in which I was, must serve as my apology.   I was
ever too quiet against suspicion, and this tranquillity
may have led me astray.   The laws speak against
me; I humbly honour their terrible meaning, and
feel that they must speak against me from the lips of
my judges.   I trust that they will lose their sharp-
ness in such mouths.   The king, my consort, must
confirm their sentence.   Oh! then my whole hope
springs into life again!   He will not repulse me, he
will not hurl me into endless misery."

The queen's tears and sighs frequently interrupted
this affecting speech; and at last she found some rest,
more in her own weakness than in any alleviation of
the painfulness of her feelings.   She addressed Uldall
with greater calmness, and arranged with him the
arguments he should employ in her defence.*

The second session of the Extraordinary Council
was held on April 2, and the following defence was
submitted:—

* " Authentische Aufklarungen."

Uldall's Defence of Queen Caroline Matilda.[*]

With unfeigned emotion I proceed to the fulfilment of the duty which the welfare of the queen, and the will of the king, impose on me.

The dignity of these exalted personages, the importance and consequences of the affair, the zealous wish to do my duty, and a reasonable apprehension that I shall not be able to do so properly, sufficiently justify my sorrow at being compelled to see the queen lay off her purple, descend from the throne, and, like the most wretched of women, seek protection from the law. Can there possibly be a more affecting example of the insecurity of human happiness? She, in whose person we do homage to the blood of so many kings, is suspected of having dishonoured it. She who gave the king her hand and heart, is accused by the man who, at that time, promised to be her lord and protector. She, who by the unanimous verdict of the nation, received the name of mother of the country, is tried by those men who at that day would have joyfully shed their blood for her. So unhappy is Queen Caroline Matilda, and she alone among all the Queens of Denmark! At an age, and gifted with all the qualities, which seemed to determine her felicity, she finds herself on the verge of an abyss, in which her honour, her dignity, and her peace may be lost. What a

[*] This state paper has never before been published in England, and is literally translated from the original text.

thought to lose her husband, her children, her throne, on the same day, and to survive the loss! Suspected, accused, in danger of leading the most wretched life for a long course of years: can there be anything more cruel for hearts that are capable of thinking and feeling? Thus the queen regards her fate, and she described it to me, when I had the honour of waiting upon her, in the following words:

"I must despair, had my intentions been other than the welfare of the king and the country. If I have possibly acted incautiously, my age, my sex, and my rank must excuse me. I never believed myself exposed to a suspicion, and even, though my confession appears to confirm my guilt, I know myself to be perfectly innocent. The law requires me to be convicted: my consort has granted me this, and I hope he will, through the mouth of his commissioners, acknowledge that I have not rendered myself unworthy of him."

I quote her Majesty's words exactly as she uttered them, but how much do I wish that I could reproduce the emotion with which they were spoken, the frankness that gave them increased weight, and the trembling voice, which justly claimed compassion. The latter, no one can refuse her without insulting humanity.

Among the charges brought against her Majesty, is the sanctity of the duties imposed on her by her marriage with her royal husband: it has been stated that the king's bed must remain unsullied, that his own honour, and the honour and prosperity of the country,

require this.   But these truths are so far from affecting
the queen, that she demands the strictest investigation
ere she can believe that she has acted contrariwise.
The more important the duties she had to perform,
the more fearful are the consequences of any infraction
of them, and the more familiar the two parties were,
the clearer must be the evidence that her Majesty
has really committed a fault. We may first ask in
which manner the honour of the king and his family
will be best promoted?   By proving the queen guilty,
or must it not be sought in her innocence?   Has her
Majesty, perchance, never known and fulfilled what
she owed to herself, her husband, and his people; or
will it not rather be allowed that from the period when
her accusation begins, she proved herself a tender
mother, an affectionate wife, and a worthy queen? Can
it be credited that her Majesty should so easily have
forgotten herself?   And can she, who at that day
sought her delight in modesty, virtue, and the veneration and affection of the king and the country, have
banished all noble feelings from her heart in a single
moment?

Advocate Bang produces, in the king's name, three
varieties of proofs against the queen: Count Struensee's
statement, her Majesty's confession, and, as he knew
that neither was sufficient, the evidence of witnesses.

Assuredly, Count Struensee, on February 17 and 25,
as the documents prove, made a statement of a most
insulting nature to her Majesty.   But that he forgot

the reverence due to the queen, that either through
unfounded alarm, confusion of mind, or the hope of
saving himself, if he could cause the queen to be
regarded as interested in his affair, or for other reasons
he has made absurd allegations, can only injure himself. For what belief can be given to the assurance
that he, if the queen thought him worthy of her confidence, should have been so daring as to misuse it in
so extreme a way, and that her Majesty should have
tolerated it? The honour of a private person, much
more that of a queen, could not be affected by it.
And how improbable it is, that such a thing should
have gone on for two whole years at court, under the
eyes of the king, and in the presence of so many spies?
They are accusations made by a prisoner not on his
oath, and are utterly destitute of probability.

Advocate Bang allows that Count Struensee's declaration in itself is of no weight against the queen,
and hence he tries to confirm it, partly by the acknowledgment which her Majesty made on March 9, as to
the correctness of Struensee's declaration, partly
through her answer that she had broken her marriage
vows and, hence, lost her marriage rights, which he
wishes to be regarded as perfect proof after the law
1—15—1. Certainly, in all civil causes, a confession is the most perfect form of proof: but in criminal
matters, and such as we are now trying, the Danish
code completely rejects this evidence, when it says:
" It is not sufficient that the accused person should

himself confess it, but the accuser must legally bring the accused before the court and properly prove the offence."

Other proofs, consequently, are requisite; and as it is his Majesty's wish that the law alone shall be followed in this cause, and the judgment be founded on the evidence, it is self-evident that the queen must have a claim to this benefit as much as the meanest of her subjects.

The letter of the law is clear, and does not admit of the slightest doubt. Hence it will be quite unnecessary to examine the motives which induced the Danish legislator to make this regulation. I will not speculate whether the respect and authority which the law grants to one sex over the other—fear of its abuse on the one hand and of excessive compliance on the other—an anxiety to prevent the dangerous consequences of precipitation and inattention, &c., may have had their share in it. As, however, the king's advocate remarks that her Majesty cannot appeal to this law, because it is based on two legal reasons, neither of which affects the queen, I must clear up the incorrectness of this conclusion. Though the law states that it is not enough for the accused party to make a confession, and adds: "Because it is often found that many persons make false statements, so that the one may get rid of the other, or injure the person with whom he or she declares to have committed a crime," I will humbly urge that these are not the sole motives why

the law rejects a confession in this case, as is clearly
shown; for it adds directly after the words quoted,
"or for the sake of other things."   Although, therefore, the law only mentions expressly some of the
motives for its regulation, it is clear that it had various others in addition to these; and hence the benefit
granted to the accused belongs to her Majesty equally
in regard of the motives alleged in the law and of
those unalleged, and she consequently claims it.*

I will now pass over to the third class of proofs,
consisting of the statements of persons summoned by
the prosecutor as witnesses.

Her Majesty has commanded me to declare that she
does not desire them to be recalled and examined in
my presence.   But as I also have her commands to investigate the nature of this evidence and what it goes to
prove, I am obliged to make some prefatory remarks.

It is a remarkable fact that not one of the witnesses
examined alleges any other motive for the first suspicion
against the queen but the town scandal which they had
heard.   It was not till it became universal that it was
mentioned to the queen.   As most of the witnesses
were constantly about the queen's person, and yet, in
her intercourse with and behaviour toward Struensee,
found no reason to believe anything insulting to her,
it is clear that the conduct of the queen must have

* What Uldall wished to say, seems to be, that the queen could not be convicted on her own confession or on that of Struensee, as the law demanded that
the evidence must be given by two persons who agreed in the facts as well as
the motives.

been irreproachable, even at the time when apprehension existed.   Everybody knows how deceptive reports are.   Such a thing is often founded on nothing; and through its universal propagation alone acquires a certain strength and credibility.   But however slippery its path may be, it leaves behind, even with the hardest of belief, the most cautious and best disposed, a suspicion which places the conduct of the persons affected by the report in a perfectly new and different light.   The reason for the rumour may be true; the curiosity to acquire a certainty about it attracts attention to things which otherwise would be most innocent, but are now seriously weighed, and if anything equivocal is detected, a verdict is at once formed without any further investigation.   It was the same with the witnesses in this case; for, although prior to the rumour they had no cause to suspect the queen, they no sooner learnt its existence than they discovered new evidence of it at every step.

This remark is the more important, as the chamberpeople of the queen, after they had been informed of the rumour, did not observe those precautions which they should have done.

Instead of at once informing her Majesty, they made all sorts of investigations; and although they found no real criterion which could have confirmed the rumour, their prejudices were sufficiently active to make them regard everything with suspicion.

When her Majesty learnt this fact, she doubtless regarded it as a want of the fidelity they ought to have displayed, and of the good opinion they should have entertained of her. She consequently removed the witnesses from her immediate presence, and partly lost that perfect confidence which she had formerly placed in them. This annoyed the chamber-people, and naturally caused them to judge the actions of her Majesty even more sharply than before.

In the evidence of Frau Schiötte, we find two special instances of this: first, when she pretends that her Majesty's amendment lasted a fortnight after the warning, but that then the thing grew again worse than ever, although Frau Blechinberg says that she noticed nothing suspicious for some weeks after the time; and again, when Frau Schiötte employs the expression that her Majesty gave herself a great deal of trouble about the bolt of a door at Frederiksberg which would not fasten. That the queen had the bolt mended may have been caused by very innocent motives, especially as Frau Schiötte herself confesses that the chamber-people had no orders to close the bolt; but the expression that the queen "gave herself a deal of trouble," or "was wild about it," is excessively improper, and displays an animosity from which a witness ought to be exempt.

As her Majesty, therefore, had such keen observers in those who were about her person, it is not surprising that they should draw different conclusions, which served in confirmation of the ideas by which they were already preoccupied. No innocence is conceivable which would not succumb under such suspicious examination, and the law has foreseen the consequences of this, and recognised the fairness that every one should be safe in his own house and among his own servants. Hence it orders that "such witnesses should not be heeded." *

If we now ask what the facts are, by which an improper intimacy carried to extremes between the queen and Count Struensee can be proved from the evidence of the witnesses, the answer is—None. That the queen showed the count favour and confidence, cannot be denied. But who ever saw or heard that they went beyond the limits of honour? Where is the man who is able to say that the queen has broken the fidelity which she owed to her consort, or can mention a single fact which would prove the certainty of such a crime? And does not the silence of all about any convincing act prove the truth of maid Bruhn's answer to question 6, " that she never witnessed any impropriety on the part of the queen"?

Regarded generally, all the witnesses appeal to their own acts. They say, they concluded that Struensee was a long time with the queen, because they were not summoned; they fancied that the queen and Struensee were on familiar terms. But on what are these suppositions founded, except on rumour, and the power which it possessed over the imagination?

* How could Colonel Keith allow such a trial as this to be carried on when the sister of his own king was the victim? And yet, it is said, he makes a merit of having saved her from the scaffold.—*Falckenskjold's Memoirs*, p. 223.

It is principally the favour which her Majesty showed to Count Struensee, that caused the suspicions of the witnesses and the conclusions derived from them. He was constantly about the queen, it is said, and in her company. But was he not also about the king, and must not the queen's confidence in him necessarily result from the confidence with which the king honoured him? In this respect the queen appeals in her justification to her consort's feelings, and what striking proofs of his Majesty's favour to Struensee are the offices which were entrusted to him, and the rank to which he was raised! He sought to acquire the queen's confidence in the same way as he had gained the king's. The fidelity which he always displayed toward the king, the attention he paid to the queen when she was unwell, and the devotedness he seemed to entertain, maintained an uninterrupted harmony between their Majesties, and more than all else the king's will, which was a law to the queen, made her believe that she could give Struensee her confidence without peril. His offices as cabinet secretary to the queen, and cabinet minister, required his constant presence, and hence it should not be surprising that he held a greater share of the queen's favour than any other man.

But, the counsel for the prosecution says, the queen is not solely accused on account of her intimacy with Count Struensee; the great point is, that it reached an extremity which dishonoured her consort, and, in order to prove this, he appeals to the evidence of the witnesses.

Before I go through the more material evidence, I must make the highly requisite remark, that a proof by witnesses, according to law, must be supported by not less than two persons on oath, whose statements agree, and who can with certainty give evidence in one and the same matter. In accordance with this, the proofs of the learned counsel must be placed in two general categories; some of them cannot, according to law, be accepted as evidence at all, while others do not prove what they are intended to prove.

To the first class belong especially the statements of Professor Berger, Count Brandt, and Fräulein von Eyben; those of the former, because they were not made on oath and before the judges; those of the latter, because they are only supported by one person, for in her answer to question 7 there is a complaint about the queen, that her Majesty appeared to regard her as a dangerous person; and lastly, because her Majesty declares that she never made such a "confidence" to the witness as her answers to questions 41 and 42 reveal, but all that the queen said to her was a remark perfectly natural for a lady who believes herself above all suspicion: "that it would be ridiculous to abandon Count Struensee on account of an unfounded report." *

---

* Mademoiselle d'Eyben had been a lady-in-waiting on the queen, and, it is said, often twitted her with her conjugal fidelity. They had a quarrel, the nature of which is not known, and Mademoiselle d'Eyben's deposition was taken

In this class must also be placed several other circumstances—for instance, that at Gottorp Castle there was a flight of stairs leading from the queen's room to Struensee's—that the 4th witness merely said that one night she heard the queen come out of Struensee's room, while witnesses 8 and 9 say "she came up the stairs," and they naturally could not know from whom the queen came, and whether she might not have been with one of her ladies—that Struensee one night at Frederiksberg put on a surtout and went in that state to the queen, for witnesses 18, 19, and 20, state they did not know where he went—that the queen·was once seen in Struensee's room, which is only asserted by witness 20—that her Majesty remarked she did not care what people said, for the statements of witnesses 6 and 20 differ as to the time when the remark was made and the words used—that Struensee obtained a *passe partout* to the palace, for it was not done by the queen's orders—that the queen was once nursed by him, when she had a pain in her side, for one witness alone mentions this—that her Majesty went to the theatre because Struensee begged her to do so, of which, however, Fräulein Trolle, who was present, knows nothing—that her Majesty used scented powder—was once once out of sight of the maids of honour at a masquerade, and so

at Lübeck. This lady was not very scrupulous in matters of gallantry, and caused considerable scandal by her open liaison with a French actor of the name of Latour.—*Falckenskjold's Memoirs*, p. 233.

on: for such trifles would never have been brought against her Majesty had not the witnesses been prejudiced.

In the proofs of the second class, we have in the first line the statements of the women Blechinberg and Schiötte, and of maid Petersen, about the opening of the door leading to the Hermitage (Mezzanine), and their experiments with wax on the key, and powder in the corridor, about the footsteps found here and in the bedroom, and the state of the bed at a time when the king had not been there, and his door was locked, on which the counsel bases his charge.

Even if all this evidence was trustworthy, it would not prove that her Majesty was guilty. But one of the facts alleged by the witnesses proves in itself how little ground for suspicion there is in all these charges. The second witness, Frau Blechinberg, says, that at the time when this occurred, the maids slept close to the queen's bedroom, and had free access to it. How incredible does it seem that her Majesty should have exposed herself so openly, as she would have done by committing any impropriety in such a situation? And if we examine the details more closely, it results that her Majesty possessed the key of the Mezzanine door since her first arrival here. Frau Schiötte is, therefore, in error when she states that the queen asked for it afterwards, and that she used it several times, though rarely; and hence it is very possible that the door remained unlocked. Although it is quite natural that the wax in the key, or keyhole, or the paper in the crack must fall out if the door was opened, the witnesses are quite unable to assert that the key was used, and the door opened, only in the night. Why could not this have happened equally well by day, before they went to look? The footsteps in the powder deserves equally slight attention; for lackey Torp declares that his post was in the Mezzanine, and lackey Hansen, according to maid Petersen, once showed her that the door leading to it was open, which proves that various men entered the corridor. It is not said, either, whence the footsteps came, or that they went to the door of the queen's bedroom, and just as little did any witnesses hear any one come to this door at night. It is the same with the footsteps alleged to have been seen on the stairs. The witnesses declare that they displayed traces of the powder, but Struensee would not have gone in such an "uncleanly" condition to the queen even at night. The marks are said to have been seen on the next morning. But are the witnesses fully convinced that these footsteps were not made on the previous day or evening, or that the king, whose servants had the key of the outer corridor, had not been there, although he might not have been seen in the queen's apartments? It is true, they state they always knew when the king was there; but on what is this knowledge based? Her Majesty declares that it was impossible for her chamber-people to be always cognisant of the circumstance, because the king did

not wish them to know it; and hence she herself went
in to the king after their Majesties had retired.   That
the door should be bolted was the usual case long before the time of the supposed intrigue; on some occasions it was caused by a trifling dispute between their
Majesties; but most frequently because the queen was
afraid lest the black boys or the dogs might come into
her room unexpectedly, by which she had been startled
several times.   If there had been any mystery in it,
the king would have been the first to notice the fact.

As this suspicion, which is the chief foundation of
the charge, is thus removed, and the rest consists entirely of suppositions, I hope to be able to deal more
shortly with the latter.

The arrangement of the apartments for Struensee in
Christiansborg Palace was not done by the queen's
commands, and the reason why the queen's apartment
was converted into a sleeping cabinet was solely not
to incommode the king at the period when the
queen was suckling the prince herself.   Her Majesty
declares that she requested the king's permission to do
so at Frederiksberg.

What incorrect conclusions witnesses 4 and 7 draw
from the queen's anger with them is proved by the
evidence of Frau Schiötte, who states that this happened in the summer before they warned the queen,
consequently in the year 1769, and hence long before
the epoch we are now discussing.

The statement of witnesses 4 and 6, that the queen

passed off Struensee for the king is equally incorrect, for the king might have been present without their observing him.

If, as some witnesses state, they saw her Majesty undressed, when she was perhaps bathing or changing her clothes; if she undressed herself without the help of her maids (which was not the case, according to witness 6, however, during the last year), and of which the queen's pregnancy was the cause,—all this is no crime, so long as no one can say that Struensee or other men were present. On the contrary, all the witnesses are agreed that the queen always required very little attendance. Equally little should we feel surprised that Struensee was at times alone with the queen, or sat by her side, if he waited upon her, either by the king's command, or for other reasons. According to the evidence of maid Gabel the chamber-people remained at such times in the room where they happened to be, and from the answer of maid Boye to question 21, and the declaration of Frau Blechinberg, it must be assumed that one of them slept before the queen's sleeping cabinet. If her Majesty jested with her servants about love, her sentiments ought not to be judged from this, for in such a way even a Cato would come short. That she intended to go away with Struensee is a fable that contradicts itself, as it was not apprehended at the time when the sailors proceeded to Hirschholm, for then, as the witnesses say,

the queen was perfectly indifferent; but in the days
when the ox was given away at Frederiksberg, when
there was nothing at all to be alarmed about.

As a physician, Struensee could be present at the
queen's accouchement equally well as Berger, and the
statement that the queen looked at him, and gazed on
his portrait after delivery, is founded partly on the
presumptions of the witnesses, partly on untrustworthy
statements, as maid Boye saw that Struensee handed
the queen an almanack, at which she looked, although
maid Boye fancies that there was a portrait in it.

That the queen purchased something of Struensee
is a matter of perfect indifference, and if she made him
presents, royal personages are accustomed to display
their favour in such a way.

That she wished to speak with him in her state of
alarm, occasioned by the events of January 17, is not
surprising, and that she on one occasion at Kronborg
inquired after him, is no proof of a "tendresse," for
many thousands who never saw him have asked the
same question.

I pass over all the rest as things which are partly
unimportant, partly do not affect the queen, or are
too improper to be answered. It is sufficient that no
proof is derived from all these things, examined singly,
that her Majesty has broken her marriage vow. The
law requires the truthful evidence of witnesses, not all
sorts of self-invented conclusions; and if it were other-

wise, her Majesty must regret that her rank and grandeur, which ought to secure her against such danger, are the very things that caused her misfortune.

I may therefore hope that I have shown the innocence of her Majesty the Queen.   Her Majesty assumes that her consort only desires her justification, and she feels assured of the caution and impartiality of her judges.

For these reasons she awaits the decision demanded by her honour, the king's dignity, and the welfare of the land.   I therefore venture most submissively in her Majesty's name to urge—

"That her Majesty Queen Caroline Matilda, be acquitted from his Majesty the King's accusation, in this matter."

ULDALL.

Copenhagen, April 2, 1772.

The defence was certainly clever, and merited the applause with which it is said to have been greeted in foreign countries.   But, on reflection, it seems as if the counsel did not touch on the best argument in the cause: that the law refuses a divorce to the husband of a woman guilty of adultery if he has been the seducer; and if, while cognizant of her infidelity, he has continued to cohabit with her.   It would have been easy to render this palpable to the king, if he had retained even a remnant of feeling and conscience. Reverdil, who, though he was fully convinced of Caro-

line Matilda's guilt, felt the most sincere compassion
for her, supplies us with an argument which might
have been used to the king :—

"Is it not true, Sire, that from the commencement
of your marriage up to the moment when the party
now in power seized on you and your ministers, you
had not the slightest respect for the marriage tie, and
that you ever testified to the queen that you dispensed
with her fidelity? Did you not invite all your successive favourites to pay their court to her? Did you
not say, and prove in a thousand ways, that her affection was troublesome to you, and that your greatest
misfortune was in paying attention to her? Your
commissioners had the effrontery to ask the queen and
Struensee who their accomplices were; in prison and in
chains the accused have had the generosity to be silent
on your account; but what they have not done your
conscience will do, and will tell you that you were the
real seducer.

"Remember, Sire, the moment when this princess,
whom they wish to make you condemn to-day, was
confided to your love and generosity. The English
left her without any adviser, or a single companion,
on your shores. Hardly emerged from childhood, she
retained its graces, innocence, and *naïveté*; but her
mind was more cultivated and mature than you expected; you were astonished at it; hearts flew to meet
her; her affability and beneficence captivated all classes
of the nation. When you had the misfortune to give

yourself up to a frivolous and reckless favourite, and
to vile companions, who led you into libertinism, she
saw herself neglected.   You displayed more than indifference toward her.   She loved you; she was silent,
and maintaining her serenity in public, contented herself with lamenting in private with the grand mistress,
whom you had yourself given her as a confidante.   Ere
long, you envied her even her sole consolation; and this
lady, whose sole crime consisted in displaying conduct
and principles too austere to please you, was dismissed
with the most signal mark of disgrace.   Frau von der
Lühe, who took her place, was the sister of your
favourite.   You, doubtless, supposed that this lady
would have as much levity and as few principles as
her brother; but she foiled your expectations.   Without expressly disgracing her, you had her duties performed by women of the most equivocal reputation.
What more could a consummate seducer have done?
This man, with whom the queen is accused of being
too intimate, yourself forced on her when she repulsed
him.   It was the hope of avoiding the annoyances which
your favourites caused her that led her to connect
herself with a man who offered his services in drawing
you back to her; it was you who removed all the bar-
riers that separated her from him, who diminished the
distance, who desired what is now called your disgrace,
who have excused and tolerated this liaison; and who,
lastly, up to January 17, talked of it as a good joke.

"Your cause is inseparable from that of your wife,

and even should the whole world condemn her, you ought to revoke this condemnation through a feeling of self-respect, if not through natural equity."

It is impossible to say whether any one of the thirty-four judges raised his voice in favour of a princess whom they were absolutely obliged to condemn, or whether not one of them dared to touch on so delicate a matter: but the sentence of divorce was pronounced after two sessions of seven hours each. It was not made public, but a rescript was sent to the provincial governors and bailiffs, in which the king informed them that he had repudiated his consort, after a solemn inquiry, in order to repair the honour of his house, and for motives of public welfare. The same tribunal pronounced that the Princess Louisa Augusta should retain the honour due to the daughters of kings. A sealed and secret document was handed at the same time to the Chanceries, which was to be read at the king's death. It doubtless regulated the regency in the event of a minority. Some persons believed that in this will the princess was disinherited: but how could that be so?*

The queen's confession was dated March 9: the king's counsel handed in his indictment on the 24th:

* According to Falckenskjold, it would have been as easy to pronounce the illegitimacy of Caroline Matilda's children, as to declare a divorce on account of adultery. Guldberg and his partisans were interested in doing so; hence it is plain that Queen Juliana Maria, and Prince Frederick would not allow it. If this be so, credit must be given them for this generosity. I fancy, however, that my earlier assertion is correct, and that Guldberg prevented a step which the queen dowager urged on behalf of the possible posterity of her beloved son.

Uldall's reply was made on April 2: and the sentence was passed on the 6th of the same month. Matters were certainly done very quickly. Baron Juel-Wind, Justiciary of the Supreme Court, received orders to inform the queen of the sentence, which he did on April 9, in the presence of Lieutenant-General von Hauch, commandant of Kronborg.

The original intention was to exile the unfortunate queen to Aalborg, in Jütland, where she was not to be imprisoned, but to have certain restrictions placed on her liberty. As early as February,* Colonel Pentz had been sent to examine the castle, and order the necessary repairs. We shall see hereafter how a change in the arrangements was made.

* This circumstance, in itself, is a sufficient proof that the trial of Caroline Matilda was solely intended to throw dust in the eyes of Europe. That her place of banishment should have been selected before her trial, is of a piece with the miserable evidence produced against her.

CHAPTER XI.

THE WOLF AND THE LAMB.

In the meanwhile, Fiscal-General Wiwet received the
king's orders on April 2 to indict Counts Struensee
and Brandt before the appointed tribunal. As defenders of the accused, Uldall was selected for Struensee,
and Bang for Brandt. The Fiscal-General appointed
April 10 for the opening of the trial. As, however,
some preliminary investigations had to be made, the
trial was deferred till April 21, on which day the
Fiscal produced his proofs, and the sentence he demanded in writing.

WIWET'S INDICTMENT OF COUNT STRUENSEE.[*]

High and well born, highly noble and well born, gentlemen: most graciously appointed commissioners in the charges against Counts Struensee and Brandt.

I laid before this exalted commission on the 10th of the present month his royal Majesty's most gracious commands to me, to proceed against Counts Struensee and Brandt for their crimes. Hence it is only necessary to deduce, prove, and hand in the indictment for sentence; and as such deduction, proof, and demand of sentence, I most submissively deliver this my memorial.

So certain and true as the proverb generally is, "that severe lords do not reign long," it is equally certain that such severe lords, during their brief authority, can produce as much harm as cannot be redressed in double the length of time.

The Danish and Norwegian subjects have been for many hundred years accustomed to be treated mercifully, as their fidelity and sincerity deserves. The affection and veneration which they feel for their king cannot be described, and they are in return beloved

[*] In Höst's "Struensee og hans Ministerium" this document is quoted, but with an omission of everything that proved the crime of high treason, and must entail the penalty of death. As this work, however, was published in 1824, or during the reign of the son of Caroline Matilda, everything had to be omitted which might appear offensive to the memory of the king's mother. But Höst did not inform his readers of this fact. The notorious indictment is now published for the first time, without any mutilations or suppressions, from the Danish secret archives. All honour to Frederick VII., who allowed it to be made known, although it casts such a slur on Danish justice.

by their regent. They generally feel a deep reverence for the Supreme Being and God's word, are all sensible, and have a feeling of shame for sins committed: they are quiet, and everybody lives securely in the country, so that foreigners said: "It is pleasant to live here," and built themselves all sorts of abodes among us, though without despising and offending the nation. But, during the last few years, this has become quite different, and has assumed a strange and confused aspect. Attempts have been made to render the king—that dearest part of everything temporal to his people—odious to his subjects, and the latter in turn to him. No one could obtain access to his Majesty unless he belonged to the party which did not mean well with him. Impudence and contempt were emboldened to rise against so highly venerable a royal house. The Almighty and His word were rendered ridiculous. People strove to drive away virtue and honour, and to open a gate to immorality, seeing no shame in it, but evidently seeking honour in it. The audacity was carried so far that the authority which the nation voluntarily committed to Frederick III. and his descendants, was solely exercised by a subject, and was even about to be extended, so that the man who exercised it might be absolute.

Like the nation, their language was despised. It was heart-torture for every honest man and lover of honour to see and hear all that which can be read in printed documents.

The ruin of families was like the deed of a fallen angel. But who was this fallen angel? It was John Frederick Struensee, the most foolhardy person who can be imagined, and who for this reason deserves the name of more than *vir unius seculi*, formerly a doctor, up to the present time a count, but of whom (as I hope), before I let him go, nothing will be left but horror, condemnation, and punishment.

Count Struensee was born at Halle, in 1737. His father is the present superintendent in Holstein. He studied medicine at Halle, passed his examination there, and lived at Gundern with his uncle, who was the private physician of Prince von Stolberg. A year later, 1758, he became city physician of Altona, where he received, as is said, *veniam occidendi per totam urbem*, which liberty he afterwards employed as cabinet minister, *per utrumque regnum*. After he had been physician for ten years at Altona, he became, in the year 1768, physician in ordinary to his royal Majesty, when his Majesty travelled abroad, as may be seen from his statement of February 25.

It required either a supernatural intellect or great daring and foolhardiness to undertake, in his twenty-first year, to be city physician and surgeon in Altona; but I believe the latter, because at the expiration of a short period he also took on himself to be the state physician; and we must consequently conclude from this, that he was as good a doctor for the city as he was in the state, and that the number of deaths in Altona, in his times, necessarily exceeded the births,

unless the number of the latter was augmented by
him in another way.* The reputation follows the
man.   I derive everything from documentary evidence, and in this his most intimate friend, Count
Enevold Brandt, said, in his reply to question 122,
" That seven or eight years ago it was generally
known of Struensee that he had no religion, and that
he had intercourse with women at an early age, which
was reproved by many respectable people."

This " medicus," of whom common report says that
he was not particularly well provided with his father's
blessing, and hence could found no hopes on the promises of the fifth commandment, formed the acquaintance of Count Enevold Brandt, at the time he was attending the late Privy Councillor Söhlenthal, Brandt's
step-father.   He revealed to Count Brandt that he
should like to be a physician in ordinary at the Danish
court, just as if Denmark had a want of clever doctors,
and required them as much as France did the Danish
Winslöw.†   Count Brandt promised him his good

---

* Well may Reverdil say about this indictment that it is impossible to read
anything more flat, more clumsy, or more disgusting. It is the style of a
lackey amusing himself in a tavern at the expense of a man who is about to be
hung.   He adds: " Ought not an unhappy man who is pining in fetters to be
spared insults useless to the cause? Ought not Wiwet to have reflected that
he could not insult the prisoner without failing in respect to the king, who
so long honoured him with his confidence, and who signed most of the orders
alleged as a crime against Struensee?"

† Winslöw, a celebrated anatomist, was born at Odense, in Fühnen, appointed professor at the *Jardin des Plantes*, in Paris, in 1742, and wrote a
work that ran through four editions: " Exposition Anatomique du Structure
du Corps Humain." He died in 1760.

offices. Count Struensee was therefore engaged to travel with his Majesty abroad, not because his royal Majesty's health required this, but in order that he might be at hand in any unforeseen emergency, and because a physician fills up the number of the suite of such exalted personages, without being exactly regarded as superfluous. I have credible information that during the journey, when he found time heavy on his hands, he mocked at religion and the word of God (just as at a later date people mocked at his and his partisans' regulations, projects, and ridiculous enterprises), and would celebrate his pretended victory by a contemptuous laugh. I should be able to prove this, and mention it here, partly because in a criminal case nothing must be forgotten that throws light on the character or conduct of the culprit, and partly to contradict Struensee's excuse, that it was not his intention to inflict any injury on religion.

When he returned home he remained with his most gracious Majesty as physician, and to read to his Majesty whatever his Majesty might order him to read; and for this purpose waited on the king every morning, mid-day, and evening, as will be seen from his answer to question 1. Count Struensee, who had already determined to acquire honour and wealth, no matter in what way, from the " respect and purse " of the Danish and Norwegian nation, clearly saw that it would not do to serve two masters in the way he intended, and that he, as a foreigner, who had just come into a country where he had no connexions, would be unable to sustain himself. He easily perceived that, while he secured his fortunes on one side, his misfortune could be founded on the other. To be constantly about his Majesty, would be so much as to neglect those plans which must remain hidden from the king. Nor could the duty of being constantly about the king's person be safely entrusted to any one.   It must be some one, in whose care he could trust as fully as in Count Brandt, who, as he was compelled by command to keep away from court, would be attached to him if he again procured him admission to it. Thus it came about that Count Brandt received leave to return to court, though he did not occupy any permanent post till the departure of Chamberlain Warnstedt, when he was attached to his Majesty, and the duty was imposed on him of so watching the king that no one reached him, and if any one came, of reporting to Struensee who it was and what was said, which Brandt faithfully carried out.   All this is to be seen in Brandt's statements before the commission on March 2, to question 8.

I will now submissively proceed to prove the nature of both Count Struensee and Count Brandt's behaviour in their intercourse with his most gracious Majesty.

After Count Struensee had, in this way, secured his position—for up to then this had not been fully the case—he writes about it in his reply to Count Brandt's warnings: "Après avoir gagné la confiance, la faveur du roi et de la reine et le crédit dans le public, et cela par mes propres forces, avec tout le risque et toutes les peines attachées à une telle entreprise que vous n'auriez certainement pas supporté: et laquelle, j'ose l'assurer, vous n'auriez pas fini, je vous appelle et je partage avec vous l'effet, et tout les agréments qui en pouvaient resulter." But what could have induced him, when Count Brandt, in his aforesaid warning, gave him to understand his annoyance in a rather harsh way, to urge the said Count Brandt to remain at his post, when he writes in the following terms: "Examinez votre position et les motifs qui vous y tiennent! Rangez d'un coté les agréments et de l'autre les désagréments et comparez cela avec vos situations passées et avec celles auxquelles vous pouvez attendre et faites alors la conclusion." When he was certain of a friend who would watch the king and pay attention to everything that happened or was said, who was to take care that none should reach the king who might repeat the general dissatisfaction at a report which wounded every honest heart, and other things which it would lead me too far to mention, he began very seriously to play the master and prove how it was his intention to become the first man, if not nominally and in respect, still in might and authority. He filched the greatest power in the most impudent way, as I shall presently prove, and he also acquired adherents, not substantial ones, but men who wished to make their fortune, and obtain something through this omnipotent *maître des requêtes.*

There was one thing, however, that prevented him from acting as he wished, namely, the High Royal Council, which was composed of respectable men, most of whom were children of the country, and all, from youth up, educated and instructed in state science, and knew the constitution, the laws, and the nation. This college must consequently be abolished; and it was done under the excuse that his Majesty was impeded by it, and could not exercise his sovereign power with perfect liberty. But the meaning of this and other things was speedily detected when the *maître des requêtes* presented himself as privy cabinet minister, and the man whom all the king's subjects, high or low, or whosoever they might be, must obey as the king's representative, and whose orders, with his signature, must be as much respected as the king's. Thus this ambitious man, through greed for gain and that he might fully satisfy his pleasures, dared to undertake the affairs of two kingdoms, and, though inexperienced in the language and laws of the country, alone do that which so many worthy men had divided among them, and had found plenty to do in managing the business of their respective departments. Under the pretext that the council impeded the king, he had the audacity to abolish it, but to assume greater authority than the council ever possessed, as I shall more fully prove.

This daring measure taken by him was regarded as the second which would, some day, break his neck, and, by his ruin, put an end to that of the country. A privy cabinet minister was seen to choose people as his advisers from whom not much good could be expected,—partly because they had been educated like him, and understood nothing about what they undertook as statesmen, or in other qualities; partly, because they were selfish projectors and persons who wished to be fattened like him, though not to so great a degree. He regarded himself as the person who was summoned to promote the prosperity of Denmark and Norway and the welfare of the king; but everything must be altered, no matter whether the changes were useful or not, so long as they were made. He and his adherents tried to turn everything topsy-turvy. The official, when he rose in the morning, did not know whether he would not lose bread and office before evening. A proof of his foolhardiness, but also of his intention to strengthen his position, is, that he proposed his brother, who was " Professor Matheseos " at Liegnitz, in Silesia, as a deputy of finances in Denmark and Sweden, a man who may be good enough as a mathematician, though there is no want of natives possessed of the science, but must be as experienced in the management of the finances as a blind man in astronomy. Hence his summons here could have had no other object but, with united strength, to attack and conquer the royal exchequer, in which Struensee

made various large and important grasps for himself
and his adherents.   He did not forget himself and his
companions.   Many thousand rix-dollars, even whole
sums of 60,000 dollars, were, with false cunning and
impudence, stolen from the royal exchequer against
his Majesty's will and pleasure, solely to enrich himself and his adherents, so that they might be in a good
humour with him.   On the other hand, he never hesi-
tated to rob other people of their income; and, in order
to make it the more painful, it was generally done in a
jeering manner.   With the cabinet orders he behaved
dishonestly; he issued them without the king's permission; and he did not bring them forward in the
order that his duty commanded, as I shall most submissively prove.   As he showed by his acts, his resolution was to treat the nation with harshness, with
contempt, and as a people that had no "sentiments."
His own words, in the answer to Count Brandt's warnings, are as follow: "Vous me reprochez que j'inspire
la peur à tout le monde, et vous m'en deviez faire
compliment parceque c'est la seule ressource pour
un état énervé, affaibli, avec une cour et tout un
public intriguant et un maître faible par respect et
qui a le même penchant pour le changement que son
peuple;" and in another passage: "Le conte et la
complaisance ont été la source du malheur de Danemarc."   But is it surprising that he should treat the
people with contempt, when he ventured to do the
same to its head, as I shall prove?

It might have been supposed that the affairs of the kingdom would have given him enough to do: but he still thought proper to play the doctor, by his own explanation, through affection for the royal family. His Royal Highness the Prince Royal was to be educated in accordauce with his (here the right expression fails me) sentiments. I shall return to this presently, for which reason I will mention it now as shortly as possible, but no man of sense could understand how this could go on well for any time, for it seemed as if the doctor first wished to deprive the prince of his health, in order to show that he was capable of restoring it,—an attempt by which the two kingdoms could not be benefited. The other amiable royal personages, whom his craft and power could not prevent from being an obstruction to him in his undertakings, he was seen to treat with a certain degree of indifference. The exalted commissioners know as well as I that I am speaking the language of truth: for I could prove by many thousands of witnesses, the universal sorrow which was felt at seeing the king's brother, who was certainly the king's best friend, separated from him in a very marked way. The king's servants trembled at Struensee; he was so harsh to his own servants, that he threatened them with the "Blue Tower:" he reproved them because they were not used to wait on great people, by which he alluded to himself, which he could do the more safely, as these people either were not aware of his former servitude,

or did not dare remind him of it, and which had been
a service with honest men, it is true, but not with
great persons. From these facts, however, his audacity
and extraordinary foolhardiness can be seen, for he
was not only harsh to his servants, (who, according to
his principles, could not expect a government post,
but must live on the means which they had saved up
after years of extraordinary roguery,) but was even so
impudent as to reprimand the servants in the presence
of the exalted person whose subject and fellow-servant
of servants he was. He not only interfered in things
which he did not understand, but also appointed persons to offices in colleges of whose duties they were
ignorant, from which many people concluded that he
wished to convert everything into a chaos, or perform
some extraordinary feat as a physician—as, for instance,
prove that land animals were best fitted to the sea; as
otherwise, this man's enterprises cannot be compre-
hended, and as they are mad things, I can only represent them in this ridiculous manner, in which I employ his own expression which he used against his
king: "that is ridiculous." He despised the language
and laws of the country. Everything must be translated for him into German, by which the work was
doubled for others, and affairs could not be expedited
so quickly, although it seemed in other respects as if
he wished everything to be done at the double.

He overturned the laws which served to maintain
honesty and respectability, but after his fall they

regained their old validity, which is a sufficent proof for me in this respect.

In addition to the exalted ministers, other persons of noble birth and rank were treated by him with contumely, whence they could not remain at court, but retired to their estates and retrenched their expenses, by which the city of Copenhagen lost considerably through the reduced value of house property, and the inhabitants through the loss of the custom of the nobles.   He did not like Copenhagen: it seemed to him too large for a city in Denmark.   Consequently, he wished to weaken its power and prestige, and he was so daring as to take away the privileges accorded to its citizens, which they gained by risking their life and blood for their king, the royal family, and the Fatherland.   On the other hand, he sought to amuse the mob by various displays of fireworks, free night toping and other jollities and carnal pleasures, which, however, he wished so contrived that they could be carried on without infection.*

It would surely lead too far to reckon up all the follies which were set in work by this foolhardy person.   And in the midst of all this he believed he had *de Daniâ bene meritus*, so it was no excessive honour for him to become a Danish count.

Foolhardiness is seen in all his undertakings.   He considers himself worthy of so great an honour, because he has had for two years an opportunity of

* I confess this sentence is quite beyond me, but it is a literal translation.

lending a horrible life in Denmark. To be raised to
this height has always been reckoned a proof of worthi-
ness, and services rendered to the king and the kingdoms. In this instance, however, it is quite the contrary. Count Struensee regarded all that which is
called rank or title as something which must not be
sought after, but be bestowed on specially distinguished
men, who have rendered themselves worthy of it
through their services,—*Exempli gratiâ*, his brother,
who was made Councillor of Justice, on account of his
knowledge of finances. If he became a count, therefore, it must be assumed how great his services had
been. The only humility he displayed in the receipt
of this dignity was, that he procured his friend, Chamberlain Brandt, the same honour, although the latter
had not taken such interest in the prosperity of the
country as Count Struensee. But as we may say of
him and Struensee, *vivimus ex rapto*, they must be
equal in the honours as in the plunder. Though the
Order (of Matilda) was so innocent when received
from the exalted hand which founded it, Count
Struensee entertained the daring design of being
honoured immediately after with the Order of the
Elephant.

All this impudence, in the midst of his most brilliant and powerful position, lowered him in the eyes
of all people: his recipes for the state were regarded
as quacksalvery; his services as dead flies in an apo-
thecary's gallipot. Both himself and his adherents

could not hold their tongues; partly, because they wished to know beforehand what people would say about this or the other design which was going to be carried out; partly, because in case of need they wished to be able to place themselves in a position of defence, or fly to Kronborg; for in Copenhagen they had nothing good to expect. But the discontent increased so greatly, that as many "one thousand million execrations" were heaped upon him, as there were brilliants in the golden shield which his running footman wears in his cap. This discontent with his conduct could not remain hidden from him. Count Brandt, who is to some extent to be pitied, on account of the friendship which he formed with Count Struensee, but cannot be excused, warned him: the daily pasquinades published about the count and his band, and of which he was informed every morning, at length disquieted him. The Horse Guards were abolished, and no longer stood in his way. The Foot Guards must also be got rid of. This was effected; but in a way which proves that Count Struensee in this affair also behaved like a villain to his king and benefactor.

The *émeute* which took place on the Christmas eve rendered him equally attentive and timid. I shall revert to the proofs of this. When the royal family, with whom he lived, came to town, such precautions were taken that people must believe that the king was afraid of his subjects; but Count Struensee, with his fellow-conspirators, intended to make himself Protector, even if he did not at once take the king's life.

The gates of Copenhagen were ordered always to stand open, so that if necessary it might be a refuge for those outside the city.

When his royal Majesty came to the capital, he drove through the streets as if flying before an enemy, so that no one might approach the king, and impart to him his well-meant thoughts.

When Count Struensee's conscience (for that is always found in a man) convinced him that his actions, judging from the value which the inhabitants of the land, high and low, attached to them, would be but badly rewarded, he resolved to venture on extremities. I must most submissively and conscientiously assert, that I do not know what his motto was; but judging from his conduct, it must be believed that it agreed with the character which is given of the Greek robbers, in the words :—

> " Fidens animi atque in utrumque paratus,
>   Seu versare dolos seu certæ occumbere morti."

After the return to Copenhagen, after the bodyguard had been dismissed, and the guard of the palace confided to other troops, the latter received rations in addition to their pay, and contrary to all custom, which reminds me of the answer given to the thief in the fable :—" Ita subita me jubet benignitas vigilare, facias ne meâ culpâ lucrum."

When the report spread in the city that the count was meditating dangerous designs, because the inhabitants were annoyed at being ruled by a *doctor medicinæ*, and as, too, the doctor was afraid of being dissected by the populace, though not *secundum artem*, and for the benefit of his colleagues, he chose another town commandant, who could terrify the whole city with his voice and gestures, and the cannon were also to be loaded for the same purpose. It may be supposed what was intended to take place at the palace. I do not believe there was any intention to lay hands on the person of his royal Majesty and take his life. But suppose an insurrection had broken out, not against the king—for everybody knows that he is innocent—but against this impudent count, this foolhardy person, it is only a necessary consequence that he and his partisans must have audaciously attacked the king in order to save themselves, and in such an event Count Struensee knew himself to be secure, as may be seen from his answer to Count Brandt.

It is certainly a proof of the peculiar consciousness which Count Struensee possessed about his conduct in Denmark being that of the most foolhardy and contemptible person conceivable, when he fears the people, among whom he tried to insinuate himself. But, on the other hand, it is also a proof that the Danish and Norwegian nation, although they at times endure what cannot be offered to any other, still love God, the king, the royal family, and good manners. Hence their wishes and sighs were raised to Him,

through whom kings reign, who did not forget the
prayers of Christian III. when the land was groaning
in the days of a former Count, and who with a mighty
arm and in an instant, put an end to the shame which
the king, the royal house, and the kingdoms, had been
compelled to endure.*

How great the joy of the people was when the
change took place, and how great its dissatisfaction at
the preceding state of things had been, was seen on
January 17, whence the count might have learned
quam caduca sit ista felicitas.   And how excessively
great the joy at this change was in other circles also,
was seen at the court held on the birthday of his royal
Majesty, where sincere anxiety for the country and
affection for the king met, and where the oppressed
man greeted the liberated man with a loving kiss, and
forgot his own wretched position in his love for the
royal family.

For the sake of future ages, when my present indictment may perhaps be seen by many, I must remark, that it is only a short narrative of all that has
happened, but, as I think, it will suffice to give a
perfect explanation of the misdeeds of this count, and
show that the sentence I demand is in conformity with
the law, and adapted to his crimes.   I must not, therefore, be reproached with having attempted to render
him ridiculous, especially in an action which demands
the utmost earnestness, for a distinction must be

* An allusion to what is called the " Grafenfehde " of 1522—23.

drawn between a minister who may have committed an error, and a mountebank who wishes to be a minister, and, as such, was an enemy of the country, and must therefore be treated with the same harshness as he displayed to others.   But, in order that Count Struensee and every one may thoroughly learn that nothing is brought forward which might be regarded as a charge without proof, I will now, in accordance with the most gracious command given me, proceed to bring my charges against him, together with the evidence.

To reckon up all the crimes committed by him would be a most useless task, the more so when we reflect that the count has only one head, and that when that is lost by a crime, the other offences would be superfluous.   I will hence close my deduction with the words—

> " ———— Longa est injuria, longae
> Ambages, sed summa sequar fastigia rerum."

First.

" Count Struensee crept into the familiarity of the highest lady in the land, to such a degree that it went beyond the limits that are drawn between persons of different sexes, who cannot and must not be connected."

As I am commanded to indict Count Struensee— and I regard the above as one of the greatest crimes committed by him, and as the first which hurled him into the others—I bring it forward first: for it is certainly the most foolhardy one, which no one forgives him, and for which he cannot be excused.

I here produce the testimony on oath of Fräulein von Eyben, not in order to prove what is sufficiently explained, but only to request it may be remarked how Struensee strove to be present at places when there was an opportunity for him to acquire what he desired, and how the indifference with which he was at first regarded by the person whose confidence he afterwards gained, proves that it was not he who was tempted, but that his " inhuman" impudence, his bold, crafty, and villanous conduct, were powerful enough to attain that which virtue and education never grant, and that he is the more criminal, because he brought others into despair, in order to acquire honours himself.*

As proofs of this most audacious deed committed by Count Struensee, I produce—(1) The examination of Counts Struensee and Brandt and Professor Berger, made on February 20. The first two hundred and eighteen questions, and the twenty asked him on the 21st, contain Count Struensee's explanations of

---

* As regards this argument, Falckenskjold remarks very sensibly: "Even supposing, which I am far from admitting, that there was an illicit liaison between the queen and Struensee, the supposition that he was the seducer is absurd. Any princess who would deign thus to degrade herself with one of her subjects, is under the necessity of taking the first steps : this is one of the inconveniences of superior rank."

his intercourse with the exalted lady, and her intimacy with him, but all of which he reckons among the things she would have so. That he could be excused as a doctor, and she also, as there is in this no confession of the crime, I need not stay to disprove, as there is better evidence. (Here follow five passages from the report of the examination.) In these passages, Count Struensee, voluntarily and with great emotion, publicly confessed the most audacious crime committed by him. The commissioners possess his signature, as well as this most important document. (2) The said Count Struensee's confession signed with his own hand. (3) Her royal Majesty Caroline Matilda's declaration of the truth of Struensee's confession, dated Kronborg, March 9, 1772. (4) Fräulein von Eyben's deposition. (5) Count Brandt's statement of February 22. These statements are confirmed by Professor Berger's deposition. From all these documents we perceive Count Struensee's atrocious conduct; how, without shame he advanced with the greatest security in his crimes, and especially in the one which can only be thought of with horror, when we look at the person hurled into shame by him, and notice how he behaved, as if he wished the whole world to learn his deeds.

His frequent unannounced running in to the queen: his lengthened stay: his riding and driving out with her: the giving and receiving of presents—all this confirms the truth of the evidence, and shows that he has not spoken falsely.

For this reason, he has in this matter committed the crime of high treason in the highest degree. He has openly acted against the fidelity which he owed the king his master, and the reverence he should have displayed toward their Majesties. He has deprived the king of the confidence, love, and personal security (*i.e.* the certainty of alone possessing the queen's person) which his Majesty had a right to expect after so sacred a promise, entered into in the sight of God; he has tried to affix a stain on the royal family, in order thus to attain dignities and power.

What honest man in the country, however mean he may be, would not feel most highly insulted by such a thing! But how awful is the thought of such an insult offered to the highest persons! a crime which the legislator has not even supposed, and which it would be improper to mention. But if a verbal insult of the king is bad, how much greater is the crime of disgracing the king and queen by an action! I do not, therefore, require to dwell longer on this head; for the facts and the confession of the deed cannot be denied, and ere I end, Count Struensee can peruse his crime and its well-merited punishment in 6—4—1 of the law. I therefore refer him to this passage of the law.

Secondly.

"Count Struensee was not only informed that his royal Majesty was ill-treated by Count Brandt, and even assaulted, but he also advised it; hence he neither prevented it, nor took measures to prevent it, and he himself also treated his royal Majesty in a contemptuous way."

From my deduction, the evidence and the indictment of Count Brandt, the court will learn how the affair happened: how his Majesty was attacked by the aforesaid Count Brandt in his cabinet, abused, and treated in an unexampled manner. As far as I am aware, there is no instance of such a thing in history—there is, unfortunately, of royal murders; but none of such treatment. That Count Struensee was not only aware of this fact, but urged Count Brandt to commit it, and approved of the crime, is proved by the following:—

Count Brandt declares that after his Majesty had threatened to beat him with a stick, Count Struensee said to him, at six o'clock on the same evening, "I have reproved the king, and he answered me, ' Brandt is a coward; he has no courage, and I will fight with him.'" Struensee then said further to Brandt, "What will you do? You must go to the king one evening and say, ' You insist upon fighting with me: here I am; if you want anything, come on;'" and he added, that this had repeatedly occurred with Count Holck. When Brandt returned from the king, the queen had begun her game of cards, and, when it was ended, Struensee stood by the stove, where Brandt told him what had occurred; to which Struensee answered, " That is right: now you will have peace; but not a

soul must know it."   Count Struensee not only confesses that he had spoken about it previously with
Count Brandt, but also that he was informed by him
of what had happened, as will be seen from Struensee's
answer to quest. 402—412.

That the count himself also forgot the respect he
owed the king, is further proved by his addressing him
harshly, as is seen by the evidence of the witness
Detlev Christopher Aabyn: "If he will not bathe, he
shall be beaten;" and the other statements of the same
witness.

In the same way, then, as Count Brandt, as I have
shown, has rendered himself guilty of the crime of
high treason by his audacious deed and harsh treatment of the king—for which Count Struensee even
promises him a reward, as we read in his reply to
Count Brandt's warnings concerning the harshness
with which he is obliged to treat the king: "la recon-
naissance que la reine vous aura, si vous reussissiez, et
les marques incontestables que vous en avez déjà reçu,
vous en recompenseront"—Count Struensee, as adviser, seducer, and accomplice, has been guilty of the
same crime, and must be punished for it by the same
penalty.

Thirdly.

"Count Struensee harshly treated the king's son,
his Royal Highness Crown Prince Frederick, so that
it seems as if it had been his sole intention to remove

the crown prince from the world, or, at least, to bring him up so that he would be incapable of reigning."

In addition to all that is known, and has been seen, by so many persons, the exalted commission learns from Hans Heinrich Majoll's declaration and Gündel Marie Schönberg's evidence, that this treatment applied to a tender child was a fruit of the brain of this impudent and foolhardy man. Had he not found it to his advantage to remain a doctor, if he had not given orders in this affair, it might be said in his excuse that the education of the crown prince in no way concerned the *maître des requêtes* or the cabinet minister. But everything was done by his orders, although he, as a doctor, must have been aware that it is utterly impossible to rear children in such a way. I am convinced Count Struensee will be unable to mention any instance of such a way of child-rearing as he recommended. He therefore ordered it thus through special malice against the innocent prince, in order, as I have already said, to get him out of the way, or try what results such a training would have. But, in either case, he offends most grievously against the royal personage, as the crown prince could not be allowed to be his "testing rag."

I will not say any more about this matter, for which there is no apology, even though Count Struensee were to appeal—as his remarks seem to indicate—to the training or keep of irrational animals. Count Struensee, who was not trained in this way, has as fat a paunch as if he were Vitellius. There is a difference between pampering children so that not a breath of air may reach them, and giving them too little food, and making them endure hunger and cold. Animals have more care for their young, and Count Struensee will not attain the honour of being placed in the same class with them. As he asserts that he possesses intelligence, all this was done by him through sheer arrogance and malice against the king's son, whose life was endangered by his advice given as doctor; and as God has hitherto held His hand over him, it is no merit of Struensee that he is still alive. But I am of opinion that any man who endangers the life of royal children, is fully as worthy of punishment as one who tries to take their life; and hence deserves to be sentenced in accordance with the law 6—4—1.

Fourthly.

"Count Struensee has grievously offended, and committed the crime of high treason, by usurping the royal authority, passing resolutions in the place of his royal Majesty, and attaching his own signature to these resolutions."

Count Struensee's evil intentions against the king and his subjects are especially displayed in this matter, even though he and some of his defenders (if he really have any) may regard it as perfectly innocent. Count Struensee considers that, as he only intended to undertake things which would prove advantageous, there was no harm in it.   But the contrary has been shown; and

it would be something incredible if a person who knew
nothing previously of state affairs, should become com-
petent, in a period of two years, to govern two kingdoms.   Who can believe that a person who considers
himself the most honourable man in the country, entertaining the best intentions for the king and the
state, but who possesses no religion, and consequently can have no other intentions but the satisfaction of his desires,—that such a man should try to
persuade a nation like the Danish and Norwegian that
he is the man who will promote everybody's fortunes
in the kingdom?   I here write what must be regarded
as incredible, if we were not so perfectly convinced of
it.   Count Struensee has committed crimes which the
meanest man in the kingdom, who has but the most
general ideas about morality and the reverence he
owes his king, will regard as the most detestable.   It
is true that an evident crime entails on the culprit the
extremest public contumely,—as, for instance, robbing
one's neighbour; seducing his wife, &c.   But it is
unanswerable, under the appearance of friendship,
fidelity, true love of the welfare of the country, disinterestedness, and sparing the royal treasury, for a
man to strive to put his fingers into everything, and
to rule with unbounded authority instead of the regent,—in a word, to make a brilliant display of his
villany (I call things by their right names).   Count
Struensee alleges that the cause of the abolition of the
council of state was partly that his royal Majesty was

not satisfied with the condition of the country and the
indebtedness in which the kingdom was; partly, that
he was impeded by the council. If his Majesty himself had the idea of abolishing the council, Count Struensee ought to have opposed it in a different way from
that which he employed in coercing the king to bathe.
But it was his duty to represent to the king his master
that his royal Majesty, having only recently ascended
the throne, required advice; and if among the councillors there were some who did not possess his Majesty's confidence, others could be found to fill their
place; that a monarch, however wise he may be, still
remains a man; that, although the King of Denmark
was not bound to retain advisers, still it was to his
honour and profit to have them; and that he who
was instructed in medical science was not fitted to
undertake the management of such affairs. Everybody knows that a king should never love hypocrisy.
But truth can be expressed in various ways. A truth
urged in a coarse manner is an insult; an attempt to
apply it sarcastically is a mockery; but when expressed with honourable straightforwardness, it is
useful, and the latter is the duty of an honest subject. Count Struensee, however, was so daring as to
take on himself the functions of many men.

In my historical preface, I have called attention to
the fact, how strange it appeared to all who are aware
that a knowledge of the welfare of kingdoms cannot
be acquired by whistling or dancing, when he attained

the most gracious royal order and instruction of July 14, 1771, to be privy cabinet minister. From this instruction, which was communicated to the colleges, we learn that Count Struensee not only exercised a power which not even the great chancellor of the kingdom possessed in former times, but exercised it as fully as only his royal Majesty could do himself. It is true there was an appearance as if everything still depended on his Majesty's approbation; but if the matter is looked into more closely, this is only delusion and juggling. For if everything in the cabinet is decided by Count Struensee, and his orders and regulations are to have the same value as the king's commands, it is clear that if anything was issued from the cabinet which opposed existing regulations and resolutions, and that this should be returned to the cabinet for alteration, the eventual decision depended on the count himself. And what assurance was given the king and his subjects that nothing wrong would be done by the cabinet minister when he possessed the power himself to examine, defend, and approve everything he had resolved on?

When Count Struensee had the fortune, favour, and honour to come to the Danish court and stand well there, he probably took the Danish and Norwegian subjects for such cattle, that they might be called together and led to the shambles by a cabinet resolution of his, without being allowed to murmur, for in no other way can we explain his daring to undertake such an

enterprise.   Any man who presumes to manage the
affairs of a kingdom, and direct them instead of the
king, must be acquainted with the duties of the king
to his subjects, and the duties of the subjects to the
king.   He must be a simple doctor who merely knows
that there is a heart in the human body, but not where
it is seated, and what parts are connected with it or
have influence over it.   Any man who did not wish
merely to play the harlequin, but maintain his honour,
ought to be acquainted with the duties of the regent
and the people.   Struensee could have seen in the
Danish and Norwegian code, and in the *Lex Regia* of
Frederick III. of blessed memory, signed on November 14, 1665, that sovereignty, but not despotism, is
granted to the king.   There is not a subject of his
Majesty who would feel offended because the king
rules with unlimited power, for that is his right.   Any
one who asserts that the king can alter the *Lex Regia* without the assent of the nation, and against the
will of all classes, is a traitor, hypocrite, and scoundrel.   The royal law, which the kings must obey, and
which is a *sine quâ non* on their part and that of their
subjects, cannot be altered by the king, without at
once overthrowing and restricting his rule, for it is
ordered (as Frederick III. could order his descendants as *primus adquirens*), that the royal law shall not
be altered, and the right to the monarchy is solely
derived from this supreme royal law, as an immutable
fundamental law for both kingdoms.

(Wiwet here quotes the two passages of the *Lex Regia*, 3 and 26, referring to this. As I have given them already literally, they may be omitted here.)

If Count Struensee was so stupid that he knew nothing about the royal law, although he undertook to be director of the kingdom, his audacity might perhaps be expiated in prison, in a mad-house, or on the pillory. But as he has declared that he was acquainted with the contents and prescriptions of the royal law, but is at the same time of opinion that there is no harm in appropriating the king's authority for the purpose of pulling the skin of the subjects over their ears, he has on this point been guilty of the crime of high treason in a high degree. Just as little as an alteration can be effected in the king's hereditary government, which insults the king, can this be done in another way, even though it might appear as if it were done in favour of the king. The royal law must so remain unchanged that Count Struensee can introduce no other form of government but that prescribed by it. The apology with which Count Struensee tries to excuse his enterprise I need not contradict, for the king cannot forgive his audacity. The honour, life, and property of the people, were entrusted to the autocracy of the descendants of Frederick III., but to no one else. Any one, therefore, who attempts to appropriate this power, offends against the reverence which he owes the king.

Fifthly.

Even if Count Struensee could be for a moment excused for acquiring, in contradiction to the royal law, such authority as was granted him in the cabinet decree of July 14, 1771, he still remains criminal, because he did not behave honestly after the contents of this instruction, from which it is plainly seen that he did not employ this power to relieve his royal Majesty, but merely to play the part which he had invented for himself and his colleagues. To mention all the intrigues of which he was guilty in this respect, is superfluous, and would lead me too far. I consider, therefore, that one example will be sufficient. Should it appear to the count, however, that I have not sufficiently convicted him of being a clumsy criminal, I have various further proofs at his service.

When Count Struensee had effected the dismissal of the Horse Guards, the Foot Guards were also to be dismissed from their duty at the palace. The matter was connected in this way: Count Struensee apprehended that he might some day receive the reward of his crimes, and therefore he must see to his precautions. The natives of the country, as a wall of defence round the royal house, were a thorn in his eye, and hence such obstacles must be removed for coming events. Consequently, he drew up a cabinet decree of December 21, 1771, concerning the disbandment of the Foot

Guards, of which his royal Majesty was not informed. These men were to be placed in other regiments, because, as the count alleges, equality ought to prevail among all officers and soldiers, as they all served the same king; while the true reason was, that the count, in the event of ill-success, did not wish to have them against him, as they might assist in seizing him by the ear. But when this order became known, and the Guards refused to obey it, he procured a royal order of December 24, by which his Majesty most graciously granted discharges to those Guards, who would not perform duty at the palace with the grenadiers. This was an extra-ordinarily foolhardy action, as will be seen from the following facts :—

First. His Majesty never knew anything about such a dismissal of the body-guard : for this reason it has been re-embodied, which proves that the disbandment took place against the king's will. *Secondly.* His Majesty did not sign the said order. *Thirdly.* Count Struensee, when he extorted his royal Majesty's approbation for the disbandment of the Guards, represented that they refused to do duty at the palace with the grenadiers, which was an evident falsehood, as the Guards only refused to enter other regiments. *Fourthly.* Although, from December 21 to 24, there were various resolutions which ought to have been approved by the king, Struensee did not lay them before his Majesty, solely from the motive of having the former orders of December 21 confirmed by the approbation of the last.

He therefore acted falsely as regards the commands and
resolutions, the drawing-up of which, and laying before
the king for approbation, depended on him as privy
cabinet minister, and thus acted contrary to the law
I—I—I.

Sixthly.

After Count Struensee had acquired the mastery
over his Majesty's treasury, both the private and the
special cabinet treasury, he contrived to turn it to his
own advantage. It would lead me too far if I mentioned all the cunning tricks done by him, and the
commission will pardon me if I do not lay all the
instances before it. Count Struensee has, therefore,
no reason to complain, for all his malversations are
not mentioned, and, indeed, they are countless. He
takes 10,000 dollars, and 3,000 at the new year, procures Count Brandt 3,000, so that he may not overthrow and betray him, and the Countess Holstein a
gratification of 3,000 dollars, because she has lost her
money at play, although her royal Majesty graciously
and justly refuses it, for the earnings of 3,000 poor
women by spinning pay for her extravagance. One
gratification after the other is granted to Falckenskjold,[*]

[*] The falsehood of this charge is best proved by Falckenskjold's own examination: "I certainly made no profit out of the 8,000 crowns given me
for my journeys, made by order of the king." When he was summoned from
the Turkish frontier to enter the Danish service he received 1,000 dollars, and
when he was sent to Petersburg on diplomatic business he was paid 2,000
crowns for his travelling and other expenses. Little enough, when we remember
that on two occasions he was obliged to stay six weeks in Petersburg.

that chosen instrument for all events, that sheet-anchor on which the whole machine (so Count Struensee calls his arrangements) depended, and who was well aware that, if the count's rule broke up, he (the colonel) would also lose his regiment. For his brother he procures money from the king's treasury, on the grounds that a financier must have money to prevent him from stealing; for such is the right conclusion that should be drawn from his defence.

That Count Struensee is as great a villain as was ever rung in and out of a German fair, any one can see from the fact that he obtained money and office for his brother. I will not refer to the circumstance that the king was obliged to pay for the journey of a person to an office of which the person summoned had no knowledge. My God, what a mockery of so many worthy men, who meant sincerely by the king and country! But to propose his brother as deputy of finances, and to give him 3,000 dollars so that he might not plunder the king in other ways of an equal sum, is so extraordinarily audacious and foolhardy, that it renders Count Struensee most excessively contemptible. Who could invent such motives without prostituting himself, and revealing that in such dealing no true honour was intended!

In the same way as Count Struensee managed to procure his brother money, he also continued to obtain considerable sums for himself and his confidants. When he acquired full authority over the king's treasury, on learning that it was by no means a matter of

indifference to his Majesty whether there was money
in the treasury or not, he requested his Majesty, upon
some money being paid in, most graciously to give
him and Brandt a trifle, probably under the same pretext as he afterwards employed for his brother.   His
Majesty therefore gave—

<pre>
      To the Queen .   .   .   . 10,000 dollars.
      To Count Brandt .   .   .   6,000   „   and
      To him, Count Struensee .   6,000   „
                                 ──────────
</pre>

        Making a total of 22,000 dollars,
which is perfectly correct.   But after his Majesty's
approval of the donations had been obtained, Count
Struensee, who was able to take the money out of the
king's special treasury—for he cannot prove that he
took it from anywhere else—hit on the idea of adding
a 0, so that the document now reads

<pre>
      To the Queen .   .   .   . 10,000 dollars.
      To Count Brandt .   .   .   60,000   „   and
      To him, Count Struensee . 60,000   „
                                 ──────────
</pre>

        Together 130,000 dollars.
As in reckoning up this did not agree with the
22,000 dollars, in order to avoid an alteration of both
the figures 2, the matter was thus arranged:

<pre>
      To the Queen .   .   .   . 10,000 dollars.
      To Count Brandt .   .   . 60,000   „
      To Count Struensee .   . 60,000   „   and
      To Falckenskjold .   .   .   2,000   „
                                 ──────────
</pre>

        Total 132,000 dollars.

Apart from the fact that any one can easily detect how the two ciphers were added, and also that a figure 2 has been altered into a 3, it is clear, as Counts Brandt and Struensee themselves, will be obliged to confess, that there is the greatest reason for regarding the affair with suspicion; and it will be proved an evident forgery, when we take into consideration the following facts:—1. His royal Majesty has himself declared that he did not give them 60,000 dollars. 2. It is remarkable that in the same document by which the king gave his two subjects and servants 60,000 dollars apiece, he granted his consort only 10,000; and 3. All the proofs brought forward by the count in this matter, hobble.

He has, therefore, in addition to the insult offered his Majesty by robbing him of so large a capital, been guilty of peculation in this instance also, and offended against the regulations of the law 6—4—10.

Seventhly.

Furthermore, Count Struensee was an accomplice, adviser, and helper, in selling her royal Majesty's costly bouquet, which was composed of precious stones, and taxed at the value of 40,000 dollars, for 10,000 dollars in Hamburg, and entrusting the sale to Etats-rath Waitz, although this concerned an article which served as an ornament to the queen regnant of the country, and ought not to have been taken from her.

(Here come eight passages from the evidence.)   In
this he has not only acted faithlessly, in allowing so
valuable an ornament to be sold for so ridiculous a
price, but it was also quite unnecessary to dispose of a
valuable in such a way "to the prostitution of its
owner."

Eighthly.

In order that this intrigue and other disgraceful
undertakings might not come to the knowledge of the
king, he gave orders that all letters addressed to his
Majesty should be delivered in the cabinet, so that he
might be the first to learn everything, and, if necessary, take those measures which his safety demanded,
and be the conductor and defender of any proceedings
that might be found requisite.

Ninthly.

At length, when Struensee perceived that matters
were not going on right, and that he was about to be
attacked, he tried to defend himself.   Those persons
whom he feared were dismissed; the citizens only remained, but these he fancied he could easily terrify.
Hence, after obtaining the nomination of another commandant, he gave orders to have the cannon field in
readiness.   It is true that he denies this, and only
acknowledges that he gave Major-General Gude orders

to hold everything in readiness which would serve for the maintenance of good order. But when we consider that this was not necessary, as such cases are always provided for in Copenhagen, we presume this unusual regulation was either the fruit of an apprehension that he was at length about to receive the reward of his actions, or that it had reference to a measure that was about to be taken and defended. That he intended to fly and take some one with him, in the event of his not being able to hold his ground, is seen from litt. F., pp. 33, 41, and 52.

I consider, therefore, that I have proved Count Struensee's enormous crimes against his royal Majesty, the royal family, and the kingdoms; and that he has been guilty of high treason in many ways. The punishment I demand consequently is—

"That Count John Frederick Struensee, for the crimes committed by him, be condemned to have lost his dignity of count, his honour, life, and property; and that, after his coat of arms has been broken by the executioner, his right hand be cut off while he is alive, his body quartered and exposed on a wheel, his head and hand stuck on a pole, and also that his fortune be confiscated to the king, and his heirs, if he have any, forfeit their rank and birth."

F. W. WIWET.

Copenhagen, April 21, 1772.

I am afraid that my translation of this unexampled

document will be regarded as extremely inelegant; but this could not be avoided, if the literal meaning were to be adhered to. The original itself is written in the most barbarous style; wherever the advocate's Danish runs short he helps himself out with a German word, which he generally misapplies, and puts in scraps of Latin here and there, which have the most absurd counter-sense. As my object, however, was to give an exact idea of charges which would not have hung a dog in this country, I have thought it advisable to sacrifice elegance to correctness.

Ere I conclude this chapter, I may be permitted to supply one example of the way in which the judges tried to scrape up evidence against the unfortunate ex-minister. On the same day when the Russian minister, Filosofow, insulted Struensee so grossly, as has been already recorded, a report was spread that the latter had quarrelled with one of the first gentlemen in the land, and treacherously assailed him, sword in hand; but this rumour died out as rapidly as it had been propagated. After the arrest of Struensee, and the difficulty felt of proving the already resolved death-sentence by credible testimony, the president of the court, Justiciary Baron von Juel-Wind, went to this gentleman, and asked him if he were disposed to bring a charge against Struensee before the commission? The gentleman nobly rejected such a proposal, and answered, that he was accustomed to pity the unfortunate, and not increase their misery;

besides, there was not the slightest truth in the rumour.

This proves that even Wiwet's diatribes were not considered sufficient evidence of Struensee's guilt, and that every opportunity was sought to bolster up the case. It is very possible, however, that the judges were more successful with other witnesses whom they tried to suborn, and therefore the evidence, such as it is, ought to be regarded with extra suspicion.

CHAPTER XII.

ON the very next day after Wiwet's indictment was
handed in to the commission, the following written
defence was delivered to the judges.

It is clear that Advocate Uldall could not have produced a reply to the indictment so quickly unless the
accusation had been delivered to him beforehand, which
was not only a breach of the law, and proves the haste
with which condemnation and execution were desired,
but also supplies a further and striking proof of the
plans of the conspirators. After they had thrown
their victims into chains, they hurried to play out
the judicial farce, and shed the blood for which they
thirsted.

Uldall's Defence of Count Struensee.

The command which his Majesty the King most graciously sent to me on March 28, orders me to conduct this cause in a responsible manner, and according to the law, on behalf of Count Struensee.

It is this duty which I shall now strive to fulfil with all the moderation which the count owes to his judges in his defence.

Among the unfortunate circumstances which beset him at the present moment, there is one which is the more painful to him, because it was unexpected. This circumstance is, that the Fiscal General tries to render all the count's actions contemptible and ridiculous.

That everything should be converted into a motive for finding him guilty is a natural, though unfortunate, result of the situation in which he finds himself placed. But that his external situation, his origin, and his first position; his mode of thinking, even in instances where it was correct, should be subjected to mockery—against this, at least, he believed himself to be protected, if not out of compassion for an unfortunate man, at any rate on account of the favour which the king had formerly shown him, and in consideration of the applause which his Majesty granted to the political principles in accordance with which he, the count, acted.

There is hardly a circumstance, however insignificant it may be, which has not been employed by the Fiscal General for the purpose of rendering Count Struensee odious.

He is called a foreigner, although through the appointment of his father as superintendent in Holstein, in Struensee's youth, the latter became a royal subject. That he was not possessed of the Danish language is certainly a defect, which, however, has also been found in other ministers, although it has never before been constituted a state crime.

If he had a share in the cabinet order which limits the granting of " characters," and which is still in existence, I believe that no patriot ever denied, or does deny, its necessity and advantage, and if the character of a councillor of justice was not fitted for a mathematician, as the count's brother was, this cannot be charged against Count Struensee, because his brother had been Justiz-rath long before he came here.

Even to religion, the only consolation left him in his misfortune, he is not considered worthy to possess it.

It would lead too far were I to examine everything which has in such a way been brought forward without ground in the Fiscal General's indictment.   Everybody knows that this mode of conviction, rendering a cause ridiculous and odious, is not conclusive, because there is nothing which cannot be rendered ridiculous in one way or the other; and, moreover, most of the

Fiscal General's imputations exceed that which, by the king's command, is to be discussed before this commission.

Count Struensee is to be charged and convicted for crimes against the laws of the land, and it is in this I have to defend him. As such, the Fiscal General alleges nine various chief points, which are said to be equally as many crimes of high treason. But as all these charges generally either concern the state arrangements, and the form and administration of the government, or are crimes against the person of his Majesty the King and members of the royal house, I will give my answers to them after the above divisions.

The first charge brought against Count Struensee, is the cabinet decree of July 14, 1771, and the authority delivered to him by it.

In order to convict him of audacity in this, the Fiscal General employs two different grounds: partly, Count Struensee's impudence in mixing himself up, though a physician, in affairs of state, and in abolishing the council, whence disorder in the affairs, oppression of the nation and the nobility, and a decrease of the prosperity of the capital, are said to have emanated: partly, that the power which he obtained was royal, as he formed resolutions, and signed in the king's name, and had it in his power to lay before the king the objections sent in against the cabinet decrees, or not to do so, which is said to be opposed to articles

3 and 26 of the *Lex Regia*, in which such a possession of power is declared to be treason.

It appears as if the first of the grounds alleged by the Fiscal General exceeds his competency to examine, and that of the commission to decide. For, as the share which Count Struensee had in affairs only emanated from the king's will, Count Struensee cannot be rendered responsible for this, because the consequences must revert to his Majesty.

An investigation, whether Count Struensee ought to give the king advice in affairs of state, and what results this advice had, is in reality an examination as to how his Majesty established the government; and Count Struensee cannot be called to account for the advice he gave, as it met with the king's approval. Still I do not see how this can be made a crime on the part of Count Struensee. It is certainly true that his original position did not seem to promise the dignity which he eventually acquired. But history offers many instances of such elevation, and, if the king fancied he deserved it, was not Struensee at liberty to accept it?

The form of the council is no material portion of the Danish constitution. That the king was dissatisfied with its arrangement, is visible from many passages in the examination; and there can be no better proof of this than that his Majesty signed the decree of its abolition with his own hand. Even though Count Struensee advised it, we find from Count

Brandt's explanation to quest. 18, that several persons considered his sentiments correct, and that the plan was that the colleges should be heard in ordinary cases, and commissions in extraordinary affairs, the final decision being left to the king; so that it cannot be asserted that the royal power was thus rendered greater or less than it should be according to the *Lex Regia*.

For a belief that affairs consequently were carried on with less vigour than before, or that the nation was unequally oppressed by the promotion of foreigners, neither the documents nor experience afford a reason.

No other noble was prohibited from appearing at court except Count Laurvig (Ahlefeldt Laurvig), who had met with the same fate once before; and if several nobles retired to their estates, and Copenhagen suffered through the declension of luxury, this may be ascribed to the hard times rather than other causes.

If we were to examine the matter politically, the prosperity of the two kingdoms could hardly be sought in the size of Copenhagen, and the value of its buildings. Nor do I believe that the wise king, Frederick IV., when he laid on Copenhagen a consumption tax double that of the other cities in the country, so much intended the increase of his revenues, as to prevent the too rapid growth of a single city, which would at last attract to it all the sources of a livelihood. France and England have long complained that their capitals

insensibly swallowed up everything; and experience
has shown that the Duc de Sully reasoned correctly,
when he, in order to prevent this, decided that those
French nobles who were not employed in the public
service should sooner serve the state and themselves
by good management of their estates, than ruin themselves and other families by indolence and extravagance.

As regards the second of the Fiscal General's
grounds—Count Struensee's authority—it cannot be
denied that his Majesty the King was at liberty to
grant his confidence to whom he pleased, and decide to
what extent he should confer it on Count Struensee.

The decree of July 14, 1771, states that the cabinet
minister shall draw up the commands which the king
gives him verbally, and either lay them before the king
for signature, or issue them in the king's name with
the seal of the cabinet, after which they shall be obeyed
by every one.

It is not, therefore, the person of the cabinet minister, but the orders given him by his Majesty himself, and which the king makes known through him,
that acquire value through this order.

The cabinet was nothing else but the king himself,
and Count Struensee was so far from apprehending
that he should be confounded with it, that, whenever
any one wrote to him as cabinet minister on business
matters, he answered that application must be made
to the cabinet or the king.   He especially remembers

that this was the case with General Huth.　In the cabinet nothing took place, and not the slightest order was issued from it save under royal authority.　The king saw and heard everything that was sent in from the colleges or elsewhere; and himself gave the decision, sometimes in writing, sometimes verbally.　Nothing could escape his Majesty's attention, because affairs were repeatedly brought before him: first, when the cabinet order was issued; secondly, when the report was sent in about it by the persons concerned; and, lastly, when the weekly extract of the cabinet orders was approved.　Everything was done in the king's name.　His Majesty signed the decree in question with his own hand, and from his own most gracious *motu proprio* appointed Count Struensee cabinet minister.

Just as there cannot lie in this the slightest supposition of a surprise, so we cannot see in it any encroachment on the royal authority.　It seems, therefore, as if Count Struensee were reproached more for what might have happened than for what really did happen, for the Fiscal General dwells more particularly on the danger which was to be apprehended, in the event of the count misusing the king's confidence in issuing other orders than those which the king gave him.

In order to prevent this, it is said the *Lex Regia* has commanded the king to sign everything himself, and declared any man guilty of encroachment on the king's supremacy who appropriated any function opposed to this.　But I trust I shall have no difficulty in proving that this reasoning is incorrect. How most unfair a law would be that punished a man because he possessed the opportunity for sinning, although he never made an attempt to take advantage of the opportunity! Hence Count Struensee cannot be punished because he might possibly have misused the king's confidence, unless it is notorious that he did so.

The royal law never desired such a thing, for the two articles quoted from it do not agree with it. It is true that article 7 orders that all letters on business of the government shall be issued in no other name but the king's, and under his seal, and that he must sign himself, if he has attained his majority (his fourteenth year). Furthermore, it is true that article 26, states that the man who acquires anything which might encroach on the king's authority shall be regarded as an insulter of his Majesty. But what is it that Count Struensee acquired, and which was injurious to the king's supremacy? The count cannot be accused of this by the first part of article 7 of the *Lex Regia;* for no one will deny that the letters and decrees of the government were issued in the king's name. But if it be true that his Majesty did not always himself sign the cabinet decrees, it must be remembered that this point concerns his Majesty, and no one else. It is clear that Count Struensee cannot be made accountable because it did not always please his Majesty to sign, and that the royal authority has suffered, or could suffer, no encroachment, as it was dependent on the king's will whether he would sign an order himself, or specially command Count Struensee to sign it in his Majesty's name.

To this argument must be added, that the *Lex Regia* does not regard it as an important part of or an insult to the royal authority to sign in the king's name, for article 9 prescribes that the regents should sign in the event of the king's minority, although article 13 orders them to take oath that they will maintain the supremacy uninjured, an oath which would be contradictory if the signature formed a material part of the supremacy: that, consequently, the *Lex Regia*, like other states, for instance, France and Spain, regards the expedition, and not the signature, as the true symbol of supremacy. Formerly this was understood in such a way, as both the colleges and other royal officials, in many instances, made the king's will known, and still do so, in his name, but without his signature. Nor did any one represent to Count Struensee that it was a thing contrary to the *Lex Regia* to do so. And, lastly, his Majesty's own special order of July 14, 1771, is sufficient to remove the responsibility from him, even if there were a crime in doing so, as it was only in accordance with his Majesty's commands, and to prove his most submissive obedience to the king's will that he acted thus, and were it otherwise, no one would be secured by a royal order.

The Fiscal General, in points 5, 6, and 7, of his indictment, brings forward several charges, in order

to prove that Count Struensee really misapplied the
king's confidence in his signature.   Of these instances,
the one referring to the dismissal of the body-guard is
the first, and it is even supposed that it was based on
dangerous designs.

What was really the motive for this operation,
namely, that the Guards were in many respects injurious to the army, is seen both from Count Struensee's
answers and from the documents, to which he appeals
in his own memorial.

That it was done, however, without his Majesty's
knowledge, or that the latter was surprised by it, is,
according to Count Struensee's assurance, incorrect.
As regards the cabinet order of December 21, concerning the reduction, he positively remembers having
read it to the king before it was sent off; and further,
that the king approved of it with his own signature,
after the college had sent in an appeal against it; and
his Majesty himself signed the order of December 24,
for dismissal, before it was sent to Lieutenant-General
von Gähler, as it was generally reported that the
Guards refused to obey the first order.

As to the crime said to have been committed in
omitting several of the extracts from the cabinet decrees in this week, so that the king might approve of
the two concerning the body-guard, I do not understand it, as his Majesty would sooner be surprised by
a long report than by a short extract, and the answers
of Panning and Morack (the cabinet secretaries) prove

20 *

that this error must be ascribed to them rather than to Struensee.

The second charge concerns the presents which Count Struensee is said to have procured for himself and others, and more especially the forgery which is said to have been committed in the accounts of the special treasury for the months of April and May, 1771. As concerns the gratifications, it is sufficient for Struensee's defence that the king himself granted or approved of them, and Count Struensee is of opinion that, if compared with those given on former occasions, they will not be found extraordinary. As regards the falsification, he learns to his deep grief that even his Majesty himself appears to bear witness against him. But, as he solemnly asserts in his memorial that he was never guilty of such things, he also hopes that he will be permitted to quote the circumstances serving to prove his innocence.

The Fiscal General employs two suppositions to prove this forgery, namely, that a cipher was added to each of the two amounts of 6,000 dollars, and that the gratification for Falckenskjold was inserted at a later date. But that this is not correct is proved by the document itself, in which the figures of all the four amounts and Falckenskjold's name are written with the same ink as the approbation, without mentioning that his Majesty (if we compare the document with the approval of other calculations written afterwards) must have signed higher up, if the line concerning Falckenskjold had not existed at the time when the royal signature was appended. It is true that the adding up seems to be written with a different ink, and the figure 3 in the 132,000 dollars to have been first a 2. But the former is of no consequence when it is remarked, that the adding up took place after the approval had been given, while the latter could easily occur through an error in casting up, as Panning has regarded it in his explanation, lit. I., p. 379.

If we add to this—1. That Count Struensee had no necessity to have recourse to such a forgery, partly because his Majesty never refused him what he asked in such matters; partly, because a hundred other ways of enriching himself stood at his service, if he wished to act dishonestly, of which not the slightest evidence has been brought forward. 2. That he never made a secret of it, which might be supposed in a dishonest action, either from Count von Schimmelmann, who paid the money, or from Count Brandt, who, on the very same day thanked the king for the 50,000 dollars which he had received, to which his Majesty replied, it was but fair that he should make him a *sort*, leading to the supposition that the sum was a considerable one (see Brandt's answer to question 44, p. 250); and lastly, 3. That it could not be concealed from the king, as credit was taken for the amount in the next balance-sheet, in which the sum was again approved— I am of opinion that this circumstance cannot be regarded as dishonesty, but that everything really is as Count Struensee has explained it.

The third charge relates to the sale of the bouquet. As this affair depended entirely on the will of her royal Majesty the Queen, and Count Struensee declares that he never knew otherwise but that the sale took place with the king's consent, and as he did not profit in the slightest degree by it, he had not supposed that this would be alleged as a crime against him.

These are the principal charges brought against Count Struensee as regards his administration. For though the Fiscal General, in his indictment, has touched on all sorts of small matters: for instance, the appointment of Councillor of Justice Struensee to the College of Finances, &c., as they all depended on the general principles which his Majesty the King had accepted in the administration, and his Majesty had given his special approval to their execution, it is unnecessary to dwell on them.

On the other hand, I will in conclusion of this portion of the indictment show, that the Fiscal General incorrectly charges Count Struensee with having formed dangerous designs, and of wishing to sustain himself in the most improper way in the post which his Majesty entrusted to him.

As a proof of this, the dismissal of the body-guard and the loading of the cannon are first alleged. It was proved in the examination that the reasons for this were perfectly legal; it is also seen from the confrontation of Major-General Gude and Count Struensee, that the intention of the latter order was only to hold the populace in check, for the sake of the public tranquillity, and that Count Struensee never ordered Major-General Gude to take the latter precaution, but the general was of opinion that it was merely a consequence of the general reminder given him, "that everything must be tranquil and in order."

Equally little probable or proven is it that Count Struensee had undertaken, or wished to undertake anything which would have procured him an opportunity for escaping, if his supposed meditated design of assuming the character of a protector had failed.

That nothing was attempted against the person of his royal Majesty is proved by the documents and the acknowledgment of the Fiscal General himself. And how could gratitude or caution have suggested so detestable a thought to the count? It was the king alone to whom he owed his fortune, and the confidence of his Majesty was the sole basis of his respect and his security.

But if he could have been so malicious as to deny all his obligations, where was the party he had formed to carry out his design? Would he have been so incautious as to announce his intention to the whole public? For such was the case with the loading of the cannon; and would he not rather have taken precautions to secure himself against such surprises as might easily take place, and really did take place, especially as we see from Christian Näses' declaration and Count Brandt's acknowledgment, that he had received some intimations to that effect?

That Count Struensee employed other illegal means to support himself is equally incorrect. It certainly seems as if Count Brandt were attached to the king in order to watch him; but the latter declares exactly the contrary, and that Count Struensee did not at all need him to support himself. Equally little can it be concluded from point eight of the indictment, that letters addressed to the king were to be delivered in the cabinet; for, without mentioning that this order was given by the king himself, and that, if it had any secret object, it ought to have been given long before, Panning and Morack's statements prove that the disorder in which letters and other papers lay about the king's apartment was the sole cause for this order, and that his Majesty, after this time, received his letters as punctually as before.

As regards the accusations, then, which have been brought against Count Struensee with respect to public affairs, I hope I have proved that he only acted according to the will of his Majesty; that it was not his intention to acquire power at the expense of his royal Majesty; and that, if he erred in one point or the other, it was not done through petulance, or deserves the harsh expressions employed by the Fiscal General, but that it is solely to be explained by the fallibility which is inseparably connected with every man. Nowhere has anything been found which raised a doubt as to the safety of the king, his family, or his supremacy, or could give cause for the supposition that Count Struensee wished to treat his king and benefactor in so shameful a way. He declares most sacredly, even now, that his only desire was to promote the king's welfare and the prosperity of the kingdoms.

I will now pass to the second portion of the charges, which relate to the insults said to have been offered to the persons of the royal house. As regards the "*éloignement*" in which her Majesty Queen Juliana Maria and his royal highness the hereditary prince were held, Count Struensee declares that he has given the true reason in his answers to questions 486 and 469; that he never attempted to maintain or increase it; that he was not aware of any other reason for a different box being given the prince at the theatre, except that the king did not wish to have the prince's suite in his box; and that, lastly, so far as he could remember, he had no share in the correspondence carried on, upon this subject, between Count Brandt and Count Scheel.

As regards the education of his royal highness the prince royal, I refer to the count's own memorial; he protests most sacredly against ever having entertained such thoughts as the Fiscal General imputes to him. In this matter, he is so conscious of the purity of his intentions, that he is willing to submit it to the verdict of experienced physicians, whether the prince's health has not been improved by it. Moreover, it was the queen's will that this course should be pursued; and Count Struensee more than once drew on himself her displeasure, by representing to her that the right measure was exceeded in it. (*Cfr.* letter F., pp. 361 and 362.)

As concerns the "passage" between his royal Majesty and Count Brandt, which forms a charge in the Fiscal General's indictment, the explanations of Count Struensee show that he could never have conjectured that Count Brandt would undertake it in so audacious a way as he did, but that the affair would be settled *en badinant* between the king and Brandt. His advice was to the effect that Brandt should keep aloof from the king; and that Brandt did not, in the remotest degree, expect Count Struensee's assent, or subsequent approval, in this affair, is seen from the fact that he not only previously kept secret the way in which he had resolved to go to work, as he merely said "that he would demand an explanation of the king," but that, afterwards, he also concealed the most aggravating portions of his deed,—the circumstance with the riding-whip; his bolting the door; and the challenging and abusive language which he employed. In so far, then, as regards the share which Count Struensee had in this "passage," he hopes the more to be excused, because his Majesty the King, in such private matters, did not wish to be regarded as king, but as a private person, which was the reason why he, Count Struensee, did not oppose Brandt's design, so far as it was known to him.

That it was never his "sentiment" to neglect the proper reverence in intercourse with the king; and that no one can mention an instance of it, strengthens his innocence in this case; for what the Fiscal General alleges to the contrary only consists of mere gossip. Equally little can Brandt's letter, quoted by the Fiscal General, serve as a proof that Brandt was rewarded for his conduct to the king, as it was written in September, 1771, and the "passage" with Brandt did not take place till November of that year. And should not all this be a sufficient justification for Count Struensee, he appeals to the kindness which his Majesty has so frequently shown him, to obtain his pardon.

In the same way he throws himself at his Majesty's feet, and implores his mercy for the crime against his Majesty's person, the first mentioned by the Fiscal General, but hitherto unalluded to by me. It is the only thing in which he knows that he consciously sinned against his king; but he confesses, with contrition, that this crime is too great for him to expect forgiveness of it. If, however, regard for human weakness, a truly penitent feeling of his error, the deepest grief at it, the tears with which he laments it, and the sighs which he dedicates to the king and the welfare of his family, deserve any compassion, he will not be found unworthy of it.

In all the rest he supposes that the law and his innocence will defend him, and that for this reason he
can expect an acquittal.   But, in the same way as in
the last point, he seeks refuge in the king's mercy
alone; he begs this high court, who have witnessed
the sincerity of his grief and sorrow, to be kind enough
to procure him the greatest possible alleviation of his
fate by a favourable representation of his repentance
to his Majesty.

ULDALL.

Copenhagen, April 22, 1772.

This defence, though neatly written, is still so weak
and lukewarm, that it cannot protect its author from
the suspicion that he had an understanding with the
conspirators, and that his defence was only intended
to throw dust in the eyes of Europe.   Falckenskjold,
who, as a native, contemporary, and adherent of Struensee, and who, as unattached to the court, is an impartial witness, expresses himself as follows on the
subject in his " Memoirs :"—

" The royal law supplied Uldall with an article
which, by formally authorising the king to suppress
or create any council or office he thought proper, consequently gave the right of proposing the suppression
of the privy council and of other offices which might
appear injurious to the interests of the monarchy, as
well as the creation of a cabinet minister.   Further,
Uldall did not develope all the absurdity of the

charge of forgery brought against his client.   He did
not make use of the means he possessed to justify him
about the ill-treatment of the king, of which Brandt
was accused: means the more easy, because there was
in this point no evidence against Struensee.   He ought
to have discussed the reforms effected by this minister,
and have shown that far from being criminal and injurious, they generally tended to the welfare of the
state and the advantage of the monarch.   This examination would have given him occasion to display the
conduct of Struensee, and show him, as he really was,
vigilant and anxious to simplify affairs, so that the
king might see and know them, and decide them himself.   It was very easy to heighten the merit of such
conduct by comparing it with that of previous ministers; by placing in its true light that royal law by
virtue of which every Danish monarch binds himself
on ascending the throne not to suffer any attack on
his power, and to maintain it in its integrity.   It was
not sufficient to say, as if *en passant*, that the will of
the king covered the acts of Struensee's administration with an inviolable defence; he ought to have
made those who attacked them feel the consequences
to which they exposed themselves; he ought to have
shown them in the royal law the sword that menaced
those who dared to condemn in Struensee the wishes
and orders of the king." *

   But Uldall had been one of Struensee's opponents

* " Mémoires de Falckenskjold," p. 190.

from the beginning, and hence was most unfitted to
be a defender; and that he consented to be so, on
being selected by the chief conspirator, throws a sufficient light on his good will as a lawyer.

But what will my readers think of the two advocates, and the legal members of the commission, when
I state that the criminal code of Christian V. prohibits
every judge from listening to or trying charges that
dishonour members of the reigning family? Falckenskjold says about this:—

" How could Uldall insert in his defence Struensee's
declarations about his relations with the queen? Was
he ignorant of the Danish law that nullified this declaration, and prohibited the judges from paying any attention to it? How, if he was versed in the principles
and duties of his profession, did he dare, in a memoir
intended to be made public, to represent his client as
demanding mercy for this pretended crime, and imploring the intercession of his persecutor? And how
was it he did not feel that by acting thus he
joined a perfidious cabal, which was abusing the unhappy Struensee with deceitful hopes of escape, in
order to drag from him the means of ruining him more
completely?"

Another witness to the shamefulness of the charges
against Struensee steps forward in honest Reverdil,
himself no admirer of the favourite, but who valued
truth above everything. He carefully analyses the
charges. The one about the queen's bouquet was most

unjust, he considers. It belonged to the queen, and
she ordered it to be sold. The price it fetched was
much lower than that paid for it, because princes pay
long prices for jewels, and sell them cheaply, especially those of great value. The purpose for which
it was sold was to get the money for making the
badges for the new Order of Matilda.

As regards the forgery, Reverdil's evidence is decidedly in favour of Struensee. His argument, which
seems to be conclusive, is to the following effect:—

1. At the time when this account was made out,
Struensee, overwhelmed with business, had no secretary
to assist him. Pleasure, audiences, races, and attentions to the queen, occupied the greater part of his time.
He was ignorant of forms and their consequences:
therefore, it is very credible that he cast up the account
incorrectly, corrected, and presented it for signature
with the erasures. The king signed without looking,
and useless crimes ought not to be supposed.

2. No other trait in Struensee's life denotes an ignoble scamp or vile man: his character was rather to
carry frankness to the verge of effrontery and hardness.

3. On the other hand, it lay in the king's character
to refuse any pecuniary favour as long as he could,
but he had no idea of the value of money, so that it
was as easy to obtain from him 60,000 crowns as 6,000.
They had the bad faith to take his evidence in this
affair, and he declared that he remembered perfectly
well having only given 6,000 crowns to each of the

counts; but, with his malicious mania and his hatred for Brandt, it was impossible to trust to the fidelity of his memory, or the truth of his declarations.

4. Struensee replied to the charge with a good deal of candour; that appearances, it is true, were against him, but they were deceitful; and that, as he had already confessed more faults than were needed to destroy him, he would not deny this one, if he had committed it. He persisted in this language, without variation, to the end.

Still, while Reverdil acquits the favourites of the forgery, he has no excuse for the affair itself. To obtain so large a sum from an imbecile king, who was not of a generous temper: to obtain it at a time when the Treasury was exhausted, the state loaded with debt, and when, under pretext of economy, the favourites were making hundreds of families miserable by arbitrary retrenchments, was no better than a swindle. Reverdil was the more revolted when the trial made the fact known, because he had heard Struensee and Brandt a thousand times upbraid the prodigalities of the old court, and the presents lavished on the favourites, especially Counts von Moltke and Holck. But neither of them had received so large a sum in so short a time. The former enriched himself in twenty years of constant favour, but a considerable portion of his fortune consisted of the savings of his income, when he lived cost free at court, as grand marshal: while the new favourites, after expelling everybody, had established themselves at court, without any apparent duties.

At those Hirschholm breakfasts, when only the elect were present, and the guests liked so much to talk about the old ministry, as an occasion to applaud the present saving, Reverdil frequently heard it mentioned, as an extraordinary instance of profusion, that during the king's stay at Paris, Bernstorff, aware that Count von Holck, the most extravagant of men, was on his last legs, promised him 30,000 crowns, so that he might not yield to the seductions of the French court, who wished to employ him in detaching the king from the Russian alliance. It would have been ridiculous for any other king to pay his favourite, lest he should propose absurd and dangerous acts to him; but this conduct, when recommended to Christian VII., was founded on reason, as a bounty of 30,000 crowns, at such a moment, might save the state.

In this case, at least, the form was decent : a perfectly upright minister solicited the king in favour of a third party, and the treasurer received his Majesty's orders to pay. But the gratification granted to Struensee and Brandt had an entirely different character. The same person solicited, decided, and countersigned. It was of no use for him to say that it was once for all, and for the purpose of securing an independent position. Who could answer that avidity was not augmented by enjoyment? and with what face could the same man, who forced the king to sign a decree that, henceforth, no retiring pension should exceed 1,000 crowns, secure, after six months' office, the capital of thrice as large an income? Such is the dangerous seduction of unlimited power. Struensee, before he attained it, was not only honourable, but noble and liberal, though his circumstances were exceedingly limited.

No time was lost in the trial of the accused minister, for on April 23 the Fiscal General handed in his reply to Uldall's defence.

Wiwet's Reply.

The order which his Majesty the King most graciously sent to me on March 23, commanded me to indict Count Struensee for his crimes, without mentioning in what they consisted: as I was able to learn them, however, from the examinations and questions laid before the court, I do not understand what Advocate Uldall means by his remarks, that most of the imputations against Struensee exceed that which his Majesty commanded this commission to investigate, for I believe I have a right to answer everything that the commissioners considered themselves empowered to ask.

Advocate Uldall also does me injustice when he carps at my historic account of Count Struensee's behaviour, and for trying to make him in every way ridiculous and contemptible. But Count Struensee finds my reasons in my brief. It is my duty to give an historical introduction to the facts, which are to be afterwards proved.

It is not creditable to discuss personal matters,
when disputing about property or things which do
not affect the persons themselves. But when a criminal has to be convicted whose head is at stake, we
must not be so sparing as Herr Uldall, as defender,
desires, especially in things which are not inventions,
but everybody knows they have happened. Everything must be brought to light. The style must be
arranged in accordance with the matter to be discussed, and Count Struensee cannot be thoroughly
convinced of his crimes, if he considers my charge
insulting to the man on whom his Majesty cast his
favour.

I have not attacked him for being a foreigner, but
because the business he undertook was foreign to him.
I will not allow with Advocate Uldall that it is no
state crime not to understand the language of the
country when a man holds such a station as Count
Struensee. Herr Uldall cannot produce any instance
of it. Perhaps one man might be found who did
not understand the language like a native, but in that
case he occupied a station in, which he did not require
to understand it.* I have alleged this, his ignorance
of the language, as a proof of his foolhardiness in ac-
cepting a post in which it was his duty to talk with
Danes and Norwegians, and to read their petitions,
without being compelled to trust to the fidelity of
a translator. The count must himself confess that

* An allusion to Bernstorff as Minister of Foreign Affairs.

he did not know the laws of the country; was he not,
therefore, deficient in the two "great things" which
are requisite to examine the demands of the nation?
and can I be blamed for mentioning that he, Struensee,
had no religion, when his friend, Count Brandt, acknowledges it, and even declares that he did not dare
propose attendance at church, solely through fear of
Struensee? Ought not every one who is about the
king to fear God, as that is made a duty of the king in
article 1 of the royal law? Can any one deny that he
was bold and impudent? If he turned his attention
to affairs of state when he was a doctor of medicine,
he was an indolent doctor, for a skilful minister of
state does not spring up like a mushroom, and in that
case how dared he take on himself to become physician in ordinary? But if he devoted himself to medicine, how could he desire to become the highest and
sole authority in the affairs of the country? Can a
man be treated mildly whose principle it is that goodness injures a country? through goodness mutual love
is acquired. Which king is the more secure—the
one who is beloved, or the one before whom people
·tremble? *Oderint dum metuant* was the consolation
of the tyrant, but he is amiable who seeks his honour
in love of his country. Therefore, I have called things
by their right name, and do not do so in order to display my courage against a prisoner—for I never took
pleasure in my neighbour's misfortune—but in order
to perform my duty.

Advocate Uldall has represented the count first from the side where his crimes find an apparent excuse, so that that comes last in his reply which stands first in my statement. I shall follow his example, and concisely answer his defence.

As regards Struensee's crimes against the royal law, the counsel for the defence entertains the same views as his principal, that the king was able to do it. It is true that the king can select any adviser he pleases, but is the man whom he selects as adviser permitted to consent to things which have injurious results? The royal law states the duty of the king and of his subjects. According to article 3, no alteration can be made in it. If anything is done to the royal law, the right of reigning is lost (I write juridically, and do not suppose that the law is maintained by the sword). The King of Denmark is sovereign on the conditions to which Frederick III. pledged himself, and, as *primus adquirens*, was able in turn to pledge his descendants and successors on the throne. In article 7 of the royal law, he commanded that all government decrees and letters should be issued in no other name but the king's, and that the king himself must sign them, if he has attained his majority. In article 26, employed against me, he determined the punishment of any man who attempted any almost imperceptible encroachment on the king's authority. Hence it was Count Struensee's duty, if he wished to be an honest adviser of the king, to represent that it was not right to make known the king's will in such a way, as it was contrary to the royal law, in which the king has no power to make the slightest alterations: that the obedience of the subjects ceases if the royal law is altered without their consent: that hence the king ran the highest risk in acting thus, and it might cost him, Struensee, his head.

That Count Struensee really misused the power which he appropriated, I have clearly proved by his conduct in the order for the dissolution of the body-guard, and also that in this instance he laid incorrect statements before the king.

The other things that Herr Uldall mentions as agreeing with the royal law, are not applicable here. I have shown that Count Struensee had impure intentions in the abolition of the council, namely, to be alone, and be able to do whatever he liked.

That he failed in the reverence which he owed his Majesty, has been proved by witnesses. The falsification is so evident to everybody, that only Count Struensee's confession of it is wanting, which he holds back, however, because he does not wish to be regarded as a forger after his death. That he afterwards brought the same sum under his Majesty's notice cannot be employed in his defence, for there was no special statement which could have reminded his royal Majesty of the incorrectness.

As regards the bouquet, it is not denied that he

was aware of the sale, but he defends himself with his sacred assurance, that he supposed the sale took place with the king's assent. The commission is aware that the ornament did not fetch its full value, as one stone alone in it was estimated at 18,000 dollars. He excuses his knowledge of Brandt's conduct to the king, and pretends that he had not been so fully aware of the affair before. All the rest consists of excuses and palliations, which are only founded on his statements, but which have been proved quite differently by me.

Consequently I refer to my former demands, and claim the verdict I proposed.

F. W. WIWET.

Copenhagen, April 23, 1772.

CHAPTER XIII.

THE TRAVELLING DOCTOR—COUNT HOLCK—THE FOREIGN TOUR
—STRUENSEE AT COURT—THE QUEEN'S CONFIDENCE—THE
MUTUAL FRIEND—THE HOLSTEIN PROGRESS—HOLCK DIS-
MISSED—THE MINISTRY—THE KING'S ADVISERS—COUNT VON
RANTZAU—THE RUSSIAN ALLIANCE—THE NEW CABINET—
STRUENSEE'S ADVICE—THE CABINET MINISTER—EDUCATION
OF THE PRINCE ROYAL.

THE two advocates for the prosecution and defence of
Struensee having thus alleged everything that could
ruin the prisoner; the first, by exciting the temper
of the judges with malicious insinuations; the second,
by most shamefully neglecting his duty, as I think
has been sufficiently proved, Uldall had a right of
reply to Wiwet's last diatribe. As he declined to avail
himself of it, however, the next step taken was to
hand in the prisoner's own defence—a defence written, be it borne in mind, under the most appalling
circumstances. It was in a dungeon, with fetters on
his hands and feet, and an iron collar round his neck,

fastened to a chain clenched in the wall, that the unfortunate Struensee drew up this hopeless appeal, only
a few days before he was dragged to the scaffold.

STRUENSEE'S APOLOGY.

Nothing is more difficult, and perhaps it is utterly
impossible to give a clear and correct account and
explanation of the motives, causes, and intentions,
which originated every single event and action in a
situation such as mine was at court. This has been
demanded of me, however, and I have explained myself
to the royal commission in my answers to the questions
laid before me for this purpose in such a way as the
nature of things permitted. But it is very possible
that now and again obscurities, mistakes, and probably
apparent contradictions, may have crept in. For this
I hope to compensate by a conscientious statement of
the motives, opportunities, and causes, that produced
the events in which I took part, or which I alone
occasioned, and I will run the risk of my narrative
either serving as my apology, or rendering me even
more criminal.

For this object, I must show in what manner I acquired the credit which established my former fortune,
how I behaved under it, and to what purpose I employed it.

I must confess that an indefatigable activity, the
most accurate attention, and the most careful use of

the opportunities and advantages which offered themselves to me, or which I obtained by my own efforts,
contributed more to my fortune than mere accident
did. Still, what is commonly called fortune was not
the chief object of my desire, or at least I regarded it
as a more remote consequence. I had chosen a path
by which to attain fortune, but was determined sooner
to let it slip than to employ improper means in acquiring it.

A desire to be useful, and to perform actions which
might have a wide-spread influence on the welfare of
the society in which I lived, alone occupied my mind.
My residence at Altona offered me but little opportunity for this, and my friends at that day, among
whom Counts Rantzau-Ascheberg, Brandt, and Holck,
were the most effective, at length succeeded in removing me to a wider scene of action.

Although some of these friends fancied they could
detect in me abilities which rendered me fitted for
other enterprises than those for which a physician has
a vocation, still I felt so great a liking for my profession that I should have permanently restricted myself
to it, had not other circumstances eventually called me
away from it.

With this opinion I came to court, and I found it
the more necessary to confirm myself in it, when I
saw that everybody at court entertained suspicions,
even if not prejudices, against me.

During the king's foreign tour I employed myself

with nothing, and turned my attention to nothing, but
matters concerning the state of the king's health,
and as his Majesty frequently gave me opportunities
to be in his presence, I tried, as far as was possible, to
render myself useful by reading and conversation.
Politics were entirely excluded, and if anything of the
sort arose it was remote, and without the slightest
reference to the posture of affairs at that day.   At
that time I was quite ignorant of them; I restricted
myself to what I had before me, and even avoided
acquiring information from the king, or other persons.
I broke off my correspondence with my friends, or it
concerned merely unimportant things.   Everything
that I did had reference to the person of the king,
and among such I reckon that during the tour I
frequently opposed Count Holck, and contradicted
him in things which I considered wrong, or which
had an influence on the king's person.   But my only
object was to weaken the count's excessive power
over the will of the king by encouraging his Majesty
to pay attention to himself, to think and reflect about
what would most enhance his welfare, without blindly
trusting to the advice of others.   However, I did not
attempt to injure Count Holck personally, although a
very convenient opportunity presented itself in Paris,
when the king was very angry with the count, when
Count Brandt came to Paris without my knowledge,
and various other circumstances at the time spoke
against Count Holck.

It is easy to see how little adapted this conduct was to make a fortune. Nor did I even use the favourable opportunity I had during the tour either to ask or obtain anything to my advantage personally from the king, or through other persons; and I only owe it to the kindness of Privy Councillors von Bernstorff and von Schimmelmann that I followed the king to Copenhagen with a salary of 1,000 dollars, and received a gratification of 500 dollars for the journey.

1769. My mode of acting, and the objects of my attention were, during the first six months after the king's return, the same as on the tour. I had attached myself exclusively to his Majesty's person, and took an interest in nothing that did not immediately affect it. I merely employed the influence which the king's confidence gave me over his mind, in drawing his attention to his real benefit, in arousing a pleasure in occupation, and in giving a certain regular course to his mode of living.

With this object I always said to the king, with the greatest conscientiousness and without reservation, everything that I considered true and serviceable, without allowing myself to be checked by the fear of losing his favour, though I frequently gained the experience, that this conduct caused him to be cool with me, which happened the more easily, because the officiousness of those who merely sought the king's favour was never idle on such occasions. The king will remember how this was more especially the case, when

I represented to him the evil consequences which arise from a premature, excessive, and unregulated enjoyment of certain sensual pleasures, and when I tried to prevent his Majesty from making certain painful, injurious, and useless attempts on his person, and attempted to bring him back from certain false, unfounded ideas which were deleterious to his happiness.

At this time I stood in connexion with nobody at court but Count Holck and Chamberlain von Warnstedt, and that only so far as they could have influence over the king. The former was reserved with me; the latter gave me from time to time his confidence, which I employed to suggest to him principles and ideas which I felt assured would prove useful to the king, if he repeated them to his Majesty on the occasions which he had.

When the court resided for the summer at Frederiksberg, I could not help making various acquaintances, being implicated in several affairs, and acquiring a more certain knowledge of the intentions of those who were at court at this time. This did not take place, however, till toward the end of the summer. There were at this time three principal parties at court: that of Count Holck, that of Count Fritz Moltke,* and that of Frau von Gabel. The first held

* Moltke, elder son of the favourite of Frederick V., had but little ambition, but he was ruled by Mademoiselle d'Eyben, first lady-in-waiting on the queen, and this lady was not without ambition, or sense, or disposition for intrigue. Moltke died suddenly, which disconcerted this party: for Mademoiselle d'Eyben, being ugly, could not easily fill up his place.—*Mémoires de Falckenskjold*, p. 181.

its ground through the favour of Count Holck and *liaisons* in the ministry, or rather through the unwillingness to injure the favourite. The second tried to procure a support through the authority of the queen, and trusted to the influence of the Russian minister, but wished to get Warnstedt and myself on their side. Of the third, it can hardly be said to have been a party, as it consisted of Frau von Gabel alone.

The latter merely sought, through the impression which she strove to produce upon the king's mind, to tear him out of the fetters of dependence, in which she imagined his Majesty was bound. The second of the parties strove, on the other hand, as may be easily conjectured, to remove Count Holck. But I must confess that under these circumstances my sense and inclination made me principally incline to the views of Frau von Gabel, as they fully agreed with mine, and I gave this lady credit for honourable sentiments. Still, I did not agree with her on two points:—(1) That she absolutely insisted on removing Count Holck, which I considered unnecessary if the king could be imbued with more correct and permanent sentiments, as in that case Count Holck's credit would fall away of itself, and, besides, an old favourite would be less injurious than a new one; and (2) I was always of opinion that the sole and right mode of rendering the king truly happy, was to do away with his *éloignement* from the queen, and to establish a mutual affection between them.

Frau von Gabel believed that she had been insulted by the queen, and seemed desirous not to seek her favour again, until she could be useful to her Majesty through the influence she had gained over the king's heart.   I tried to convince the Moltke party, as far as they granted me their confidence, how little hope they could have of overthrowing Count Holck, or of deriving any advantage from it; and to how many unpleasantnesses the queen would be exposed if they employed their power in removing the count before the king's confidence was gained; and hence I considered it the best course to live in unity and peace.   In any case, I did not consider myself at liberty to act against Count Holck, and though I was not satisfied with his conduct, I thought that this ought to be left to the king alone.

1770.   Even in the following winter when, owing to the misunderstandings between Count Holck and the Russian minister, it would have been an easy task to overthrow the former, I did everything in my power to support him; and, in this affair, always spoke to the king in Count Holck's favour, although, in other respects, I told the king the truth of the affair, and Count Holck gave it a *tournure* which I could not approve.

In the year 1769, when, toward the end of the summer and afterwards, I had frequent opportunities of speaking with the queen, and her Majesty confided to me her thoughts about her situation, I found that she was excessively discontented with it; had no hopes of ever being happy with her consort; and could expect no peace or contentment from the existing state of affairs.

This condition of mind was maintained, and even more excited, by the continued reports and repulsive representations which the queen received of everything that occurred. The object of her repugnance, however, was not the king, but solely Count Holck, whom she regarded as the originator of all the unpleasantness that befell her. What she personally suffered from the king did not affect her greatly; and she merely tried to protect herself against it by a greater reserve, which, however, only heightened their mutual coldness and estrangement. My situation, under these circumstances, was extremely embarrassing; while, on the one hand, the queen confided to me her dissatisfaction, on the other I was a constant witness of the discontent, anger, and desire of the king to free himself from everything that was repulsive to him. I therefore followed the principle which I have ever entertained, that their mutual felicity depended on their union; for I was obliged to give them both advice, and I considered myself bound to do everything that lay in my power to promote their satisfaction. Although I had but little hope of effecting it, I acted accordingly. I sought to make the queen understand, and firmly impress on her mind, that it was to her own good, and the sole way of making her situation agreeable, if she strove to acquire the king's confidence, and this could only be

effected by kindness, counsel, attention, and exertion
to make her company as pleasant as possible to the
king. I begged the queen not to listen to insinuations
against the king, however slight they might be, and
though made with a good purpose, but to be quiet,
and watch and examine for herself. I strove to reduce, or entirely remove, her repugnance to Count
Holck. The latter, also, did all he knew to render
himself agreeable to the queen; but his exertions
generally produced an opposite effect, and the pre-
judice against him was so strong that nothing could
overpower it. On the other hand, I strove to induce
the king to be polite to the queen, without considering
it necessary to be so ceremonious and respectful with
her as he had grown to be since his return from the
foreign tour, and which often degenerated into irony,
to which the queen was more susceptible than to want
of attention and of familiarity between them. There
was one point on which the inclinations of the king
and queen agreed, and this aided the most to maintain
the concord in which they afterwards lived. This
consisted in the circumstance that both were excessively wearied of their mode of life at the time, and
wished that they could lay aside their rank. This was
the reason of many of the alterations introduced at
court eventually. Count Holck had lost his credit
long before the journey to Holstein, and only maintained himself by old associations, and because no one
exactly tried to injure him with the king. He dealt

himself the last blow, when he appointed young Hauch
as page of the bed-chamber to the king, in order to sup-
plant Warnstedt.   From this time forth, the favour of
the latter increased; Count Holck proposed the Holstein progress, in order, as I believe, to sustain himself,
and this very thing caused his downfall.

The queen was constantly of opinion that no peace
or security could be hoped for at court so long as
Count Holck remained at it, although I tried to convince her that it was not advantageous for the king's
character and mind to try and remove on the first
favourable opportunity that offered itself those persons to whom his Majesty had granted his favour and
confidence, but that it would be better that he should
become thoroughly acquainted with these persons, and
that this was the surest way to disarm all favourites.
Moreover, I did not consider Count Holck dangerous
for the king's person, because he no longer possessed
any influence over the king's mind.

In order, however, to pacify the queen, I proposed
to her two remedies,—to have Count Brandt at court,
and to recall Privy Councillor Count von Rantzau to
Copenhagen.   Both gentlemen were agreeable to the
king; and the latter would be useful in balancing the
power of the ministry, whom the queen feared, because
she thought they might restore Count Holck's credit,
by the removal of those persons who stood in his way.
All this was designed to acquire security at court,
without forming any intentions or plan for the even-

tual changes in the ministry. The queen had not the slightest inclination for governing or interfering in affairs of state; she merely wished for peace and security. Count Brandt joined the court in Schleswig; Count Rantzau at Traventhal. Count Holck received his dismissal because the king wished it; but the persons about his Majesty did their share in effecting it.

From this time, other scenes took place, and changes occurred the motives and reasons for which I will state presently. But I will first remark, that the credit I had hitherto enjoyed merely consisted in the king's personal confidence in me; that I employed the influence I possessed solely in matters which had immediate reference to the king's person, and that my private fortunes were of the following nature:—I was Councillor of Conference and Reader, with a salary of 1,500 dollars. I had debts amounting to between 4,000 and 5,000 dollars, which I had formerly contracted in Altona and upon the foreign progress, and had never received any extraordinary present from the king, except the before-mentioned 500 dollars and a horse. I had not asked anything for my friends, except an addition of 400 dollars for Count Brandt, unless I take into consideration that I had twice aided in inducing the king to make Count Holck a present of 10,000 thalers.

On the recall of Counts Brandt and Rantzau, no one, as I have stated, of those who took part in it thought of the changes that afterwards took place, or that any of the ministers would be removed. As concerns myself, however, I do not deny that I, without feeling any personal aversion or repugnance to any one of the ministers, was rather disposed against, than in favour of, the administration. Long before I came to court I had been filled with thoughts against it, and I had never found a reason to doubt the trustworthiness, integrity, patriotic will, and disinterestedness of the persons and reports from which I derived them. I was also confirmed in my opinion by what I heard in this respect in Copenhagen, and partly remarked. The following points were the chief ones alleged against the administration of that day.*

1. It had grown into a principle, through habit, to keep the king aloof from affairs, and try to deprive him of all inclination for them, by increasing his governmental labours by superfluous mechanical tasks, and by not bringing matters forward simply and distinctly. Every matter of importance was wrapped up in long-winded phrases and declamations, which led the king into unnecessary details; he was rarely left the choice between two opinions, but was led to

* The repetition was unavoidable here without breaking the entire sequence of the report of this remarkable trial. I was obliged partly to incorporate Struensee's apology with my text in the first instance, and now find that I am compelled to make room for it here again. I hope my readers will forgive me, in consideration that I have really made very few attempts at "padding" throughout my narrative, and have rather let facts speak for themselves than take advantage of the constant opportunities for fine writing which have presented themselves.

decide for the one which had been previously adopted by the ministers; and lastly, his attention was drawn to trivial matters, and for this reason more important ones produced less impression upon him.

2. The king had so little personal authority, that he had no will of his own, even in the poorest trifles, and was even ruled in his domestic life. Hence those persons were always ruined who attached themselves to him, and possessed his taste, inclination, and confidence; while, on the other hand, others held their ground for whom he entertained exactly opposite feelings.

3. Favour and intrigue were mixed up in everything. The most important dignities and offices were given to courtiers whose sole merit was having been pages, and the other appointments were bestowed on creatures and lackeys of personages and families who supported each other in power.

4. A perfect anarchy prevailed, as no one would, or dared, to use his authority, for fear of injuring himself. Everybody was striving to acquire influence in other departments beside his own. Subordination was nowhere to be found: everything resolved itself into consultations, giving advice, investigations, modifications, and expedients. The subordinates, instead of carrying out the orders they received, only strove to raise difficulties, objections, and counter-propositions.

5. The finances were ruined—not through the ex-

penses the king incurred (although many of the latter
were unnecessary, as, for instance, the colonists, the
costly factories, the forced development of the arts,
taste, and luxury, far beyond the resources of the
country, the disproportionate augmentation of the
army, and the support of a commerce which was not
adapted to the nature of the country, while its true
and natural industry was neglected), but in consequence of the prevalent disorder, the worthless opera-
tions, and the manœuvres so often carried on for private
objects.

6. The influence of foreign courts and their ministers had been for some time past great and oppressive.
As the mainspring in negociations is complaisance,
nought but a dependence could result from this, which
could not be compensated by any resulting benefit.
As a rule, more expense and attention was devoted
to this portion of the business of the state than the
nature and circumstances of the country required.

7. Lastly, the great and small offices, distinctions,
and honorary titles, were too numerous for the size of
the state, too oppressive for the country, and, at the
same time, valueless. Everybody wished to live and
enrich himself at the cost of the king; there was no
impulse among the nobility to serve his Majesty with
their fortune and strength, and in the other classes no
inclination to seek self-support in industry.

I will not decide how far these reproaches are
founded, but for my part I was convinced of their
truth by everything I afterwards experienced, though

without accusing one or the other minister personally
of being the cause.   In matters of state, success in
most cases decides the value of an administration, in
the present case it decided against it.   When I acquired
influence in affairs through the king's confidence, my
design merely was to induce his Majesty to examine
into them himself, and for this reason I believed it
was necessary that the king should have about him
other persons holding opinions opposed to those of the
then existing ministry.   If, afterwards, alterations and
resolutions with this object followed more rapidly, this
was caused rather by the personal sentiments of the
king, and by accidental circumstances, than by any
regular resolution or plan—at least, as far as concerned
myself.   With regard to the king's wishes successive
steps were necessary, for his Majesty was more than
too willing to undertake such changes.   On my join-
ing the king, I found his mind, temper, and inclination full of aversion from the ministry, and this always
remained so.   If, for my part, I did not try to change
his sentiments so far as my conviction admitted, on
the other hand, prior to the Holstein progress, I did
not strive to imbue the king with any favourable idea
of the persons belonging to the opposite party.   It is
well known that his Majesty, from the beginning of
his reign, desired changes in the ministry.   In addition
to the above-mentioned dislikes, which were more or
less impressed on the king's mind, his Majesty had
others which he felt personally, as—1. The ministry
attracted to themselves the prestige of the government,

and nothing was left him but the title and burden of representation.   2. Affairs in Denmark were so confused and damaged, and the want of money was so great, that nothing good or great could be effected. 3. The influence of the foreign ministers was excessive, of which his Majesty had on several occasions obtained personal experience.   4. The Holstein negociation was onerous in the way it was carried on, and it had been employed at various times to divert the king from certain resolutions, when other reasons would probably have been sufficient and better.   5. Nothing could be more embarrassing to the king than to preside at the council twice a week, and I believe the reason for this lay in the fact that his Majesty, from his childhood, had felt a certain respect and sort of fear of it, which, in the course of time, had grown into a habit. As this feeling was not based on his confidence, while his real sentiments and the impressions received contradicted it, such a dislike could be easily aroused. The king would say at times, "When I am of a different opinion from the council, I at once notice a restlessness on all faces; solemn representations ensue, and I am obliged to hold my tongue."   6. The king had been spoken to at times about economy in matters affecting him personally, such as comedies, hunting, &c., and his Majesty believed that such an economy ought to be commenced in other outlays.   And 7. The king was excessively displeased with the results of the Algerine expedition.

Such was the disposition of the king on his return from Holstein, and it may be easily supposed that those persons who had his ear did nothing to alter it. Their attention was principally directed to the effects and measures which the presence of Count von Rantzau would produce. Count von Bernstorff had handed in a memorial to the king on this subject at Traventhal. Count von Rantzau answered it, and declared that he would not interfere in the Holstein negociations, or attempt to oppose them; while, on the other hand, the former (Count Bernstorff) would seek to remove disagreeable impressions at the Russian court. Unfortunately, Count von Bernstorff alluded in his speeches, and on other occasions, to the enemies of the Russian alliance. This occasioned his dismissal, and the changes ensuing from it. I cannot remember that any special steps were taken to bring the latter about. With the king, as I have remarked, there were no difficulties to overcome: those persons to whom he listened at that time were prepared for the changes, and agreed in them. Nor can I state how far the remarks of those who were for the measure had an effect on the king's mind, especially with reference to Count von Rantzau. This I know, that at the time I read to his Majesty several letters and memorials about the general position of affairs; that I received considerable encouragement and support in the matter, and employed it in accordance with my convictions; that no one was formally consulted on the subject, and that the king prepared its execution and the arrangements himself in my presence. The king drew up all the measures in his own hand. At times I previously prepared rough drafts on the principal heads of an affair, which his Majesty altered or retained as he thought proper. More frequently, however, his Majesty wrote them out of his own head. The cabinet secretary corrected, and the king read, the document through once again ere it was copied and completed. I sealed the letters in the presence of the king in the cabinet. I rarely showed the rough drafts to any one beforehand, and if it took place, it was to Counts Rantzau and Brandt. People now entertained the best hopes that everything would go on well. The king worked with pleasure, and read everything connected with the affairs of state. In order to keep his Majesty to this, and to arrange the mode of his occupation in accordance with his taste, the following principles were adopted, and I always strove to act in accordance with them so far as it depended on myself:—

1. The king would retain the final decision in affairs.

2. All reports were to be made in writing, and the king's resolutions made known in the same way.

3. The officials would try to render their reports distinct, short, and free from divergences, in order that they might contain the material points alone, so that the different matters in which the king was to decide

might be distinctly expressed and explained in the extract.

4. In cases where the king found it necessary to ask the advice of others, his Majesty would either take the opinion of the colleges, or appoint a commission for the purpose, but everything, as far as possible, was to be done by the ordinary departments.

5. The colleges would try, so far as the nature of the matter allowed, to discuss and report affairs in a similar form.

6. As the king did not wish to interfere in the details of carrying out affairs, but expected this to be done by the colleges, the latter were invited to follow the same style in business, to urge their subordinates to do the same, and to make the latter responsible.

7. Everything would be decided upon settled principles.

8. Finally, the business of the departments would be kept distinct, so that each would manage its own affairs for itself, and one department have no influence over the other, save through the king alone. Their number would also be reduced, so that there should be only one department for each branch of business.

As regards the affairs, the king laid down the following general rules:—

1.—*The Foreign Department.*

(*a*) The king would seek no further influence at

foreign courts than the position of his kingdoms and their commerce required.

(*b*) He would save all the expense which the ostentation of numerous ministers at foreign courts entailed; and

(*c*) Tolerate no influence over the internal affairs of his kingdoms or elsewhere.

(*d*) He would adhere faithfully to the Russian alliance, but did not wish the latter court to found its security on accidental circumstances, but trust to the integrity of his conduct, of which the king had given the empress very evident proofs recently.

(*e*) His Majesty would not expend more money on the Swedish affair than was stipulated by treaty, and not interfere in the private quarrels in that country.

With regard to the last two points, the king himself read everything that could be urged for and against them, and afterwards decided himself, as his Majesty previously possessed no settled opinion or conviction.

2.—*The Finances.*

(*a*) There was to be only one college, which would expedite all the business connected with the department.

(*b*) Order and economy were the sole means of restoring the finances, to the exclusion of all projects which were not based on those principles.

(*c*) All the royal resources would flow into the general treasury, and thence be distributed to the other departments, so that the king might more easily survey the state of his revenues.

(*d*) Efforts would be made to simplify the collection of the taxes for the relief of the subjects.

(*e*) The usual payments in kind would be converted into pecuniary payments, in order to encourage the industry of the countrymen, and remove the existing abuses.

(*f*) The expenses of the state would be kept entirely distinct from the private outlay for the king and the royal family.

(*g*) Those factories which, owing to the nature of the country, were not self-supporting, would not be maintained at the expense of the king, and the support of others would merely be reduced to bounties, so that the king might not have any share in them; which was also regulated with reference to commerce.

(*h*) The crown domains would be farmed out.

(*i*) At the beginning of each year the budget expenses would be settled, and not exceeded during the year.

(*k*) The pensions, which were quite disproportionate in comparison with the amount of the king's revenue, would undergo a certain reduction.

If in this branch reforms and reductions have taken place or are intended, it will be easily discovered how greatly the nature of the finances requires such.

3.—*Justice.*

(*a*) The king would not decide in any cause until it had been properly tried by the courts of law.

(*b*) The number of law courts would be reduced, as every man, no matter his rank, must be regarded as a citizen in the sight of the law.

(*c*) The judges would receive no fees, and the forms of proceeding would be abridged.

4. Concerning the army, I refer to the memorial found among my papers, which alludes to it.

5. As regards the navy, it was arranged:—

(*a*) That the strength of the fleet was not to be sought in an increase of the number of vessels, but in those existing being kept in a good state and thoroughly equipped.

(*b*) That the storing up of everything required for a bombardment is correct in principle.

6.—*The Court.*

(*a*) Everything superfluous and only belonging to ostentation was to be cut down, and only that retained which served for amusement.

(*b*) The amusements and parties would be arranged after the taste and opinion of the king and queen, without regard to other considerations.

In addition to these there are many other principles which I repeated to the king, and strove to impress on his mind. I will mention some of them, as they will serve to clear up several points.

1. It is injurious to occasion a great affluence of persons to court through the hope of making their fortunes, for it ruins private individuals, renders the provinces poor, and the royal treasury in the end has to bear the loss.

2. It is better for the nobility to live on their estates if they wish to be idlers, and if they seek government appointments they must pass through the lower stages. Only valid reasons could produce an exception, but not favour or several years' residence at court.

3. The king, in filling up posts, ought to trust to the proposals of the departments, but pay no heed to supplications and recommendations at court.

4. His Majesty would grant no reversions, survivorships, exclusive privileges, or other liberties, which encroach on the rights of the subjects; and

5. At least for the first year grant no " characters " and distinctions which were not really connected with the office held.

6. No pensions should be granted except in extraordinary cases, and no alms bestowed at court; but instead of it, the poor should be liberally remembered.

7. Copenhagen could not be made great and prosperous by luxury and an increase of the number of consumers to the detriment of the provinces, but by real industry and promotion of the foreign trade. Rich people must be attracted to the capital by the agreeable mode of life there.

8. Morals cannot be improved by police laws, and such are opposed to the liberty of men, as their moral actions, in so far as they have no immediate influence on the peace and security of society, should be left to education and the lessons and exhortations of the clergy; for the secret vices produced by coercion are frequently the worst, and create hypocrites.

These principles can be employed in forming an opinion how far it was useful or injurious to the king's affairs that his Majesty granted me his confidence.   I readily acknowledge that after the time when the council was abolished affairs were not conducted in the proper form.   But this was the very thing which some of those who gave advice desired; for it was hoped thus to give the king a prestige if a great many orders were issued from the cabinet, and cabinet orders passed without consulting the colleges. Others, on the contrary (Lieutenant General von Gähler,) were of an opposite opinion, and disapproved of it.   The former advisers pleased the king; but I found that the latter were in the right, and hence I tried to draw his Majesty's attention more especially to the regulation of the departments.   Equally little could I give my approval to the proposition (especially of Count Rantzau) that the affairs prepared by the heads of departments should be forwarded to the cabinet, and issued thence without making the author's name known.   On this head countless insinuations, memoirs, and propositions, were sent in.   I tried, as far as I could, to prevent this mode of conducting business, and only those orders emanated from the cabinet which concerned the form of the colleges, or established great general rules. In some cases it was also done in order to please the king's taste, and, as I willingly acknowledge, to give a prestige to the cabinet. Of such a nature were the instructions of Baron von Gyldencrone and Falckenskjold's mission, of which no one knew anything but the cabinet before they were determined on, except that I spoke with the latter officer generally about the affair. If afterwards so many decrees were issued from the cabinet, this had its origin in the ordinary course of business, and the representations of the colleges, or they concerned matters about which a report was requested in the cabinet. It was my wish to regulate the cabinet business after a certain form and rule, and to reduce it. Hence I calculated that no one ought to have any influence over it, except in so far as his office gave him a right, and that this should be effected by the representation of his department, or a direct report to the king. I understood to what confusion it would give rise if I listened to all the insinuations and suggestions laid before the king, and carried them out through the cabinet. I was therefore induced to take great care not to speak with any one about affairs unconnected with his department, and I directed my attention solely to information that reached the cabinet through ordinary channels. This conduct injured me personally, though it might be advantageous to the affairs, for it drew on me a suspicion that I was distrustful and reserved, and unwilling to accept any good advice. By degrees several persons were suspected of exerting an influence over me, but I can declare that no one ever possessed such an ascendancy, and that the only person to whom I gave unlimited confidence was Count Brandt. Still, I can assert that I said but little, even to Count Brandt, about the affairs, and the rest shared my confidence only in isolated instances. In the affairs I had no secrets affecting myself, and the other matters I could not and would not confide to any one but Count Brandt. I wished that persons in business matters should act according to their convictions, and not look to me. For this reason, I believed it requisite for the king formally to declare that his Majesty had entrusted the cabinet business to me, so that it might not appear as if I had usurped it. This occasioned the cabinet decree of July 14, 1771, which is so greatly brought against me, and is said to be opposed to the *Lex Regia*. I will honestly declare my intentions and principles.

1. I am free to confess that I tried to concentrate the royal authority in the cabinet, in accordance with the above-mentioned form and principles.

2. I had frequently remarked that royal orders were given by persons who had an opportunity to approach his Majesty, without having any other justification for doing so, than the fact that they had spoken with the king on the matter. This might give rise to

many abuses, which I tried to prevent by having every direct order copied in a register. The persons who executed them were thus rendered secure, and the king knew who was answerable for the execution.

3. Instead of such orders not being brought under the king's notice, as was formerly the case, his Majesty saw them three or four times.

4. The king signed them in the extract, which was kept in the cabinet, or on the representations of the department, which reported receipt of the order.

5. No department could have any influence over another, except through the king, and there was a copy of it in the cabinet.

6. The king found no difficulty in carrying out what he pleased, and I was ever of opinion, and had always heard, that in a sovereign state the form should be kept as simple as possible: that good principles, and the desire to act well, were the best means to keep a king from abusing his power: and that other difficulties impeded the execution of great and useful plans, without preventing the results of a bad appliance of the authority.

7. All the time I was minister, the cabinet orders were sent to the colleges and heads of departments. The latter could then raise objections especially in cases where such regulations were contrary to the laws and earlier royal resolutions.

8. I thus acquired no personal authority, except in so far as the king granted me his confidence.

9. I thus deprived myself of the means of mis-applying the king's confidence to designs opposed to his interests, and if I had any such designs, of which I am not conscious, however, they can be very easily detected in the copies preserved in the cabinet.

10. As regards the king's signature, several persons, especially Councillor of Conference Schumacher, know what his Majesty thought of it, and that this was the reason why all the cabinet orders were not signed by the king.

Although I have thus declared with the greatest truthfulness the sentiments with which I employed the king's confidence, I do not venture to decide how far, on the whole, the changes that resulted were advantageous or injurious. The result must prove this, and for this the time during which they have existed is too short.

So much, however, I believe I may assert, that the economic arrangements at court, as well as the management of the royal privy treasury, were advantageous, and will produce considerable savings: and further, that the financial system is established on a sound basis, as the price of corn in Copenhagen this winter will prove, how far correct measures were taken in that matter;—that all the expenses of the last year have been paid, and the resources which the extraordinary ones required, were not oppressive for the country;—that the arrangement of the Chanceries and Colleges of Justice is advantageous;—that the persons whom I

proposed as officials, three or four excepted, as I might
be mistaken about them, possessed the requisite ability
for what they were employed in;—and lastly, that
there has been no delay in the settlement of business.
It was unavoidable that defects should have crept in
here and there, which I certainly felt, but could not
possibly prevent.   If private persons have suffered,
the intention always was to employ such persons again,
and give them compensation.

If the undertaking has failed through incorrect
measures, or want of support, I will confess that I deserve all the reproaches that may be made me in consequence, as it is sufficient that it has not been carried
out.   The king alone can decide how far my advice
has had an influence on his personal comfort, and the
examination will prove how far the results have been
injurious on the whole.   At the beginning I was encouraged by my friends: but when it had grown too
late to draw back, I lost them. If it be possible in such
a situation as mine was, for a man to act without personal motives and impartially, I tried to do so, and so
much the less did I believe that I should deserve the
general hatred.   On this account I was indifferent to
all the menaces that were spread against me in public.
I suspected even less, that I should be seriously
accused of wishing to sustain myself against the
opinion and will of the king, and of entertaining dangerous designs against his Majesty's person.   As concerns the first charge, I do not know whether the

king ever had the wish, or formed a resolution of discharging me.   Everything I could employ to sustain
myself in the king's favour was that I strove to be
agreeable to his Majesty.   Besides this, the influence
of the queen was the only thing on which I could calculate.   During the last half year, Count Brandt lost
the king's confidence.   Etats-rath Reverdil had no personal *liaisons* with me, and would assuredly not have
allowed me to support myself in an improper manner.
I did not know page Schuck personally, before he was
attached to the king: the king said but little about
Berger, and, besides, all the valets were still attached
to his Majesty whom I found there, and they were
under very slight or no obligations to me.   These persons will know whether I asked of them information
as to what the king said, or services to my advantage.
If I had wished to prevent his Majesty from forming a
speedy decision (about my dismissal) in consequence
of insinuations made to him, I could only trust to the
repugnance which such a thing would meet with in
his mind, because there were countless opportunities,
which I could neither prevent, nor attempted to prevent, and at least I ought to have made more certain
of the sentiments of the persons who were about the
king. Besides, the king had formerly dismissed several
persons who were about him, and it would have been
very easy for him to find means for doing the same
with me, if he had wished it, and how could I have
opposed it?

Equally improbable is the other charge that I entertained designs against the king's person. With every one prejudiced against me, without a party, even hated by the public, how could I have formed the idea of undertaking such a thing? and if I had formed it, how could I take such bad measures? All my security consisted in the person of the king and his authority. Whose authority could have been substituted for that of the king? The regulations which aroused suspicion were hardly sufficient to check the disturbances and a revolt of the populace if such had broken out; and it would have been quite impossible to carry out a plan which must displease the people. At least, there is no political probability in all this that such an idea existed. And what moral reason could arouse suspicion against those persons, who must necessarily have been acquainted with it, that they would have been capable of forming such a detestable resolution? A careful investigation, on the contrary, will prove the excellent sentiments all my friends entertained for the king's person. I do not deny that measures were taken to check any violent attacks of the people; and I do not believe that a government would be justified in allowing changes in its administration to be effected by such means.

If everything which I have said conscientiously and in accordance with the truth about the intentions and motives of my actions be carefully examined, more political faults and moral errors will be found in my conduct than crimes worthy of punishment. Those persons who knew me, and watched me closely, can judge and bear witness how far I have spoken the truth. If I had sought money and personal distinctions, my situation afforded much easier ways of acquiring them than the one I selected. The desire of making my fortune was a more remote impulse, and I merely wished to owe it to the services I rendered the king. My readiness to carry out whatever the king desired, and his Majesty's willingness to accept my advice, cannot justify me, but they serve as my excuse, even if, through my error, evil results for the king's interest were produced by them.

I appeal to the memory and feeling of the king whether the changes I carried out or occasioned produced an unpleasant impression on his Majesty, and I know of no disorders which originated from them. For the dissatisfaction of individuals is of no effect in this matter. It was ever my opinion that I owed the king alone an account of my actions, and it was easy to explain them to the king as the affairs came so repeatedly before him. Not a trace will be found that I wished to exercise an influence over the representations of the departments, or give a false appearance to affairs, as in my time every deputy of a college was allowed to give his vote. The first changes occurred in the vicinity of the king, and it would certainly not have been wise to begin with the council and the court, if his Majesty's conviction, will, and assent, had not agreed with it.

No one was prevented from attending court but Count Laurvig; nor was any one sent from Copenhagen with orders not to return; or any dismissed minister prevented from having an audience of the king.

All those persons whom I knew to have lost their liberty through their employment about the king's person, or who were forbidden to reside in Copenhagen, were liberated on my representations. No private cause was ever decided or protected by the cabinet. Count Rantzau's affair with the agent Bodenhoff will prove how little influence friendship had. If, in custom-house disputes, in royal contracts, and in cases which were clear, the royal resolution was carried out on the representation of a college, any man who considered himself injured by it was at liberty to seek justice in the ordinary course. I do not believe that in this any inclination to despotism will be found. Despotism, in my opinion, consists in the king deciding about the rights, liberties, fortunes, and lives of his subjects arbitrarily, without examination, and without regard to established forms. Those royal officials who were dismissed through the changes received pensions, and would have the first claim to vacancies. If any one was dismissed from a college for proved negligence, unfaithfulness, or other offences, I did not believe that a judicial process was requisite, which could only take place if he deserved further punishment; and every man was at liberty to defend himself legally, if injustice had been dealt to him by the college.

I have the following remarks to make about the education of the crown prince. I derived the principles on which it was established from the king's wishes, and the queen desired and herself carried them out. The crown prince, when the system was commenced, had a weak constitution, a tendency to rickets, a great deal of obstinacy, continually cried, would not walk alone, but must always be carried, attached himself to certain persons, would not play by himself, but must have people to sing and dance to him, and had been taught a certain fear of the queen, as his nurses used to threaten that his mamma would come if he were not good. In order to prevent all this, the following means were employed:—his royal highness only had simple food given him, gruel, bread, water, rice, milk, and afterwards potatoes, but all cold. At first, he was bathed twice or thrice a day in cold water, and at last went daily into his bath of his own accord. Last winter, he remained in a cold room when he was not with the queen, was only lightly clad, and went nearly the whole of the previous winter without shoes or stockings. He was allowed to do everything that he could effect with his own strength, but when he cried or obstinately desired anything which was not absolutely necessary, it was not given him, but he did not, on that account, receive any punishment, scolding, or threats; on the other hand, he was never pacified by soothing. He played alone with his companion, and no distinction was made

between them, and they helped one another at meals
and in undressing. They climbed, broke, and did
what they pleased, but everything with which they
might hurt themselves was kept from them. They
generally remained alone, even in the dark. If they
hurt themselves they were not pitied, and if they
quarrelled, they made it up between themselves, for
the lackeys were forbidden speaking or playing with
them. The prince's education was to begin in his
sixth or seventh year. Up to that time it was considered sufficient to allow his ideas and abilities to be
developed by habit and experience. The result has
been, that the crown prince's constitution is now as
strong and good as might be naturally expected.
His royal highness has never been ill, except in a
few trifling cases; he got over the inoculation for the
small-pox with the greatest ease; he knows the use
and employment of his limbs, as is suited to his age;
he dresses and undresses himself, can go up and down
stairs without assistance, and knows how to guard
himself from injury. He has none of that timidity
which arises from repeated warnings, is not shy in
society, obstinate, or capricious. If mental knowledge,
or a morality which is based on assumed customs, is
left out of the question, little will be missed in the
prince royal, which can be demanded from a child of
five years of age. If it is advantageous that a prince
should have his first education in common with that
of all other men, that he should acquire the strength

which such a ripe training produces, that he should know how to do little matters for himself, without growing accustomed to be dependent on others; that he should not at too early an age learn the external insignia of his rank, which might render him lax in his duties, or imbue him with a vanity which would have eventually to be checked by moral principles; and if, lastly, that mode of education is the best in early years which is nearest to the natural one, I believe that the one applied to the crown prince will not be considered absurd. The only punishment inflicted on him was that he had no breakfast, or was left by himself in a room if he was naughty.

As regards the alleged forgery of the document to prove the receipt of the 60,000 dollars from the king, I declare most sacredly that I intended no fraud in drawing it up, and was not guilty of forgery; that, before his Majesty signed the document, I wrote the whole account in his. presence, and that I expressly asked the king for 50,000 dollars for Count Brandt and for myself, and his Majesty granted them; and that I could not notice at this time, nor when he signed the document, the slightest disinclination on the part of the king to our receiving such a sum. With the same certainty I can declare that everything which this memoir contains relating to the motives and inducements of my actions, and the occurrences in which I took part, has been most conscientiously recorded by me, as well as my memory enabled me to

recall it.   This was not the place to speak about
morality, hence I shall not be suspected of having
wished to bring forward anything in my excuse in this
respect.

Postscript.

Perhaps it will not be superfluous to add an accurate and definite explanation of my sentiments with
regard to the Russian alliance.   I was ever of opinion
that the king ought to maintain it, and although I was
not at first so convinced as I afterwards was of the
advantage of the Holstein negociation, still my advice
was not to listen to any other propositions in this
matter, and to carefully avoid arousing any suspicion
of the sort at the Russian court.   The insinuations
and opinions of others, especially of Count Rantzau,
produced but slight impression on me, and much less
did I follow them.   They were to the effect that we
ought not to trust solely to the Russian court, but
draw nearer to others, especially the Swedish.

I never noticed any inclination of the sort in Lieutenant-General von Gähler.   Since Easter of last year
I have never spoken on the subject with any one
but the minister of foreign affairs.   As regards the
Swedish alliance, I believed that it was advantageous,
if the king only took that part which the treaty with
Russia obliged him to do, but not seek any other influence, especially the influence of money.

These are the true principles on which I acted, although I at times thought and said that the Russian alliance is not the only resource for Denmark, and that it was not well to sacrifice all other considerations to it.

STRUENSEE.

April 14, 1772.

This apology, though obscure in some parts, is decidedly clever and modest.   In any ordinary court of justice it ought to have produced its effect, and the minister who could not be condemned for mere errors of judgment, ought to have been acquitted.   But it was the old story of the wolf and the lamb, and the bought judges were of opinion that any rope was good enough to hang a dog.

END OF VOL. II.

INDEX TO VOL. II.

HISTORICAL AND BIOGRAPHICAL.

C.

D.

E.

F.

G.

LONDON:

LEWIS AND SON, PRINTERS, SWAN BUILDINGS, MOORGATE STREET.